### *Kate felt her mouth go dry.*

She saw the photo of the familiar farmhouse, her parents holding hands by the porch, and then the snapshot of the three of them taken beside the barn. Her brother, Michael, standing so tall and straight, Hannah looking more serious. And there she was, a little towhead alongside Rex, the family sheepdog. Kate blinked back a sudden rush of tears. And then she saw her....

She was tall and slender, her dark hair worn shorter now. Her mother—older of course, but unmistakably Julia Richards. With a gasp, Kate's hand moved to her chest to press against her thudding heart.

"They told me you died," she whispered.

Dear Reader,

Fall is in full swing and so is Special Edition, with a very special lineup!

We begin this month with our THAT'S MY BABY! title for October. It's a lesson in instant motherhood for our heroine in *Mom for Hire,* the latest story from the popular Victoria Pade.

Three veteran authors will charm you with their miniseries this month. CUPID'S LITTLE HELPERS is the new series from Tracy Sinclair—don't miss book one, *Thank Heaven for Little Girls.* For fans of Elizabeth August, October is an extraspecial month— *The Husband* is the latest emotional and compelling title in her popular SMYTHESHIRE, MASSACHUSETTS series. This series began in Silhouette Romance and now it is coming to Special Edition for the very first time! And Pat Warren's REUNION series continues this month with *Keeping Kate.*

Helping to round out the month is *Not Before Marriage!* by Sandra Steffen—a compelling novel about waiting for Mr. Right. Finally, October is premiere month, where Special Edition brings you a new author. Debut author Julia Mozingo is one of our Women To Watch, and her title is *In a Family Way.*

I hope you enjoy this book, and all of the stories to come!

Sincerely,

Tara Gavin,
Senior Editor

Please address questions and book requests to:
Silhouette Reader Service
U.S.: 3010 Walden Ave., P.O. Box 1325, Buffalo, NY 14269
Canadian: P.O. Box 609, Fort Erie, Ont. L2A 5X3

# PAT WARREN
## KEEPING KATE

Published by Silhouette Books
America's Publisher of Contemporary Romance

This book is dedicated to my son, Dave—
with love, pride and affection

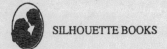 SILHOUETTE BOOKS

ISBN 0-373-24060-0

KEEPING KATE

Copyright © 1996 by Pat Warren

**Printed in U.S.A.**

---

## PAT WARREN,

mother of four, lives in Arizona with her travel-agent husband and a lazy white cat. She's a former newspaper columnist whose lifetime dream was to become a novelist. A strong romantic streak, a sense of humor and a keen interest in developing relationships led her to try romance novels, with which she feels very much at home.

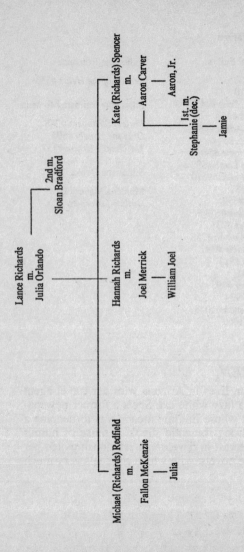

Lance Richards
m.
Julia Orlando

2nd m.
Sloan Bradford

Michael (Richards) Redfield
m.
Fallon McKenzie

Julia

Hannah Richards
m.
Joel Merrick

William Joel

Kate (Richards) Spencer
m.
Aaron Carver

Aaron, Jr.

1st. m.
Stephanie (dec.)

Jamie

## Prologue

*Mexico—September 1978*

Finally, I find a moment to write a quick entry in this journal that I've carried with me these many miles. We are safe and sound in a motel in California, the ordeal in Mexico at last over. Though I tried to keep a positive attitude during those arduous weeks, inside I worried we would never complete our journey, never return.

My beloved Sloan, however, wouldn't let me lose heart. Every night, he would encourage me to talk about my children, Michael, Hannah and Katie. He knows that I never sleep without praying for their safety and for the day they will be reunited with me. Because of Sloan Bradford, I have a second chance at love and renewed hope that he will help me locate my three little ones now that his nightmare is over.

It was fate, I believe, that led me to Sloan, a man who'd spent years tracking down children lost to their parents. Ironically, before he could assist me, he had a mission of his own to complete: to rescue his seven-year-old son from his ex-wife, Monica, and her lover, Al Torres. The two had kidnapped the boy from his home in Michigan and taken him deep into the Mexican hill country, demanding money for his release. In exchange for Sloan's help, I agreed to go along with him to search for Christopher as interpreter, for I speak fluent Spanish.

The way has not been easy, but it seems there are benefits to everything, for Sloan and I have fallen in love.

I've never been so frightened as the day we reached the mountaintop cabin where we'd been told they were holding the boy. It was dusk when we arrived. A skinny cat was the only sign of life, so we dared to peek in through a dirty window.

Sloan tensed as he saw Christopher looking listless and pale, lying on a filthy cot. Al was nowhere to be seen in the one room visible, but Monica was seated at a wooden table drinking, an open bottle nearby. Sloan had bought guns from a man we'd run across the second day, with me negotiating the sale in Spanish, and later he taught me the basics of how to shoot. But, as it turned out, we didn't need to use them, thank God. Armed, we rushed in and saw right away that Monica was drunk and her boyfriend not at home. Sloan tied her up as she howled protests, then we scooped up the boy and left hurriedly.

Even now, we don't know where Al had gone, though Monica screamed that he'd be right back. We never ran across him on our rush back down the mountain. Christopher rallied as soon as he saw his father. By the time we cleaned him up in a stream and got some food and water into him, he appeared fine, though Sloan wants an American doctor to check him over.

The race back to the border was frantic, but having Christopher safe lightened our steps. He is a sweet child, the image of his father, whose love and protection for both of us is evident in everything he does. The boy's gentle ways remind me of my Michael at that age, and my heart yearns for my own son, my firstborn, and his two sisters. Finally, I believe that soon I will hold all three in my arms again, for Sloan promised he would find them no matter how long it took, and he is a man of his word.

Although I'm exhausted, I sit here watching the man I've come to love with all my heart and his brave little son sleep, so grateful that things turned out all right.

Now at last, the search for my three children will begin as soon as we're settled back in Michigan. May God grant us the same sweet success in this, our second mission.

# Chapter One

*St. Clair, Michigan—December 1995*

Putting the children to bed was something Kate always enjoyed. Just one more drink of water, one last story, a final hug and kiss. Smiling, she skipped downstairs just as the phone began jingling, and picked it up on the second ring.

"Are you watching television?" Pam asked.

Always glad to hear from her cousin, Kate flopped onto the family-room couch. "No, just finished the bath-and-bedtime routine. Why? Should I be?"

"Yes. Turn it on right away. Channel 7. Call me later." Pam hung up.

Puzzled at the abrupt call, Kate reached for the remote and clicked on the set across the room, tuning in the channel as directed. It had to be something important, since Pam wasn't one to order anyone around.

Kate recognized the television show immediately, a weekly program she often watched, called "Solutions." It was one of those programs that encouraged the viewing audience to call in if they had any information on the reenacted crimes that were presented or if they could help reunite families torn apart by a variety of circumstances. This evening's segment was just beginning, the handsome host talking about a search for three siblings who'd been separated over twenty years ago.

Her curiosity aroused, Kate leaned forward as the man went on to inform the audience that the Child Protective Services had taken the children from their farm home in Frankenmuth, Michigan, after their father had been killed in an accident and their mother had to be hospitalized due to a life-threatening illness. Her eyes growing wider, Kate felt her mouth go dry.

She saw the photo of the familiar farmhouse, her parents holding hands by the porch, and then the snapshot taken by the barn of the three of them, her brother, Michael, standing so tall and straight, Hannah looking more serious. And there she was, a little towhead alongside Rex, the family sheepdog. In her dresser in the bedroom, she had copies of both pictures, treasures she'd kept all these years as the only tangible evidence of her early life. Blinking back a sudden rush of tears, Kate wondered who had brought these photos to the attention of the show's producers.

Then she saw her, tall and slender, her dark hair worn shorter now and those deep dimples. Her mother—older, of course—but unmistakably Julia Richards. With a gasp, Kate moved her hand to her chest to press against her thudding heart. "They told me you died," she whispered aloud to the empty room.

She listened as the woman she'd cried out for so many long years ago told how she'd been searching for her children ever since she'd been released from the hospital two years after the separation. The still-attractive woman's dark eyes were shiny with unshed tears as the host implored the viewing audience to call the number at the bottom of the screen if they knew the whereabouts of any of the three Richards children, which he went on to name, listing the ages they would be now. Next followed a computerized rendition of how the three might look today, and Kate was shocked to see how accurate her picture was.

With trembling hands, Kate reached for a pad and pencil, jotted down the station's phone number, then leaned back into the soft comfort of the couch, feeling numb. She kept staring at the screen as the segment ended and they shifted to a commercial, then she clicked off the television.

Her mother, Julia Richards, alive. How could that be? Why had the authorities, and everyone else she knew, lied to her? Where were Hannah and Michael after all these years, and had they, too, seen the show tonight? She'd cried for them, too, until she'd finally given up the dream of ever finding them. It had all happened so long ago. She'd been only six that fateful summer day. So much had happened since.

Closing her eyes, Kate let herself remember.

*St. Clair, Michigan—September, two years earlier*

Fog. Kate had always loved walking in the fog along the boardwalk that trailed the edge of the St. Clair River.

She liked it best in the early-morning hours, when the area was generally deserted. She enjoyed the swirling mist that hovered, eerie and mystical, winding and twisting itself around her, head to ankles. The gossamer haze lent itself to romantic imaginings and foolish fantasies. How often Dad had smiled at her fanciful strolls when, as a young girl, she'd sworn she'd seen ghosts and vampires and mythological heroes on horseback wandering the murky riverside.

She felt a tug at her heart as she thought of Dad, gone too soon, and Mother, too. Just a month ago, she'd seen them off on vacation, one of the few they'd taken, for George Spencer had been a busy surgeon and Carol had owned a successful real-estate agency in Grosse Pointe. Days later, the call had come, informing the Spencers' adopted daughter that there'd been a boating accident and both her parents had been killed.

And now she'd never see them again.

Kate strolled along the railed walkway, her eyes on the horizon where a weak sun was trying to break through the morning cloud cover. Indian summer, a lovely time in Michigan. Remnants of heat competed with an autumn breeze, often creating the fog that lingered over the lake until midmorning. But this year, everything looked sad and lonely to her, bittersweet memories of summers spent at the cottage causing her throat to clog with grief.

Coming to a lamppost casting an amber glow, Kate paused, wrapping her arms around herself against the slight chill that seeped through her heavy sweater. It was hard to imagine that she'd never see Dad's warm smile again or Mom's blond beauty. Finding a tissue in the pocket of her wool slacks, she dabbed at her eyes, wondering how long before these unexpected emotional rushes would end.

She had to make a plan, Kate decided, to take her mind off her loss. She had to determine what to do next. She couldn't stay in the summer cottage much longer. She needed to fill her hours, to get a job, to get on with her life.

By most people's standards, the life she'd lived thus far had been charmed—until a month ago, when everything had fallen apart. She'd been raised in a lovely home, graduated from her mother's alma mater, the University of Michigan, and traveled in Europe for two years afterward. She'd had all the creature comforts and many of life's advantages.

Yet today, she felt as if she had nothing, and this wasn't the first time she'd experienced such a wrenching feeling.

A capricious wind rearranged Kate's shoulder-length blond hair as she stood lost in thought, listening to the foghorn of a distant freighter making its way south from Lake Huron. It was time to go back, to get herself moving. There was no point in dwelling on the might-have-beens or indulging in wishful thinking. She'd faced difficult times before and somehow she'd survive this, too.

Determination had Kate lifting her chin a notch and turning. It was then that she noticed the man.

He stood about thirty feet from her, his dark hair ruffled, a frown on his face as he studied her. He was tall, well dressed, his expression intense. Without speaking, he started out, heading straight for her.

Groaning inwardly, Kate turned away and began walking. The last thing she needed right now in her particular state of mind was to encounter a stranger who looked as if he intended to start a conversation. She wasn't afraid, for St. Clair was hardly a high-crime area.

She'd strolled this same shoreline dozens of times and felt no danger.

The sky was lightening, and North Riverside Avenue, which paralleled the walkway, was in plain view with traffic moving steadily. Still, she picked up her pace.

"Wait!" the man called out. "I need to talk with you."

A chill raced down Kate's spine. She didn't stop but glanced over her shoulder, trying to determine if they'd met and she'd forgotten. The past few weeks seemed something of a blur. But no, she was certain she'd never seen the man before today. She kept on going.

His legs were long, and he was soon much closer. "Miss Spencer, wait, please," he said, his voice deep but nonthreatening.

He knew her name. Perhaps he was one of Dad's friends or patients. Kate stopped, turning to face him as she slipped her hands into her pants pockets, her fingers curling around the Mace attached to her key chain. A little caution was called for. "Do I know you?" she asked as he came to a halt a few feet away.

"No. I apologize if I frightened you. My name's Aaron Carver." With a nod of his head, he indicated a large brick home across Riverside up on the hill. "I live just over there."

Kate waited, uncertain why he'd called out to her. She was in no mood to make new friends just now.

Aaron wasn't used to feeling awkward. As a rule, he was always in control—of his office, his staff, his life. But the past six months had taught him that control was a nebulous thing, elusive and as hazy as the morning fog slowly burning off. "I learned from Henry Hull at Riverview Drugs that your parents recently died." Who knew better than he about grief, the soul-shattering kind that eats away at the very fabric of your existence? He'd sensed that same emotion in her as he'd stood watching her stroll along the boardwalk. "I'm so sorry."

Kate swallowed down the lump that seemed to arise at each and every new offer of sympathy. "Thank you. Did you know them for long?" She still couldn't place his face or his name.

Aaron ran a hand through his hair, again feeling clumsy with the task he knew he had to complete. He hated being at the mercy of the fates. "Actually, I didn't know them at all, although my father might have. But Henry tells me they were wonderful people. He also told me that you might be at loose ends, perhaps thinking of relocating." The pharmacist had mentioned that Kate Spencer lived in Grosse Pointe, about an hour's drive south of St. Clair.

Kate had chatted just yesterday with the friendly druggist she'd known most of her life, confiding that she was thinking of getting a job, something different, perhaps in another town. "I guess you could say that. It's difficult adjusting to such a sudden loss. I thought a change of scene might help." She had no desire to take him further into her confidence. He was still a stranger, even if he knew Henry Hull.

Besides, she couldn't imagine how what she might do would be of interest to this stranger. There seemed nothing further to say. "Thanks for your concern." She turned, about to walk away.

"'Difficult' isn't strong enough," Aaron said, his voice suddenly thick. "Overwhelming, maybe. Devastating. Debilitating. I know just how you feel." He watched her slowly swing back to face him and saw renewed interest in her eyes. "I lost my wife six months ago," he finished, hating having to say it out loud, the finality of the words.

He was quite tall, so much so that Kate had to look up to study him. He was very attractive, but looking closer, she saw more than that, saw the pain on his face, the sorrow in his dark eyes, and felt her heart swell with sympathy. He was young to lose a wife, in his early thirties, most likely. Yet could it hurt any less at a later age? "A sudden loss makes you want to strike out, doesn't it? At fate, at life in general, the fickle gods, anyone."

Aaron nodded, seeing that she understood perfectly. "Yes, and then you feel guilty for having those feelings."

"Exactly." Kate thought she knew now why Henry had told him about her misfortune. He was very kind and probably thought the two of them might find some common ground, since they'd both experienced a recent tragic loss. "How did your wife die?"

Aaron moved beneath the lamppost, thrusting his hands into the pockets of his jacket, his eyes focusing on the clouds overhead. "A viral infection. Four days and she was gone." He shook his head as if he still couldn't quite believe it himself. "Stephanie was so healthy. We'd been married three years, and she'd never been ill. All through her pregnancy, she didn't even have morning sickness."

Pregnancy? Kate stepped closer. "You have a child?"

Aaron cleared his throat and sat up, nodding. "A little girl, Jamie. She was eight months old yesterday." Getting a grip on his emotions, he turned to her. For a moment, he didn't speak, just stared.

From afar, he'd thought the woman resembled Stephanie. True, the hair was the same, but up close, he saw many subtle differences. Kate's eyes were deep blue and fringed with thick lashes, while Stephanie's had been a warm chocolate brown. Kate was smaller, more slender, where Stephanie's figure had been more womanly, especially after giving birth. And the voice was all wrong, husky rather than sweetly feminine like Stephanie's.

But the biggest difference was that Stephanie had looked confident and unafraid, always smiling, certain the world in general would accept her, and it had. This young woman seemed hesitant, uncertain, vulnerable, with a haunted look about her.

No, Kate wasn't Stephanie, and Aaron was glad. The slight resemblance was hard enough to handle. A more exact facsimile would have been impossible. He pulled out his wallet and showed her his daughter's picture.

Jamie looked to be about six months old in the picture, with blond fuzz for hair and huge brown eyes. She was seated on the floor and surrounded by several stuffed animals. She was not smiling.

"She's beautiful," Kate said softly. The poor little thing. No child should have to lose a parent at a young age. The premature loss affected their whole life. She knew that better than most.

"Jamie's the reason I came looking for you," Aaron said, finally getting around to why he'd approached her. "Henry said you might consider taking a job as a nanny."

Taken aback at the unexpected suggestion, Kate glanced up. "Did he? A nanny. Well, I don't know. I've never given child care much thought."

Henry had confided to Aaron that Kate Spencer had come from a very good family, but she suddenly found herself financially strapped. He'd gone on to explain that Kate had taught Sunday school, had started a children's reading hour at the local library, and had babysat Henry's own two children often on summers spent in St.

Clair. "I'd been led to believe that you were good with children, that you liked them. Do you?"

Of course she did, but liking children and caring for them full time were two separate things. "Yes, but I just never considered being a nanny. Of course I babysat in my neighborhood in my teens, like most of my friends." And her mother had bristled each time she'd done it, for small children had frightened Carol Spencer, which was why she'd adopted a six-year-old. "I was raised as an only child and had nannies of my own so of course, I learned from them." A couple of the women Carol had hired had been so-so, but Glynis, the one who'd stayed the longest, had been wonderful. "Still, I'm not sure how good I'd be."

"The job isn't difficult," Aaron went on, feeling the need to reassure her. "The pay's negotiable and the position comes with room and board." He was getting desperate and hoped it didn't show. Kate Spencer was the best candidate he'd run across in months of interviews. "We've had college girls helping out this summer, but they're all back in school. Fitz is getting on in years and just can't keep up with an active child."

"Fitz?"

"My housekeeper. Her real name's Margaret Fitzmaurice, but everyone calls her Fitz. She's been with my family since just before I was born, first as a nanny, then later she kept house for my father. She moved to my house after the wedding to do light housekeeping and cooking. Stephanie was head nurse in the cardiology unit and worked long hours. You wouldn't have to do anything except care for Jamie, and she's no trouble, really."

It was all happening too fast, Kate couldn't help thinking. She'd been wondering how she'd manage when she'd set out for her walk, and now here was this tall stranger offering her a solution. Still, she felt a little overwhelmed.

Aaron Carver was obviously a man who saw what he wanted, then went after it with every confidence that he'd be able to persuade one and all to do his bidding. But life had taught Kate to be more cautious, to go slowly. And even then, she'd run up against some truly tough hurdles.

The position he offered sounded too good to be true, under her present circumstances. But she needed to know more. "Tell me about your daughter."

Aaron was unaware that a smile at the thought of his daughter changed his face, softening the harsher angles that sadness had etched into his features. He wanted to be fair and honest with this woman who was struggling through her own loss. "Jamie's very independent and insists on feeding herself, which can wind up pretty messy. She still drinks from a bottle. She crawls everywhere and she's trying to walk holding on to tables and whatever else she can reach. She's a little small for her age, but very healthy, or so Dr. Benson tells me. Frankly, I think Jamie needs the stability of having the same woman mothering her." His eyes met Kate's. "I wouldn't want you to take this job unless you really want to make a go of it. Jamie can't keep losing people."

Kate wasn't offended, was in fact impressed with both the man's sensitivity and the depth of his feelings for his daughter. "I agree. I wouldn't want her hurt, either." When mentally listing her options for job hunting, child care hadn't even made the list. A degree in fine arts hadn't really prepared her for the job market. The only work experience she'd had was running her father's bookstore. But that option had been taken away from her after Dr. Spencer's death.

Perhaps Aaron Carver's offer wasn't so outlandish. He obviously wanted someone reliable, and she'd always been that. Since she needed a place to live, a job and a change of scene, maybe being Jamie's nanny would solve all three of her immediate problems, and she'd also be able to help someone in need.

Kate looked up at him again. "Before I decide, could I meet Jamie and Fitz?"

"Absolutely." Aaron felt a sense of relief, albeit temporary, and a wave of hope. Maybe, just maybe, Jamie would take to this woman, and she to his daughter. Lord, he hoped so. He'd spent entirely too much time away from his desk the past few months. But he couldn't concentrate fully until Jamie was in good hands.

Aaron again pointed to his house, visible from where they stood. "It's a short walk, or I can get my car."

Kate shook her head. "I like walking." She fell in step alongside him. "I hope you don't mind my asking, but what do you do for a living?"

He slowed his longer stride to accommodate her shorter steps. "I'm an architect in my father's firm, Carver and Associates. Made full partner last year."

He'd had it all, Aaron couldn't help thinking, with a by-now familiar pang of regret. A wife everyone liked and admired, a beautiful baby, a lovely home and full partnership. Then, from out of left field, had come a hit he hadn't dreamed of in his worst nightmare. Stephanie gravely ill, then suddenly gone forever.

Kate couldn't help noticing his sudden silence and knew he was remembering something painful. She, too, was given to those unexpected and hurtful memories.

Automatically, Aaron took Kate's elbow as they crossed the busy road, then started up the hill. The leaves were already changing, several falling to the ground and rustling underfoot as they walked. It wasn't quite eight. With any luck, he could be in the office by nine. Although everyone had been wonderfully understanding, Aaron hated not carrying his share of the work load.

"As I mentioned," Aaron went on, "you'd have your own room and private bath, of course. We could work something out with Fitz about days off. Naturally, you'd take all your meals with us. We're sort of informal." Stephanie had loved to entertain, supervising elaborate dinner parties in their large dining room, filling the house with laughter and friends. He hadn't had anyone over since her funeral, not even his father. "We can discuss salary and any other questions you might have after you meet everyone. If you decide to take the position, how soon would you be available?"

She needed to vacate the cottage, which was up for sale. There seemed no point in lingering where memories lived in every room and popped up regularly to sadden her. "Right away, actually," Kate told him.

Perfect, Aaron thought, refusing to believe she would turn down his offer. Still, a little help couldn't hurt. *Please let this work out,* he prayed to a God he was no longer sure was listening.

Kate slowed her steps as they entered through the open wrought-iron gate into the large, fenced yard. Impressive, she couldn't help thinking. English tudor, two stories plus an attic, a three-car attached garage and a long screened porch that faced the river. The lot was huge and very lovely with several old elms and maple trees, and flower beds neatly edged with angled white bricks. "Did you design the house yourself?"

Aaron nodded, not trusting his voice. He recalled the day he'd brought Stephanie here after it was completed, how her eyes had danced, how she'd squealed with delight. He'd built it for her, and now she was no longer here to share it with him.

Again, Kate saw the signs and knew he was remembering something upsetting. She'd seen the same expression on her own face in the mirror. Maybe it was a good thing, this sharing of grief. Maybe Aaron would understand her as no one else had been able to thus far because he, too, was trying to adjust. And perhaps a child was just what she needed in her life right now. It was truly difficult to be downcast around a happy child just discovering the world, she was certain.

With hope in her heart, Kate followed Aaron onto the porch.

Since her picture had been taken, Jamie Carver's hair had grown into gold ringlets, but she still wasn't smiling as Aaron led Kate into the yellow-and-white kitchen. Aaron chided himself for too often presenting such a forlorn face to his daughter that she reflected his own sorrow rather than the joy of childhood that she should be feeling.

"How's Daddy's girl?" he asked, walking over to her high chair, where she sat picking up bits of cereal and putting them in her mouth.

Solemn brown eyes stared back at him as she chewed.

"She's a bit under the weather, I think," Fitz explained as she sprinkled more cereal on the child's tray. "Teething, you know." The housekeeper looked the newcomer over, taking her measure, wondering if Aaron had found yet another candidate for nanny. She was way behind in her work, what with looking after Jamie and trying to get some nourishing food into the still-grieving father.

Aaron introduced the two women. "Fitz's like my right arm around here," he went on. "She knows all about the running of the house, about Jamie—and even me."

"It's pleased I am to meet you," Fitz said, her smile welcoming.

Kate was charmed by the woman's Irish accent. Fitz was a study in gray from her short-cropped hair to her sweater and wool slacks on through to sensible oxfords tied with bright green laces.

"Have you had breakfast, then? It won't take me but a jiffy to get you some." Her blue eyes shifted to Aaron. "You, too. I've just made a fresh pot of tea."

Aaron's smile was affectionate. "I might be coaxed into having one of your scones," he told her before turning to Kate. "Fitz convinced me ages ago that tea's better for you than coffee. She also makes the best scones you'll ever taste."

Kate had had only juice before setting out for her walk, and a bowl of soup last night, since her appetite was not what it used to be these days. Suddenly, the aroma of fresh-baked scones in the warm kitchen had her mouth watering. "That sounds good. I haven't had scones since I was in England two years ago."

While Fitz went to get cups and Aaron removed his jacket, Kate sat down at the table alongside the high chair. "Hi, Jamie." Chewing cereal, the baby watched her with a serious expression. Kate picked up the sippy cup that she noticed contained milk. "How about a drink?" She held the cup toward the high chair.

After a moment, Jamie opened her little mouth, inviting the drink. Kate touched the plastic spout to her lips and tilted up the glass. Watching her, Jamie drank. "That's a good girl," Kate told her.

Fitz brought over cups and the red teapot she favored, along with a plate of scones, and Aaron sat down, observing the interaction between Kate and his daughter.

Kate concentrated on the child, wondering if she could win a smile. "Can I have one of those?" she asked, pointing to the cereal on the tray.

After a thoughtful couple of seconds, Jamie picked one up and held it out toward her. "Thank you." Kate ate the piece and smiled. "Mmm, that's good. Your turn." She handed one to Jamie, who took it from her with chubby fingers and crammed it into her mouth.

A wobbly clown figure was attached to the high-chair tray by a suction cup. Kate batted at it gently, causing it to weave. "Oh, look, Mr. Clown wants to eat." She held a cereal piece toward the clown's red mouth, then bobbed the head and made the piece disappear. Jamie's eyes grew wide. "Where'd it go?" Kate asked. Jamie continued to stare.

Kate pretended to search all over for the cereal piece tucked in her hand, then suddenly pulled it out from the baby's shirt pocket. "Here it is!" That earned her a small smile as Jamie took the cereal from her. Not a great victory, but a beginning, Kate decided.

"The poor dear's been through a lot," Fitz explained as she poured tea for all three of them. "We've had a parade of sitters all summer long. She's not real quick to trust anyone just now."

"I can't say I blame her," Kate replied before taking a sip of tea. It was dark and hot and most welcome after the chill of their walk.

Aaron picked at his scone. "Kate's been highly recommended as a nanny, Fitz, and I'm hoping she'll decide to help us out."

"That would be nice," Fitz answered. "Are you from around here, dear?"

"My parents have…*had* a summer cottage near the St. Clair Boat Harbor. They died recently, in an accident."

"Oh, I'm so sorry." So that was why she looked on the sad side. Fitz watched Kate break off a tiny piece of scone and taste it. No appetite, she'd wager. The sweater she wore just hung on her. She needed some looking after, same as Jamie. And Aaron, too. Fitz sighed as she got to her feet, turning to the employer she'd helped raise. "Would you be wanting to show Kate around while I clean up the little one?"

Aaron drained his cup and stood. "Good idea. Let's start with the nursery upstairs, Kate."

The tour took quite a while, for the house was large. Either Stephanie had been wonderfully talented or they'd hired a decorator, Kate thought as Aaron walked her along the wide, carpeted upstairs hallway, opening doors to show her the baby's room, two guest rooms, including the one that would be hers if she took the job, and finally the room that was his directly across the hall.

The door at the far end was closed, and he hadn't mentioned it, had in fact avoided stepping near. Kate gazed at it curiously, but decided that it would be rude to ask.

Aaron caught her look and cleared his throat. "That's the master suite, but I decided it was too large for one person."

She understood all too well that the room held too many memories. "I had to leave my parents' home. Every time I walked by their room, I began to cry."

He touched her elbow, leading the way back downstairs. "We have a piano, if you like to play. There's a tennis court out back, which you're free to use." He took her into a room paneled in oak. "The library. Help yourself to anything that catches your eye. There's a stereo built in over there." And the terrazzo floor where he and Stephanie had ended many an evening with a slow dance in front of the fire. He felt his eyes fill and turned aside, blinking.

He had to leave, Aaron decided suddenly, to get out and get some air, to drive to the office, where workplace distractions would take over. He usually had himself under control fairly well, but today, for some reason, was worse than most.

Pointedly, he looked at his watch. Past nine. "I have to leave." He glanced at Kate and saw her avert her eyes. Somehow, she'd guessed that he hated anyone to see him struggling with overwhelming emotions. "Do you mind if Fitz finishes the tour?"

Kate was already walking back toward the kitchen. "Not at all. You go ahead."

His briefcase was on the table in the foyer. He paused, wishing she'd tell him she was accepting the position so he could stop worrying about it. But he knew it would be unfair to rush her. He didn't want someone with Jamie who wasn't going to give her all. "I imagine you want to get better acquainted with Jamie before you decide. Why don't I call later, and you can let me know your decision?"

"That sounds fine. I'd like to stay awhile, if Fitz doesn't mind." She needed to talk more with the only other person who'd lived in this house for years, to make sure they'd get along. Two women at odds in a house would only create tension, and Jamie definitely didn't need more of that.

"I'm sure she won't. Do you want to give me your home number so I can phone you later?"

Kate glanced into the family room and noticed that Jamie was on the floor playing with a pile of building blocks while Sesame Street characters jabbered on the television. "Why don't you just call here, say around lunchtime?"

"Fine." Aaron signaled Fitz to join him as Kate strolled to the family room. Moving slowly so as not to frighten the child, he noticed, she sat down and began making a tower. His daughter's solemn gaze watched the newcomer.

"She's lovely, isn't she?" Fitz commented, coming alongside. "Seems to like children."

Aaron stood observing as the tower grew. Finally, Kate took Jamie's little hand in her own and deliberately knocked over the tower. To his amazement, his daughter laughed gleefully and immediately began stacking blocks again. "Yes, she does," he answered. Now, if only she would turn out to be as good as she appeared on such short acquaintance...

"However, even if she decides to stay, let's keep a good eye on her. I want to be sure she's what Jamie needs, you know?"

"Of course," Fitz replied. "There is one thing I couldn't help noticing."

His hand on the doorknob, Aaron turned back. "What's that?"

"I don't see how you could have missed it. She's the image of Stephanie."

# Chapter Two

By lunchtime, Jamie was obviously getting sleepy, but her appetite had improved, Kate thought as she managed to sneak in spoonfuls of chicken noodle soup between bites of cheese that the child was feeding herself from her high-chair tray. "You're sure an independent little thing," Kate commented as the baby dodged the spoon and instead crammed a piece of cracker into her mouth.

"She is that," Fitz agreed, seated at the table observing. "She's got her mother's spirit, may God rest her soul."

It was the opening Kate had been waiting for. After Aaron had left, she'd played with Jamie on the floor awhile, then the two of them had bundled the baby into her stroller and gone for a walk in the morning sunshine. She'd found the chatty housekeeper to be quite friendly, with something to say about each neighboring home they'd passed, but precious little so far about the Carver household.

"I understand that Stephanie Carver died quite suddenly. Her death must have been a shock for all of you."

"That it was, and her so lovely with everything to live for. I lost my own husband early in our marriage, so I know how sick at heart Aaron is, even to this day."

"Oh, I'm so sorry." Kate had a strong empathetic streak, fostered in part by her recent loss. "Were you living here at the time?"

Fitz nodded. "We'd just arrived from County Cork the previous autumn with our little one. Peggy was barely two, a real handful. Sean took sick the first winter and died of pneumonia. He couldn't handle the fierce cold. We weren't used to it, you know."

Kate gave up on getting more soup into Jamie and let the child finish her cheese. "Does your daughter live nearby?"

"That she does, thank the Lord. She's a grown woman now, married with two husky boys, both redheads like Peggy's husband. They live in Lansing, where Terry's a teacher at the college there."

Kate wanted to return the focus to the Carvers. She'd noticed something odd while being shown around the house. "I've wondered . . . there aren't any pictures of Aaron's wife upstairs or down, at least none I've seen."

Fitz shook her gray head. "Not a one. Aaron tucked them all away the day of the funeral. Said he couldn't bear to look at them. The grief was eating away at him." She dabbed at the baby's chin with a washcloth, then tackled her sticky little hands. "It's time now, I told Aaron just the other day. He needs to put it all behind him for the sake of the little one, and get on with his life."

Everyone grieved differently, Kate believed. Still, would she be moving into a house with no joy, no laughter? The thought held little appeal. "How did he respond to your suggestion?"

"It's only because I've known the family since before Aaron was born that I even dared speak my mind, you understand. Oh, he agreed with me, but saying the words and doing the deed are two separate things. He's trying, though. I'll give him that. He's a good man and he loves this child dearly. I've been hoping he'd be on the mend by now."

Kate knew there was no timetable for overcoming grief. Perhaps she could lighten his worry load and hasten his recovery. She touched a finger to the baby's nose, making her laugh, then seized the opportunity to pop in a final bit of cheese. "She's such a beautiful little girl."

"Isn't she, just? Beautiful and bright and curious. Already, she crawls every which place and soon she'll be walking, then running. Like I told Aaron, I just turned sixty-two my last birthday. Caring for the house, working at my own pace and doing a little each day, I can manage just fine. But the little one wears me out. Mostly, I fear she'll hurt herself if I can't keep up with her."

Holding Jamie's sippy cup to her lips, Kate smiled at the little girl as she drank thirstily. "Aaron works long hours?"

"That he does. Scarcely home, even knowing Jamie misses him. I believe he buries himself in his work to take his mind off his grief, you know." Automatically, she cleaned off the tray as she spoke.

Kate found it difficult to imagine such a strong love. Certainly, she'd never experienced one herself, nor had she ever witnessed such a relationship. What a shame that Stephanie had been taken from her family.

"I think someone's sleepy," Kate commented as Jamie rubbed at her eyes. She took the child from her high chair and grabbed Elmo, the well-loved stuffed dog that Fitz had said was Jamie's favorite. "May I take her up for her nap?"

"Of course. I'll go with you and show you her routine."

"It would be mostly you and me running the place," Fitz told Kate as they sat with a cup of tea after putting Jamie to nap. "I'm not a fancy cook, but then, Aaron doesn't eat at home much these days. Fixing for just the babe and me isn't hard."

"I love to cook," Kate volunteered. "Maybe I could help out some days."

"That would be lovely." Fitz's curiosity about the woman Aaron wanted to entrust his child to hadn't been satisfied, not by a long shot. "You're all alone, then?"

"Since my parents died, yes."

"And you were an only child, I imagine."

"Adopted, actually, when I was six. I'd lived on a farm in Frankenmuth until my birth parents died."

"Lord, you've lost *two* sets of parents." It's a wonder she wasn't sobbing her heart out, Fitz thought as she reached over to squeeze Kate's hand. Something else troubled her. Before he'd left, Aaron had mentioned that Dr. George Spencer had been a highly respected and successful surgeon. Why, then, was Kate needing work and a place to stay, as Aaron had told her?

Fitz searched for the right words so as not to offend. "Surely your folks left something for you. I shouldn't be asking, I know, but doctors are usually well paid. If I'm being too nosy, just say so and I'll not question you again."

Kate couldn't blame Fitz for her inquisitiveness. Still, she couldn't bring herself to detail the mess that was her family background at the moment. It was too raw a wound to keep reopening. "It's a long and not very interesting story, but believe me, as of right now, my worldly goods consist of my clothes, my car, a little jewelry and a few books."

While the older woman digested that, Kate glanced around at the lovely kitchen, the sloping lawn just outside the back windows, the quiet neighborhood beyond the high shrubbery. It would be pleasant living here. Fitz was a genuinely kind and caring person, and the baby was wonderful. Jamie needed someone to make her smile more, to give her undivided attention, which would be no hardship for Kate. And Aaron Carver needed to stop worrying about his only child so he could begin to heal. "You know, this may just work out," she said thoughtfully.

The ringing phone kept Fitz from having to answer.

In his office, Aaron sat at his desk with the phone in his hand, wondering what Kate Spencer's answer would be.

He'd spent the morning trying to concentrate on the final design for the shopping mall he'd been laboring over for months. The work had gone slowly because his attention span was grossly limited since Stephanie's death. When he wasn't remembering and grieving, he was worrying about his daughter and about their future without the woman around whom he'd built his dreams. He'd had to drag his mind back repeatedly to the project.

But today, with one worry hopefully about to be eliminated, he'd gotten quite a bit accomplished. Now, if only

Kate would take the job, he could settle down and let his work absorb him once again.

Kate Spencer was right for Jamie. He'd seen it from the minute she'd sat down at the table, drawing his daughter's interest almost immediately. And when he'd watched them play with the building blocks, he'd actually heard Jamie laugh out loud, a sound heard all too infrequently.

Kate was young enough to have lots of energy for Jamie, keeping after her as she learned to walk and run, taking her on walks, to the park with the swings, to the harbor to watch the boats. He certainly didn't have the time, and Fitz had difficulty walking, since her arthritis was acting up after years in a cold climate.

It wasn't true, what Fitz had said, that Kate looked just like Stephanie. A little, perhaps—the same blond hair. But otherwise, they were very different. And he certainly wasn't eager to hire her because of some vague resemblance. He wanted her because Henry Hull had said she came from a fine family and was a good person who'd be a positive influence on Jamie. Her looks had absolutely nothing to do with his decision.

Aaron cleared his throat as Fitz answered the phone. He asked if Kate was still there.

"That she is, right here," Fitz replied. "I'll get her for you." She held the phone out to Kate. "Aaron, for you."

Feeling calm after arriving at her decision, Kate said hello and waited.

Aaron kept his voice level, not wanting to appear anxious. "You asked me to call at lunchtime, so here I am. Have you decided?"

"I'd like to accept your offer," Kate answered. "Perhaps we should do it on a trial basis. Say, for one week, just to make certain we all get along."

He tried not to release a relieved sigh into the phone. "That's fine with me." He had no doubts that Jamie would win Kate over long before the week was up. "When can you move in?"

The next day was Saturday. Kate was certain she could have all her loose ends tied up by then. "Tomorrow morning, if that's all right with you."

"Terrific. Will you need help?" He wasn't certain just what all she'd be moving over. The room he'd indicated would be hers was furnished.

"Thank you, but no. I can get all my things into my car. I'll be here by late morning."

"Great. Please have Fitz give you a house key. Now, about your salary and days off..."

"We can discuss all that when I return. I'm sure you're a fair man." She'd trusted before and found herself with regrets. But if this job didn't work out, she could always leave. Living in the home a week should tell her all she needed to know.

Aaron said goodbye, and Kate hung up.

Fitz stepped over and slipped an arm around the young woman's slender shoulders. "Welcome, dear. I'm so very glad you've agreed to give us all a trial run."

"Thank you, Fitz." Kate felt a rush of emotion she tried to swallow down. At least she was wanted in one home.


"A nanny? You're kidding, right?" Pam Spencer's usually calm voice was bordering on incredulous.

"Perfectly serious," Kate told her. Holding the phone to her ear with an upraised shoulder, she emptied the medicine chest into a cardboard box. "Why are you so surprised? I like children."

"Yes, so do I. My own, should I have any one day. But being a substitute mother for someone else's child? I can't believe you're serious. Weren't you the one who said you could write a book telling the world all that a nanny *shouldn't* be?"

Kate smiled, picturing her cousin's pixie face wearing a worried frown as she shoved her specs higher on her nose, a nervous habit. "That's true, and I could. Which only means I know ahead of time what a nanny should and shouldn't do, right?"

"I suppose. What's the baby's father like?"

"Very tall, quite handsome and still grieving over the death of his wife six months ago."

"Swell. What a cheery house to move in to. Listen, Kate, I have a better idea. Come live with me. My apartment above the shop is plenty big enough for the two of us and—"

"No! Absolutely not." Kate was surprised at her quick refusal, but she had to make Pam see. Her cousin was sweet but almost painfully shy, bookish and very non-assertive. At twenty-four, the same age as Kate, she was still doing her father's bidding, afraid to make him angry. Of course, Tom Spencer, George Spencer's only brother and Kate's uncle, was a formidable man to oppose, as Kate had only recently discovered.

"I'm sorry, Pam. It isn't that I wouldn't enjoy living with you, because I would. But, with the way things are between your father and me, it's simply not a good idea. You've told me that he's always dropping in at the shop or your apartment. I couldn't handle that, not now." Pam operated and now owned The Book Tree, the upscale bookstore in Grosse Pointe that until recently had belonged to Kate's father. It was the same shop Kate used to manage for him. No, returning there would be far too difficult.

"I hate all this." Pam's soft-spoken words reflected her frustration. "I feel like I'm in the middle of you two."

Kate closed the door to the medicine chest and sighed. "Please don't feel that way. None of this is your fault."

"Well, it's not your fault, either. I feel like a traitor saying this, but I think you should sue Dad. He's wrong and..."

Kate carried the small box and placed it by the front door. "We've already talked about this. I simply don't have the energy for a long, nasty court case. And you know that's what it would turn out to be."

Pam's voice held a hint of tears. "I know. But he's stealing from you. He's my father and I love him, but you shouldn't let him get away with it."

She probably shouldn't. Her father's attorney, who'd read the will in his office that dreadful day, had taken her aside and told her he could recommend a lawyer if she wanted to take Tom Spencer to court. But even then, she'd refused.

"Listen, I'm going to leave the keys to the cottage on the table. Will you please tell your father?" She hated involving Pam, but she had no intention of talking with her uncle again.

"I'll tell him. Kate, are you going to be all right?"

"I'm going to be fine." At least, she prayed she would be. Still, there were days when she thought that maybe Uncle Tom was right and she was entitled to nothing from her parents' estate, not being blood and all. Other days, she was furious at the fates for robbing her of a second birthright. Between the crying jags, missing her folks and the angry bouts, she was an emotional mess.

So the best thing to do was to make a new life for herself, to leave the past be. The only family member she didn't want to lose touch with was Pam. "This doesn't mean we won't see one another. I'll be only an hour's drive away."

"Why does it feel like you're moving out of my life, then?" Pam's question ended on a sob.

Kate refused to resort to tears, not over this. She'd cried until she had no more tears left over her parents' death. But she wouldn't waste tears over her uncle and his ruthless maneuverings. She would make her own way and not look back. If she didn't, she'd wind up like Pam, stuck right under her father's thumb, just where Tom Spencer wanted her.

"I promise you, Pam, I plan to stay in your life. Let's wait until I settle in, and maybe you'd like to take a drive to St. Clair and visit me. The baby's adorable, and the housekeeper, Fitz, has this wonderful Irish accent."

Noisily, Pam blew her nose. "I'd like that, but we'd better not tell Dad."

Kate drew in a steadying breath. Pam would never be her own person until she shook free of Tom Spencer's influence. They'd had this discussion many times, but Pam still hadn't found the courage to stand up to her father. For her cousin's sake, Kate hoped she would soon. As difficult as she found her current situation, she felt she was better off than Pam. "I'll call you."

Feeling let down by the call, Kate went into the bedroom and pulled her suitcases out of the closet. Tomorrow would be a new day, she promised herself.

Rain. It had started during the night and was a regular downpour by morning. Kate stood in the open doorway of the cottage, gazing out at the wet walkways, the sodden grass and accumulated puddles, hoping that this wasn't an omen about this new fork in the road she was about to try.

Dodging the raindrops, Kate pulled her white BMW close to the front door. She loved the racy little convertible that her father had given her two years ago. George Spencer had been generous to a fault, often surprising her with no-occasion gifts, all expensive, all things he'd picked out himself. A Limoges candy dish, a Piaget watch, a Hermés scarf. He'd been equally, if not more, extravagant with his wife. Mom had scolded him frequently for his lavish spending sprees, but no one could stay angry with Dad for long. He'd loved life. He'd liked and trusted everyone.

If only he hadn't, Kate thought, thinking of Tom Spencer.

It took her only twenty minutes to load the car and take a last look around the cottage where she'd spent many a happy summer. They'd gone boating, fishing, swimming. Dad's boat was still anchored at the nearby marina, and it was also for sale. Tom seemed in a big hurry to liquidate every asset Mom and Dad had left behind. He was welcome to the lot, Kate decided. Fighting her uncle wasn't worth the hassle.

Shaking off old memories along with the lingering bitterness, Kate removed the key from her key ring and placed it on the kitchen table. For a moment, she studied the new key to the Carver house that Fitz had given her yesterday. Off with the old, on with the new.

A brand-new start, Kate told herself as she made sure the front-door lock clicked in before she climbed behind the wheel. No looking back, no regrets. The best was yet to be.

She almost believed it as she turned on the windshield wipers, then swung out of the circular driveway.

Ten minutes later, she stopped in front of the black wrought-iron gate leading to the Carver house. Fitz had said it was seldom closed and hardly ever locked. She drove on through and paused by the front door.

In the gloom of a rainy day, with wet autumn leaves clinging to the grass and winding driveway and the wind whipping about the trees, the place didn't look terribly inviting. Kate squared her shoulders. No negative thinking, she told herself as she followed the path around to the back entry.

Fitz had told her she could park in the third stall of the attached garage. But the door was down, and she had no opener. So she got out and hurried onto the small stoop and was digging in her jacket pocket for the key when the door swung open.

"There you are," Aaron said. "I was beginning to think you'd changed your mind." Actually, he'd walked out front several times, hoping to spot her. He didn't have her phone number, nor did he know exactly where she'd been staying. He'd had half a thought to phone Henry at the pharmacy but had decided to wait a bit longer. He was glad she'd shown up and saved him the embarrassing call.

She was standing beneath the overhang, and he was two steps higher. The additional height, added to his own six feet, made him appear quite large, Kate thought as her eyes traveled up. He had on a black turtleneck and stone-washed jeans with white running shoes. His dark hair was unruly, as if he'd only recently crawled out of bed, or maybe it was mussed from his blunt fingers thrusting through the thickness in frustration because he couldn't sleep. He hadn't shaved; the dark stubble gave his lean face an incongruously dangerous look. His eyes were hooded, assessing, as they'd been yesterday morning in the fog.

She slid up the sleeve of her leather jacket and checked her watch. "I told you midmorning, and it's just ten. Am I late?"

"No, you're right on time." He held the door wider, motioning her inside. "Fitz is in Jamie's room changing her outfit. She managed to get the top off her cup and spilled juice all over her clothes. Go on in while I get your things."

She didn't want to be a bother and she was far from helpless. "I can manage, really."

The black leather jacket seemed a size too large for her, Aaron thought, as if she'd recently lost weight. Beneath it, she wore a pink sweatshirt and designer jeans. Everything about her spoke of money, from her gold watch to the antique pearl ring to the Bass loafers she wore. Yet here she was, needing a job and a home. A story there somewhere, Aaron thought as he held out his hand. "Give me your keys and I'll get your bags."

A man used to being in charge, Kate thought as she pulled her keys from her pocket and placed them in his open palm. In doing so, her fingers brushed his. She felt a slight jolt, a sudden awareness. Quickly, she looked up and met his eyes and saw that he was both surprised and annoyed that such a brief contact could cause a reaction. Also a man used to controlling his feelings, one who disliked surprises, Kate decided as she brushed past him and went inside.

In three trips, Aaron had all her things deposited in her new room and bath. He opened the spacious closet. "I see that Fitz has supplied you with plenty of hangers. The bed's just been changed, I'm sure, and fresh towels are kept in the linen closet at the end of the hall when you need more."

"Thank you. I'll unpack and go find Jamie." She slipped off her jacket.

Aaron stuck his hands in his back pockets, feeling strangely disconcerted. Having a woman other than Fitz in the house was unnerving. Kate Spencer was a lovely woman. Any other man would be thrilled to have her under his roof. But he was different, dead inside, unable to feel anything. That brief awareness downstairs had been a nervous reaction and nothing more, he assured himself.

On the table by the window, Kate spotted an African violet in full bloom in a lovely little pot. She wandered over and picked it up. "These were Mother's favorites. She used to have them all over the house. They're difficult to grow, but she had a way with them."

"Did she talk to them?" Aaron asked, moving to her side. "That's what Stephanie used to do. She often said that plants could hear you, identify the tone of your voice and respond to praise. Silly." He almost smiled at the memory.

"Perhaps, but it does seem to work."

"Well, then maybe you can say a few words to our plants. Fitz has been too busy to tend to them, so most are in pretty bad shape." He watched her set down the pot with great care. "If you have time, that is." He'd hired her for Jamie, not to resurrect his plants, he reminded himself.

"I love working with plants and flowers. I'll check them out." She turned to him then, wondering why he was still hanging around. He seemed nervous, fidgety.

Her scent reached him, something softly feminine. Aaron found himself inhaling deeply. Then he noticed she was watching him with a questioning look in her eyes. Clearing his throat, he turned. "If you need anything, I'll be in my study. I've brought some work home."

Kate followed him out into the hallway just as Jamie came crawling out of her room. Gazing up, her eyes skimmed over her father and landed on Kate. She gave a little happy sound and headed straight for her new nanny.

Stopping in his tracks, Aaron watched his daughter reach Kate, sit down on her little padded rump and stretch up her arms to be picked up. He heard Kate's soft "Hi, sweetie," then saw her hoist Jamie into her arms and cuddle her close.

For an instant, he envied his daughter the simple affection of that childlike embrace and craved the comfort Jamie sought and found. As he studied the two of them, Kate's eyes met his over the baby's head. At that moment, seeing the warmth in their blue depths, Aaron was certain he'd found the right person to take care of his daughter.

Aaron parked his black Mercedes by the front door and stepped out. Stretching, he rolled his shoulders, trying to get the kinks out. He'd spent hours bending over his drawing board, then driven to the shopping-mall developer's office to drop off the set of revised blueprints. By then, it had been after five, and he'd opted to drive home rather than return to his own office.

He wasn't checking up on how Kate was doing, not really, he told himself. In the two weeks she'd been with them, there'd been no problems. Jamie seemed happy enough, and Fitz had had no complaints, had in fact said she was much happier with Kate around. Of course, Aaron was home very little, leaving around seven most mornings and rarely returning before seven or eight in the

evening. Which was why he'd thought that arriving home
earlier than usual would give him a clearer picture.

Using his key, he entered and looked around. No one
in sight. He set his briefcase by the front door, removed
his jacket and tie and dropped them on a chair, then
wandered toward the back of the house. He heard a voice
coming from the direction of the kitchen and headed that
way. In the dining room, he paused, gazing at the scene
through the archway.

Jamie was in her high chair, and Kate was seated
alongside her. He leaned forward to listen.

"Here comes a pretty red snake," Kate said, placing
the item in question on the baby's tray. As Jamie reached
for it, Kate stole it from her fingers. "And zoom, into
your little mouth."

Jamie giggled, then clamped her lips together and
chewed.

"Next, we have a bright yellow worm," Kate went on.
"Look how it wiggles and squirms on your tray." She
waited until Jamie swallowed, then picked up the worm
and popped it into her mouth. "All gone!"

Snakes? Worms? Aaron stepped into the kitchen, not
bothering to muffle his footsteps. "What have we here?"

"Oh, hi." Kate saw that Jamie was still absorbed in
trying to pick up another worm. "Look, sweetie, your
daddy's home." But the baby was too absorbed to greet
her father.

Aaron bent to place a kiss on her sweet head, then
checked out the colorful assortment on his daughter's
tray. "What is all that?"

"Worms and snakes and even wiggly spiders." Kate
showed him the two bowls. "Macaroni and cheese in
here, and gelatin cutouts in this one." To demonstrate,
she picked up a daddy longlegs and held it out to Jamie.

"Here comes a green spider." With a laugh, Jamie closed her mouth around the offering.

Aaron slipped his hands into his pockets, obviously puzzled. "What brought this about?"

Kate held the cup for Jamie to drink as she explained. "Your daughter's a bit of a picky eater, especially when she's teething. She kept spitting out her baby food. She's got six teeth. So I thought I'd make a game of it with table food that's good for her. She likes the bright colors and she thinks it's great fun when the bugs and things I cut out wiggle into her mouth." She smiled at the baby as she wiped her chin. "Don't you, sweetie?"

Jamie smiled back, then went to work trying to pick up another red snake.

Impressed with Kate's ingenuity, Aaron pulled out a chair. "I thought girls were afraid of bugs and snakes."

"They are, of the real thing. But Jamie's too young to recognize these as replicas of something harmful." Kate slipped another spoonful of macaroni and cheese into the child. "They really keep her busy."

"Mealtime takes quite a while that way, I imagine."

"Yes, but I believe that if you make mealtime fun, children eat better instead of picking at dinner, then filling up on cookies and sugar-coated cereals." She dropped another green spider on Jamie's tray.

Aaron cocked his head at her. "I thought you said you didn't know much about kids."

Kate shrugged. "I don't. But I used to manage a bookstore, and the children's story hour was my favorite time. I read up on how to hold a toddler's interest at mealtime and bath time and story time. Kids will cooperate with most anything you want them to do if you make it appealing in some way at their level."

Aaron had to admit that Jamie was eating more happily than he'd seen before. Actually, the bowl of macaroni smelled good and looked awfully inviting. He hadn't tasted that particular dish in years. Earlier, he'd grabbed lunch on the run and had told Fitz this morning to not count on him for dinner. But his plans had changed, and suddenly he found his mouth watering. He went to the cupboard, took down a plate and spooned himself a generous helping.

Kate glanced at him and frowned. "Oh, you don't have to eat this. Fitz is lying down with a headache, but I can fix you something more substantial."

Aaron swallowed a savory spoonful. "Why, is there something wrong with this?"

"No, of course not, or I wouldn't be giving it to Jamie."

"What were you planning to eat?"

"The same thing. But you must be used to..."

"Gourmet meals?" Aaron shook his head. "Not really. When Stephanie was alive, our schedules were always at such cross-purposes, hers at the hospital and mine at the office, that we didn't share that many dinners. We ate on the fly quite often. She had no interest in cooking, so Fitz was in charge of the kitchen. This—" he pointed to the pasta "—is a real treat. My mother used to make this when I was a kid." Realizing what he'd said, Aaron stopped. He rarely mentioned his mother. All these years later, and it still hurt.

Kate noticed his sober expression and wondered what he was remembering.

Chewing, Aaron screwed up his face thoughtfully. "There's something different about your version, some taste I can't quite identify."

"Mushrooms. I love mushrooms, so before baking, I added some fresh ones chopped fine so the baby wouldn't have trouble with them."

"Ah, yes, mushrooms. It's great." Finished, he scooped another helping. "Aren't you going to eat?"

"I usually wait until Jamie's finished."

He glanced at the baby, who was finger deep in squiggly gelatin worms. "She's happy." He rose to get another bowl and some silverware. "How about a glass of milk? I'd like some."

"Yes, thank you." Funny, she'd been picturing him preferring more-adult fare or possibly something foreign, coq au vin with a glass of wine or beef bourguignonne. Certainly not a bowl of macaroni and cheese with cold milk eaten at the kitchen table. Oddly, the fact that he liked a simple meal made him more approachable to her.

Kate gave the baby another drink, then turned to eat her own dinner. "I should at least have made you some rolls or..."

Aaron shook his head. "This is fine."

As she ate, she couldn't help stealing glances at him from under lowered lashes. This impromptu meal seemed so homey, so normal. It was reminiscent of occasional evening suppers she'd shared with Dad when he'd come home after a long day of surgery and Mom was still at her office. He'd made pasta with clam sauce, his favorite, and the two of them had discussed their day. Kate swallowed down a sudden lump in her throat.

"You miss them still, don't you?" Aaron asked softly. He'd been watching her, noting how quiet she'd become, realizing she was remembering her parents.

Kate blinked. It was amazing how he knew without her having said a word. She looked up at him, her eyes moist. "You too, eh?"

He nodded. "Yeah, me too." Without giving it much thought, he covered her hand with his and squeezed in a gesture of sympathy.

Kate looked down at their joined hands, his fingers long and lean and strong, hers fragile by comparison. And she couldn't help noticing the gold band on his third finger. Seven months after his wife's death, and he still wore his wedding band.

Aaron followed her gaze and sighed. "I can't seem to make myself take it off. It seems so...so final."

"I understand."

He drew back his hand and rose, reaching to clear the table. "Listen, why don't you take Jamie up for her bath, and I'll clean up here?"

"You shouldn't have to. I'll clean up here first and—"

He swiveled toward her, his face looking strained. "Just go, please." He turned to the counter and opened the dishwasher.

Uncertain why he seemed upset, Kate took Jamie from her high chair and left the room. Climbing the stairs, she hoped she hadn't said anything to bring on Aaron's sudden mood shift. More likely, he was struggling with memories that refused to retreat, as she was.

In the kitchen, Aaron braced his hands on the edge of the sink and leaned forward, his eyes closed. He realized that, as much as anyone could understand what he was going through, Kate did, for she bore her own grief. But she seemed to be handling her pain better than he was, perhaps because she was younger, only twenty-four. He was nine years older and, tonight, felt every day of it.

Her hand had been soft, her skin silky smooth. How long had it been since he'd reached out to touch a woman? Too long, yet even that small gesture had him feeling guilty and disloyal. He'd loved Stephanie, deeply, completely. He didn't want to forget her and he hadn't.

But it was damn difficult living in the same house with a lovely woman and not having some thoughts about her. He didn't want to think about Kate, and she certainly didn't invite the smallest intimacy. But on weekends, he'd be working in his study and he'd hear her explaining something to Jamie in that throaty voice or the two of them laughing. And his mind would wander.

She dressed in loose tops and baggy sweaters, never in anything enticing. Yet he noticed her, her scent, her walk, her smile. Drawing in a shaky breath, he bent to load the dishwasher.

Damn, it wasn't fair. His wife was gone, and he missed her terribly. But his body longed for a woman's touch, and that wasn't all. Another part of him wished he could sit with Kate in his study by the fire after Jamie was in bed, and they could talk. Not in a sensual way, just discuss their day, the cute things Jamie had done, a book one of them had read. He yearned for the return of those times he'd shared with Stephanie.

Yet he had no right to want to curl up by the fire with Kate. He loved someone else, someone lost to him forever. He had no right to look at Kate as a man free of entanglements might. He had no right to be disloyal to his wife's memory. What kind of a man began thinking about another woman when his wife was barely cold in her grave? Aaron dropped the last of the silverware into the tray and slammed the dishwasher door shut.

Fair or not, he had no right to touch Kate. He would watch himself in the future, avoid cozy moments together. The last thing he wanted was to hurt this vulnerable young woman.

Turning out the light, he went up to his den.

Work. He would bury himself in work.

## Chapter Three

"The presentation is less than a month away, Freddie. I had the prototype in your office weeks ago, and you *still* haven't completed the layout." Aaron felt his anger rising and tried to keep it in check. "I don't know if you understand the importance of having this model of the shopping mall finished in time for the show."

"I *do* understand, Aaron. But I've told you that I'm shorthanded, and this isn't the only job we're working on with everybody wanting everything yesterday. We can only work so many man hours." Freddie's voice was filled with exasperation.

Aaron glanced over at his father sitting calmly in the chair opposite his desk and drew in a slow breath. "All right. Just when can I reasonably expect delivery?"

"Like I said, a couple of weeks."

"That's not good enough!" Aaron's patience had been stretched to the limit. "I need an exact delivery date."

Freddie sighed heavily into the phone. "All right. November 7 is the best I can do."

"The seventh? The presentation's set for the tenth. This is the twentieth of October. That gives you over two weeks to finish and us only a couple of days to repair anything that might be wrong."

"You won't need more than three days, because there won't be anything wrong. We do good work, Aaron. You know that."

Aaron wished he could tell Freddie to forget the whole thing and he'd take his business elsewhere. But the man was right. They did good work. Slow but good. "All right, but Freddie, if there's a screwup, I'm going to hold you personally responsible. Goodbye." With monumental effort, he refrained from slamming the phone down. "Did you hear that?" he asked his father as he picked up a pencil and began tapping it on the desk.

"Yes, I heard." William Carver crossed his long legs and studied his eldest son. Aaron had always been the steady one, the dependable one, the even-tempered one. His younger brother, Johnny, was the carefree sort, charming but irresponsible, the one William worried about. However, since Stephanie's death, Aaron had changed.

First, he'd been inconsolable, which had been understandable. Then he'd been guilt ridden, something many experienced—the guilt of the survivor. But recently, just when William had thought Aaron was well on the road to healing, he'd become edgy, short-tempered, often irritable. And William wasn't the only one who'd noticed the changes.

Why, William wondered, had his son had this relapse in his recovery?

"We'll have three days to go over everything and make sure it's up to snuff. That should be enough time unless they truly mess up."

Aaron snapped the pencil in half and threw down both pieces. "And what if they do?"

"We've been using Freddie for fifteen years or more, Aaron. He's made a few mistakes but nothing major. I think we need to trust him a little on this."

Even his own father didn't understand. "Dad, I've put six months' work into this project." On and off, of course, for some days he'd been able to work very little. "Can you blame me for worrying just a little that something that's out of my control might cause it all to go down the drain?"

William stroked his mustache thoughtfully. "Aaron, are you having trouble sleeping?"

"What?" Aaron was stunned. "What's my sleeping got to do with Freddie's delivery date?" He ran an agitated hand through his hair, wondering if his father were turning senile.

"Maybe a great deal. You seem to be overreacting. Is everything all right at home? I thought when you hired that nanny for Jamie that your situation would improve."

Aaron had thought so, too. "My problem has nothing to do with my sleep habits or my home. My problem is with this project, the hours I've put in." Forcing himself to simmer down, he leaned back in his chair. "I admit I'm a little short-tempered these days, what with working twelve, fourteen hours a day lately. Who wouldn't be?"

William didn't buy that. Aaron had always been a workaholic, as he himself was. But he'd never been so high-strung. "You're entitled to an occasional blowup.

But, son, you've been stretched tighter than a drum for weeks. Is there anything troubling you?"

"Like what?"

"I don't know. You tell me." William narrowed his gaze. Usually, when a man was this strung out, it had to do with a woman. But as far as he knew, there'd been no women in Aaron's life since Stephanie. Except... "How's that nanny working out?"

"Fine." Aaron straightened. "Look, Dad, I've got to get back to work."

He'd hit on it, William was certain. "She's good with Jamie?"

"Very." He pulled out his side drawer and rummaged through the files, searching for one in particular.

"And how is she with Fitz?"

"They get along just fine." Giving up, Aaron swung back to look at his father. "What are you getting at?"

"How do *you* get along with her?"

Aaron frowned. "What's that supposed to mean? She's my daughter's nanny, that's all. I hardly see her." He fanned through a stack of folders on his desk. "Where the hell's the Compton file?"

"I'll leave you to your work." Slowly, William stood, then paused to gaze down at his firstborn. "Is there anything you want to talk about?" Troubled dark eyes just stared up at him. "You've nothing to blame yourself for, you know." Quietly, William let himself out of the office and closed the door.

Nothing to blame himself for. Easy for Dad to say.

Aaron swiveled his chair around to stare out the window. A stiff October breeze whipped at the flag on the pole. The river looked cold, and the sky was thick with dark clouds. The somber day suited his mood exactly.

How did he get along with Kate Spencer? his father wanted to know. Like a man living on a precipice, wanting to reach out yet afraid to make a move and riddled with guilt at being there in the first place. Kate's presence in the house could be felt in every room, whether she was present or not. It was disturbing, to say the very least.

Little things. She'd brought the plants back to life and added fresh potted flowers here and there. They were blooming and thriving, the house regularly filled with color and fragrance. She played the piano beautifully, and often, when he'd open the front door evenings, he'd hear music coming from the library, sometimes Chopin, sometimes show tunes. And laughter. Kate had the remarkable ability to push back the sadness he knew she still felt over her parents' death and put on a happy face for Jamie's sake. The child smiled more and laughed often. It was a welcome change.

Yet when he found himself joining in, smiling in response, in minutes, he'd be overwhelmed with guilt. It was as if he could picture Stephanie looking over his shoulder, asking how he could be laughing with someone else when she'd died in the prime of life a mere few months ago. His wife had never been vindictive or critical, so he knew the scenario had come from inside him. Yet he couldn't seem to turn it off.

Swiveling back toward his desk, he picked up the card his secretary had given him only yesterday. Marge was in her forties, an excellent assistant with the kindest eyes he'd ever seen. The card listed the phone number of a grief support group, one Marge had joined when her sixteen-year-old daughter had died in a hit-and-run auto accident. Apparently, Marge had noticed his mood swings, too.

He tossed aside the card. A group held no appeal for him. He'd get over this on his own. He was a strong man, one who controlled his life, sometimes by sheer willpower. He'd been in a terrible accident himself not all that long ago. That was where he'd met Stephanie, in the hospital he'd been taken to after they'd pried him out of the wreckage that was his car, before she'd been assigned to cardiac care. The doctors had said he might never recover fully. But he'd made up his mind and, a year later, he was playing tennis and running five miles a day. Six months later, he'd married Stephanie.

It hadn't been easy, but then, what was? He'd manage this, too, somehow.

Opening his day planner, Aaron glanced at his appointment schedule. Three o'clock was circled in red. Jamie's checkup at the doctor's office. He frowned, recalling that he'd discussed the appointment with Kate earlier in the week. He'd asked Fitz to take Jamie the past two visits. He couldn't keep passing on his obligations. Kate was too new on the job to go alone with Jamie. He'd have to make the time.

Straightening, Aaron bent to his work, since he'd have to leave early today.

The traffic was heavy, and Aaron was annoyed. They'd be late for Jamie's doctor's appointment if he didn't get home soon. Impatiently, he swerved around a car full of tourists dawdling along gazing at the autumn leaves, and turned onto his street. Minutes later, he was hurrying inside and calling for Kate.

"In here," Kate answered from the kitchen.

He heard Jamie's little giggle as he made his way back. In the doorway, he stopped, stunned at the scene before him. Fitz was removing a cookie sheet from the oven while Kate was icing cookies at the table, and Jamie, seated in her high chair, was apparently helping out. She had icing and cookie dough all over her face, her hands, on the sleeves of her shirt and even in her hair.

A big orange blob was on the end of her nose, making Jamie giggle. She gave Aaron a messy grin as she stuck a gooey finger into her mouth.

"You're home early," Kate said as she finished icing a pumpkin cookie. "Come join us." Hearing no response, she glanced toward the doorway, noticed his stormy expression and felt the smile slide from her face. "Is something wrong?"

"Plenty." Hands on his hips, Aaron marched in. "Jamie's doctor's appointment is in half an hour. I reminded you on Monday to have her ready."

"Oh, no," Kate whispered. "I forgot. I'm sorry." Quickly, she wiped her hands on the dishcloth and reached for the baby. "I'll clean her up and have her ready right away."

"Do you know how hard it is to get these appointments? You have to wait weeks sometimes. I left an important meeting so I could go with you, and I come home to this...this unholy mess and my daughter sugar-coated from stem to stern." His voice was louder than he'd intended, but damn it, he needed her to know how badly she'd upset his schedule. Pointedly, he looked at his watch. "Now we'll never make it."

Unused to yelling, Jamie started to cry. Kate had the protesting baby in her arms, her own face pink with embarrassment. "I'm truly sorry. We'll be right back."

Aaron watched her leave, then slammed his keys on the table. "Damn! Now I'll have to take another day off for this because she forgot."

Fitz stood by the oven, hands on her hips, listening to the man go on. "I seriously doubt that Dr. Benson won't take you if you're a bit late. He's not that sort of man, and besides, you've known one another since boyhood."

"Yeah, well, it's wrong to take advantage of a friendship by showing up late for a professional appointment. Personally, I hate it when my clients are late."

She'd had about enough of his childish behavior. "I've no doubt you do. How do you punish them, refuse to deal with them again?"

Taken aback, Aaron just stared at her.

"You know, when you were rude as a boy and I was watching after you, I'd send you to your room so you could think over what you'd done. What, I wonder, would make a grown man change his ways?"

It took a lot to set off Margaret Fitzmaurice, but she had no fear in speaking up when she saw a wrong that needed correcting. What could he do, fire her? Not likely.

Fitz saw the beginnings of a look of chagrin on Aaron's face, but it wasn't yet enough. "I can't imagine you'd take out your bad temper on that sweet girl. Forgetting something you told her four days ago is hardly a crime where I come from. It's thanking her you should be doing, for watching your little one night and day. She doesn't even take her days off, did you know that?"

Aaron's collar felt a little tight. "Maybe I was a little rash." Angry with himself, he went to stand by the window, looking out but seeing Kate's flushed face. Just hours ago, his father had told him he'd overreacted in a business situation. Now he'd managed to do it again at home.

"'Rash' doesn't cover it. You owe the girl an apology, Aaron. The man I raised would make mistakes but always admit it when he was wrong." She saw his back stiffen and hoped she was getting through to him. "You've a right to grieve, no one will deny that. But you've no right to take out your unhappiness on the people who try to make your life easier."

The oven bell rang. Fitz bent to remove the last batch of cookies, set the pan on the rack to cool and left the kitchen. She'd given him a bit to think about. Now she'd wait to see what he'd do.

He heard her soft, soothing voice before he reached the doorway to Jamie's room. Feeling uncomfortable, for he rarely had to apologize, Aaron paused.

"There, there, sweetie, it's all right," Kate told the sniffling child as she tugged a clean shirt over her head. "Daddy didn't mean to yell and he wasn't angry with you. Never with you, sweet baby." She kissed the curly head and smiled as she noticed that Jamie had stopped that awful hiccuping cry. "Another minute and we'll be finished here." She hurried to change her diaper.

Aaron bit the bullet and walked in. "Kate, I'm sorry." He saw that she didn't turn around, so he stepped nearer. "It's no excuse, but I've had a messy day at the office. I apologize."

Kate blinked as she snapped Jamie's corduroy pant legs together. Why was it that apologies so often made her want to cry along with the guilty party? "It's all right," she told him.

"No, it isn't." He saw his daughter eye him suspiciously, probably wondering if he would start raving again. "I was wrong to yell, wrong to take my mood out on the two of you. I should have called to remind you of the appointment." He touched her arm as she finished diapering and waited until she looked up. "I won't do it again, I promise."

Kate managed a smile. "No harm done, and we're ready. I'll just get her jacket. Her diaper bag's packed."

Cautiously, he picked Jamie up, hoping she wouldn't start to cry again. He was in luck, as his red tie grabbed her attention.

"I hope you don't mind going with me. I've never taken her to the doctor alone." Frankly, he was worried that Benson would ask him a question about his daughter that he couldn't answer. "It's just a wellness check. Shouldn't be a problem."

Kate stood in the doorway with bag and jacket. "We'll be fine. Let's go."

Aaron nuzzled Jamie's warm neck, inhaling her baby-powdery scent. "I'll make it up to you, sweetheart," he whispered.

Dr. Ronald Benson stuffed his stethoscope into the pocket of his white lab coat, pushed his black-framed glasses higher up on his nose and turned to his old friend standing at the foot of the examining table. "She's a healthy little specimen, Aaron. I see no major problems."

Aaron watched his diaper-clad daughter play with the tongue depressor the doctor had handed her to divert her attention during the exam. "Well, that's good news."

"There is one thing I want to ask. Does she ever pull at her ears? Do you notice any drainage on the crib sheets?"

Puzzled, Aaron turned to Kate, who was standing at the head of the table. "I don't think so. Do you?"

"No drainage, Doctor," Kate answered, "but occasionally she tugs at her right ear. I always swab both ears out after her bath, and she doesn't act as if she's in pain. No fever, either.''

Benson nodded. "Good. Yes, that's the ear. It's a little sore looking, though I don't believe it's infected, not yet anyway.''

"Infected?" Aaron asked. "Jamie has an ear infection?''

"She may be developing one. We'll keep an eye on her. I don't want to put her on an antibiotic too soon, since her system might get immune to it and water down the effect later." He saw Aaron's frown and patted his shoulder. "It's not unusual for children to get ear infections, Aaron. If they persist, we often insert a tube to help drainage and prevent injury to the eardrum. Most kids outgrow them by age five. I just wanted to mention the possibility, but I'm not concerned yet. It appears to me that she's well taken care of.''

Subdued, Aaron looked at his daughter, who'd given up on the tongue depressor, crawled to the far side and was holding out her arms to Kate to be picked up.

Kate could see that Aaron was a little hurt that the baby had reached for her instead of her father. It was only because Jamie spent nearly every waking moment with her, while Aaron was rarely around. She held her a moment before turning to Aaron. "Would you like to dress her?''

Feeling oddly left out, Aaron shook his head. "No, you go ahead.'' He walked out with Ron Benson. "So you think there's nothing to worry about, right?''

"Absolutely." The doctor stopped in the hallway. "And if Jamie did have a problem, I have a feeling that young lady you've hired would manage just fine. She seems to care a great deal for the child.''

"Yes, she does." And she also knew far more about his daughter than he himself did. That didn't set well with Aaron. He'd been so preoccupied trying to overcome the loss of his wife that he hadn't bothered to get to know Jamie.

That would have to change, Aaron decided as he waited for Kate to join him.

Kate tried not to laugh out loud. She totally lost the battle not to smile. But it wasn't every day that she witnessed a grown man down on all fours playing horsey with his little girl. If only his partners could see him now, she thought, her mouth twitching as she stood in the doorway of the family room while Aaron jogged around the big, free-form coffee table with a giggling Jamie on his back.

He'd been quiet on the ride home from the doctor's. Jamie had fallen asleep in her car seat, and Kate had respected his mood, occupying herself by looking out the window at the colorful leaves drifting down and covering the lawns. At home, she'd put the baby down for a late nap, then gone in to start dinner.

Ever since discovering that Fitz didn't much care for cooking, Kate had spent some time going through Stephanie's collection of cookbooks. Gradually, she'd taken over most of the cooking chores and found she enjoyed experimenting in the kitchen. Aaron still rarely ate dinner with them, but she always made enough and left a plate for him.

Today, because he didn't return to the office and said he'd have dinner at home, she'd made a special meal. She'd had Fitz buy the ingredients some time ago and had been waiting for the right evening. The aroma of Cornish game hens baking had soon filled the downstairs.

She'd served them with stuffing and sweet potatoes, baby peas and cucumbers in dill sauce.

She'd surprised Aaron, who'd eaten with a healthy appetite for the first time since her arrival. Even Fitz had taken seconds. Jamie had become less fussy at mealtimes, as well. It had turned out to be a nice dinner.

And she'd noticed that Aaron had moved his chair close to Jamie's, had cut up her food and coaxed her to take bites of game hen when she wanted to play with the peas on her tray. Kate was pleased to see his increased interest in his daughter. She'd known all along that Jamie would blossom with more attention, and she had, no longer looking so sad and lost, smiling often and beginning to happily chatter away in her own language.

Kate had enjoyed the dinner hour, thinking that the four of them seemed like a family. Oh, she knew she wasn't really a part of the Carver family, not even as much as Fitz was. She knew, too, that one day Aaron would be bringing someone home, that special woman who would be his second wife and Jamie's stepmother. He was far too young and handsome to live out the rest of his life alone. After just a little over a month caring for the adorable little girl, already Kate felt a sharp pain at the thought of having to turn Jamie over to another woman.

Now, watching Aaron roll his daughter from his back to the floor and begin to tickle her, listening to their mingled laughter, felt another, more confusing emotion as she gazed at the father. Aaron Carver was a very attractive man, one who easily could set any woman's heart to beating rapidly. He was kind and thoughtful, and he was man enough to apologize when he was wrong. He was very much the type of man she'd hoped one day to find.

But he was still in love with his dead wife.

Which was why Kate had to keep her distance as much as possible, considering that they lived under the same roof. She mustn't get her hopes up or her heart involved. Certainly, one day he'd get over Stephanie, but he'd undoubtedly reach out to a woman who was more like his first wife had been. A strong, successful career woman who could decorate a house and give fabulous parties with as much ease as she could head up the cardiac-nursing staff.

Still, she could dream, Kate thought as she watched Jamie muss her father's hair. It would feel soft, she imagined, and silklike threading through her fingers. He was still wearing his white dress shirt, the sleeves rolled up on muscular arms, his shoulders seemingly a mile wide. Her fingers itched to trace those strong muscles, to caress those shoulders and the vulnerable nape of his neck before getting lost in the thickness of his hair, and…

With a start, Kate straightened, her face heating. What on earth had come over her? she wondered as she stepped into the room, hoping Aaron couldn't read her mind. "Hey, guys, I think maybe it's time for Jamie's bath."

Aaron picked up his daughter and got to his feet. "Is everything all right?" he asked Kate. "You look a little flushed." The heightened color looked good on her, actually. Sometimes she seemed so pale, but lately, the sad bouts were fewer and further between.

Kate touched her cheeks and knew he was right. "It's warm in here, that's all. Do you want to bathe her?"

"I'd like to help." He wasn't sure he could manage alone just yet.

"All right. Follow me."

\* \* \*

Though he'd rolled up his sleeves and knelt on a rug alongside the tub as he washed his squirming child, by the time Jamie's bath was over, Aaron was nearly as wet as she was. Nevertheless, he smiled at his daughter as he bundled her into a soft pink bath towel with a hooded corner, which he slipped over her head. He carried her to her room and laid her down on the change table, then began patting her dry.

"No wonder Fitz couldn't keep up with this little dynamo," he commented as he struggled to keep her from squirming off. "You have to be in darn good shape to cope with her day in and day out."

"You can say that again," Kate said, handing him a diaper. Next came the footed pajamas. Aaron looked at the pajama top as if it were a foreign object. "Do they snap in front or back?"

"Back. Then snap the bottoms to the top. Next comes the blanket sleeper, but that zips up."

"Won't she be too hot?" he asked, trying to stuff an uncooperative arm into a sleeve while Jamie jabbered at him and pulled at his nose with her other hand.

"Not really. Don't you sleep in pajamas and cover with a blanket?" The moment the words were out, she regretted them. For the third time this day, her cheeks flamed as she turned aside to search for Jamie's blanket sleeper. "Forget I said that," she muttered.

Aaron was enjoying her discomfort. "Actually, I don't wear pajamas, and a sheet's usually plenty for me. I'm warm-blooded so, naturally, I thought my daughter would be, too."

"Perhaps she will be when she grows up. For now, she tosses off her covers, which is why a blanket sleeper is best. She won't catch a chill, because she can't remove it.'' Lord, when would she learn to control her runaway mouth?

Finished dressing his daughter, Aaron gathered her into his arms. But he wasn't finished teasing Kate. "Do *you* sleep in pajamas?" he asked, an innocent look on his face. "Inquiring minds want to know."

"I think that's probably irrelevant." But she was smiling, not at what he'd asked, but at the fact that he was in a kidding mood. It was the first time, ever, with her. With no small effort, Kate pulled her gaze from his laughing face to the sweet-smelling baby. "Are you ready for your ba-ba?" From behind her back, she produced Jamie's nighttime bottle. Sleepily, she reached for it. Kate let her take it, then stepped back to switch on the night-light and turn off the overhead light.

Aaron moved to the crib and laid her down, arranging her stuffed animals around the foot of the crib and tucking Elmo the dog to her side. He smiled at his daughter as she began to drink her milk, her eyes already heavy. "See you in the morning, sweetheart." He backed out the door, leaving it slightly ajar, and found Kate in the hallway.

"I'll say good-night, then," Kate said, walking toward her room.

"Wait." Picking at his damp shirt, he followed her down the hall, then stopped in front of her. "I just want to thank you."

"For what? I didn't do anything."

"Yes, you did. You and Fitz forced me to look at myself and you put me back in touch with my daughter. I want you to know I'll try not to let so much distance build between us again."

He was close enough for her to recognize the distinctive masculine scent he wore. Close enough to cause her to take a step back. "I'm glad, Aaron."

"She's not the child she was when you arrived. You've made her happy. It's wonderful to hear her laughing. I . . . I'd let my problems take over, and it seemed I had nothing left for Jamie. I mean to do better."

"That's good. She adores you."

"You're very good for her." And very bad for me, he thought. In the dim light, she looked pale once more and very lovely. No matter the hour, early morning or late evening, she always looked serene and very beautiful. He envied that in her. He envied the man who would win her heart.

"Thanks for saying that. I truly enjoy being with Jamie."

"Well, it shows." He shuffled his feet, glanced at his own room across the hall. He didn't want to leave her, yet he had no right to remain with her. Guilt washed over him more surely than Jamie's bathwater had, and he felt as if he were drowning.

Abruptly, he turned. "Good night." Swiftly, he left her, going into his room and closing the door quietly behind him.

Kate stood for long minutes staring after him, wishing he wasn't so troubled, wanting badly to make the pain go away, for both of them.

*Fall 1981*

*It is three years since we left Mexico with Christopher in tow, Sloan and I. We returned to Michigan and made a family. Chris turned out to be quite healthy, despite his ordeal, and just as bright as his father. True to his word, although he returned to his work, Sloan works long hours daily trying to locate my three missing children. The waiting is a living nightmare.*

*Running down leads obtained through painstaking work can be devastating as each ends in failure. False hope, followed by frustration, begins to be a way of life. It eats at the fabric of a relationship. It is to Sloan's credit that he is so understanding, so very patient with me. At times, I weep with the futility of our search and I question my faith. But Sloan never allows me to give up.*

*We lived together over a year with Sloan begging me weekly to marry him. I loved him then as I do now, but I wanted the wedding to take place after we located my three. It was not to be. Finally, I could hold out no longer. I had no right to continue refusing this good and kind man, nor his son, who sorely wanted a real mother that he could call his own. We were married last year. The absence of my own children was the only damper as I became an autumn bride, making me Julia Bradford.*

*Sloan has taught me the meaning of faith and patience and a love that never gives up. He claims that I've taught him to trust a woman again after his terrible first marriage. In many ways, God has blessed us with a second chance at love and happiness and a true partnership.*

*Yet there is still something missing. Or rather someone—three someones. Despite all my present treasures and my new family, I will never truly draw a happy breath until Michael and Hannah and Kate are reunited with me and become a part of this wonderful union.*

*I pray daily, hourly, that it will happen soon.*

## Chapter Four

The days were getting shorter, Aaron noticed as he drove toward home. Five o'clock and it was already almost dark. Of course, it was the last day of October.

He hadn't intended to leave the office quite so early. He'd been putting in long hours lately for several reasons. To make up for the weeks he'd been only half-there, feeling numb and useless; to catch up on work that had waited for him; and more important, so he wouldn't spend too many cozy hours with Kate.

The family scene worked on him as nothing else could have. He'd grown up in a household with only one parent, his father doing the best he could to raise two sons, with Fitz's help. Aaron had wanted more for his child, for his marriage. And he'd had that, for a while, with Stephanie and Jamie.

Of course, he and Stephanie had argued now and then. All couples squabbled occasionally, especially if both parties were Type-A personalities. The major disagreement he and Stephanie had had was about her job. Aaron had wanted her to ease up on the hours she worked, especially after Jamie had come along. His wife had insisted she had as much right to a career as he did. Stalemate.

Aaron's jaw clenched as he remembered with deep regret a quarrel they'd had shortly before Stephanie had taken ill. To this day, he wished he hadn't said the hurtful things he'd told her, wished he hadn't stormed out and left her there crying. Soon after, when she'd gotten so sick, he'd realized belatedly that their argument hadn't been so very important after all, and his temper tantrum had left him with even more guilt.

Basically, though, his memories of their marriage and the home life they shared were good. Which was why the recent dinners around the kitchen table—with Fitz telling one of her long-winded but humorous stories, Jamie jabbering in her high chair and the wonderful cooking smells filling the room—made him wistful. Wistful at all that he'd lost, sad that the bright, smiling woman who'd been his wife all too briefly was no longer in their home and guilty that he was alive and enjoying himself.

Aaron turned onto his street, chastising himself for feeling as he did. Mentally, he knew better. The living had to get on with their lives, as his father told him all too frequently. But emotionally, he was caught in a web of his own making.

Since that evening when he'd made up his mind to be a better father to Jamie, he had made improvements. These days, when he walked into the house, if she was still awake, Jamie would come barreling toward him, crawling as fast as she could, jabbering a greeting. He'd kept his temper in check at work and even more so at home, being deliberately considerate of both of the women who worked for him.

Fitz was the only woman who'd ever been able to point out the error of his ways to Aaron and make him feel like a small, delinquent boy again. He could see she approved of the change in him. But it was Kate who worried him.

Or rather, his feelings for Kate.

He enjoyed her, plain and simple. Being around her, talking with her, listening to her, laughing with her. Always, when they were together, Jamie was with them, and often Fitz, too. They were never alone. Why, then, did he feel disloyal to Stephanie for even entertaining warm thoughts about Kate? Damned if he knew.

In the approaching dusk, he saw that several children in costume, followed by their parents, were going from house to house. A jack-o'-lantern next door to his home sat atop a thick post covered with a sheet. Porch lights were ablaze, and childish voices were calling out "trick or treat" threats to all who opened their doors.

It was Halloween night, and both Fitz and Kate had implored him to be home early for Jamie's first beggars' night. He pulled into his circular driveway and hurried inside, slipping off his jacket and tie. As usual, he found them in the kitchen. Walking in, he had to smile.

Jamie was seated on the counter wearing a billowy white clown's costume, the shiny material liberally sprinkled with pink-and-purple dots. A pointed silver hat was fastened to her head with a chin strap. And much to his surprise, she was holding very still while Kate finished applying red circles to her cheeks and adding a bulbous nose.

"Hi," Kate called out. "You're just in time. We're almost ready." She straightened, examining her handiwork. "What do you think?"

Aaron grinned at his daughter as he grabbed his suede jacket from the back hall closet. "Gorgeous. Absolutely gorgeous."

"And what a good girl she is, holding still while Katie made her beautiful," Fitz added. Then, hearing the doorbell ring, she picked up the basket of popcorn balls and candy bars, carrying them to the front to greet the little visitors.

Aaron lifted his daughter from the counter. "No mask?" he asked Kate.

"She wouldn't leave it on even if we had one. Besides, they're dangerous. She couldn't see very well with it on and could fall." Jamie was walking now as long as someone held her hand.

"I'll stay here and hold down the fort," Fitz said by the front door. "You three go on now and bring home some new goodies."

"Wave bye-bye," Kate reminded Jamie, and she did, though she was busily eyeing the candy basket on the hall table.

"I didn't know you could wave bye-bye," Aaron admitted, settling her more comfortably into the crook of his arm. Every week, it seemed, she learned something new.

"For a couple of days now." Kate smiled at a ghost and a ballerina coming up the walk toward Fitz. "Are you going to carry her?" she asked Aaron.

"I think so. The houses around here are far apart. She'll get too tired. I'll set her down when we get close to the doors." He fell in step with Kate as he gazed up at a cold but clear evening sky. "Nice out."

"Yes. I can hardly wait till it snows. Jamie's never played in it. Do you have a sled?"

He hadn't given it much thought, but the idea of playing in the snow with his daughter, maybe making a snowman, appealed to him. "No, but I'll get her one, maybe for Christmas."

Christmas. He'd been dreading the holidays, remembering last Christmas with Stephanie pregnant, the future looking so bright. Aaron swallowed hard and walked on.

There was that look again, Kate thought, glancing up at Aaron. Probably brought on by the mention of Christmas. This would be a difficult holiday for her, too. Maybe they could help each other through the bad moments.

Gazing around, she spotted something that she hoped would make Aaron smile. "Look at the two coming toward us." She pointed out the little girl dressed like an angel, complete with a halo that was tipped sideways on her head. The boy was the caped crusader and wore tights on his skinny little legs and a blue shirt with a big red *S* emblazoned on his thin chest. He had a protective arm around the girl as they passed them. The father trailing after nodded to them as he puffed on his pipe.

"Cute," Aaron commented. "You know, it occurs to me that I don't know my neighbors, not hardly a one." Several had sent notes of condolence, and a few had stopped by when Stephanie had died, but that whole time was like a blur. His father and Fitz had handled visitors for him.

"Well, you work long hours." She turned toward the first house and held out a bright orange plastic pumpkin with a black handle for Jamie. "Go get 'em, sweetie."

Aaron carried her up to the porch, then set her down and, holding her hand, rang the bell. He called out, "Trick or treat." In moments, a tall, bearded man came to the door with a large bowl.

"Mr. Carver. Good to see you." He opened the screen and stepped out, offering his hand. "Matt Bennett."

"It's Aaron, and thank you, Matt."

With a smile, Matt bent down. "What a pretty little clown. What's your name?"

"Jamie," Aaron answered for her as he helped his daughter hold out her pumpkin.

Matt placed a generous handful of packaged jelly beans into the pumpkin. "Don't eat all those at once." He looked past Aaron at Kate standing on the sidelines, his expression filled with curiosity.

"Let's go back to your nanny," Aaron said pointedly as he hoisted up his daughter together with her loot. He didn't owe the man an explanation about Kate, yet he gave one anyway. He wanted no gossip to get started that he was dating and his wife barely gone.

Yet strolling from the house, he felt silly having rushed to justify Kate's presence, as if they'd been doing something wrong. It was none of his neighbors' business whom Aaron chose to see. Annoyed with himself, he walked on.

Kate had to hurry to keep up with Aaron's long strides. What had set him off this time? she wondered. Aaron was like the walking wounded, always ready to take another self-inflicted hit. He would never recover if he continued to be so hard on himself.

Eventually, he cooled off and slowed down. They made their way along the street, both getting a kick out of the children dressed in a variety of costumes. A couple more neighbors recognized Aaron and stopped to say a few words. He was not unfriendly but not very warm, either. He felt oddly out of place and wished he could join in wholeheartedly.

It wasn't until they'd crossed the street and begun their journey back toward home that he had his first hearty laugh. They were on the porch of a wide Colonial when Jamie decided she'd had enough of everyone putting treats in her plastic pumpkin yet allowing her to eat none. She sat her solid little bottom down on the walk and refused to budge, holding a piece of candy tightly in one little fist while she shook her head at her father as he tried to coax her up.

Kate couldn't stifle a laugh. "I'd say she knows what she wants and she wants to eat that *now.*"

Aaron looked skeptical as he watched the boy go back inside. "Do you think it's all right to let her eat that? I mean, you read all these stories about pins placed in apples and poisoned candy. We don't know any of these people."

Kate, too, had her misgivings. There were so many crazies out there. "It looks all right, but it's probably best not to take a chance. Let's give her something that's wrapped from the manufacturer, and she'll give up the candy corn. She just wants to sample something."

A good compromise, Aaron thought as he found a small, soft candy bar, peeled back the wrapping and held it out to Jamie. She immediately dropped the one she'd been holding and took the open bar, taking a huge bite. Giving a chocolaty grin, she allowed Aaron to pick her up.

He laughed out loud. "Stubborn little thing got her way."

Kate decided to take a chance with a teasing remark. "Wouldn't take after her father, would she?"

His eyebrows rose in mock surprise. "Who, me, stubborn? Surely you jest."

The curb was high at this end of the street. Carrying Jamie, Aaron took Kate's hand to help her down and across. Her fingers were like ice. "You're cold. We'd better head back."

His fingers were warm. She wanted to curl hers around and keep the contact. "I'm fine, really."

He noticed she wouldn't meet his eyes. Reluctantly, he dropped her hand. "I think this little one's had enough Halloween anyhow."

They passed the tall shrubs and came to the winding driveway leading to his front door. Aaron smiled as he noticed the gray Lincoln parked behind his Mercedes. "Looks like Grandpa had to come over and share in Jamie's first Halloween."

Following him up the walk, Kate wondered what Aaron's father was like and how he'd view her caring for his only grandchild.

There were five seated around the large oak kitchen table that seemed to be the heart of the house, Kate thought. In her high chair, still wearing her costume, her makeup a bit smudged by now, Jamie sat happily munching on her candy between sips of milk. After snapping half a dozen pictures, the adults had their own treat, courtesy of William Carver—fresh doughnuts and cider.

"Jamie has the makings of a chocoholic like her father before her," Fitz commented as the child licked her messy fingers.

"And his father before him," William admitted. Finishing a chocolate-iced doughnut, he wiped his hands on a napkin. "Chocolate is nature's most perfect food, right, Jamie?'' He smiled at his sticky-faced granddaughter.

"I'd heard that was milk," Fitz interjected, and poured herself a cup of tea, which she much preferred over cider.

"Not true," William insisted. He turned to Kate, who was urging the baby to take a drink to wash down her candy. "What about you, Kate? Are you fond of chocolate?"

"Certainly. It's un-American not to be, isn't it?" She'd liked Aaron's father on the spot, thinking that his son would look exactly like him one day, a not unpleasant forecast. Only, William had tiny laugh lines at the corners of his eyes, and Aaron had none, which she doubted had much to do with age. Maybe in time, Aaron would learn to laugh more.

Aaron had told his father all that he knew about Kate's background, and William sympathized with the young woman who'd lost both parents so suddenly. "I understand your folks had a cottage around here somewhere. I'm wondering if we ever met."

"The cottage is on Pine near the boat harbor. You might have met my father, Dr. George Spencer. But Mom didn't come up as often. He liked to get away from the hospital weekends, but she was a realtor, and weekends were her busiest times."

"Of course," William said, recalling an immaculately groomed blonde. "Carol Spencer. She was a member of the Symphony League, right?" He'd been a symphony patron for years.

Kate nodded. "Yes, that's right."

"That's where I met her. A lovely woman. You resemble her a great deal."

Everyone said so, even the ones who knew she was adopted. "Thank you. You never met Dad?"

An astute observer and a very good listener, William thought he detected more warmth in her voice when she mentioned her father than her mother. He was seldom wrong. "I'm afraid not." He eyed a second doughnut, made up his mind and chose one without icing this time.

Fitz shook her head. "Will you look at the man? Two doughnuts and he hasn't gained a pound since I've known him."

William smiled, then glanced at his son. "You're finally picking up some of the weight you'd lost, Aaron. Looks good on you."

"It's due to Kate's cooking," Fitz interjected. "She's got all of us looking forward to mealtime, even the little one."

"Yeah, she's a terrific cook," Aaron chimed in. He noticed a small streak of lipstick on Kate's cheek, undoubtedly from when she'd applied Jamie's makeup. Incongruously, only half listening to the table conversation, he'd been thinking he'd like to take her aside and clean off that small spot. He was smart enough to know that cleaning the smudge was just an excuse to touch her. He dropped his gaze to his glass, hoping his thoughts didn't show.

"You must enjoy cooking," William went on to Kate, knowing that meal preparation wasn't exactly in the job description for most nannies, although Fitz had certainly done her share.

"I do. I experiment with recipes while Jamie naps." Taking the washcloth, she swiped at the baby's hands as the child yawned expansively. "And speaking of naps, I think she's ready for a quick bath and bed, if that's all right with everyone."

"Of course." William rose and went over to plant a kiss on his granddaughter's blond head. "You make a lovely clown, Jamie. Where'd she get this outfit? Did you make it, Fitz?"

"Not I," the older woman answered. "I'm quite clumsy with a needle these days. Katie bought the material herself and put it together."

William watched Kate remove the high-chair tray. "You are indeed talented."

Kate hefted Jamie into her arms. "I had a nanny named Glynis who taught me to sew. She was very special." She smiled at the smeared little face. "Shall we go around and say good-night to everyone?"

While Kate toted Jamie to each person for a sloppy kiss, William stood back watching. Kate had had a nanny growing up, and now she *was* a nanny. A doctor's daughter. Interesting. He wondered if his son knew the story behind the woman who cared for his child.

"I'll be up in a bit to tuck her in," Aaron told Kate.

"Fine. It was good meeting you," she said to William, then left with the still-chattering baby.

"She's a wonder, that girl," Fitz commented as she began to clear the table. "Aaron, you haven't had your dinner. There's chicken salad in the fridge that Kate made this morning. And homemade soup. Can I heat you some?"

Aaron drained his cider and shoved back his chair. "Later, maybe."

William reached for his coat. "I think those doughnuts *were* my dinner."

"Look at him, Fitz," Aaron teased, "the minute his grandchild leaves the room, he's ready to go home."

"Maybe Johnny will give you a couple more one day," Fitz added, though she doubted that Aaron's younger brother would ever settle down.

"Now, that would be a real shock," William said with a laugh.

"Where is Johnny these days?" Aaron asked, walking to the door with his father.

"Let's see, I believe he's working on an oil rig that he bought into," William answered, not bothering to disguise his skepticism. "Or perhaps an old gold mine. I forget, offhand."

Aaron was a cynic when it came to his irresponsible brother. But he tried not to let it show. "Well, I hope he makes it."

"Don't we all." William said good-night to Fitz, then turned to his son. "It's good to see you looking better, Aaron."

"Yeah, thanks." Now, if only his attitude were better.

Kate was in the kitchen pulling off Jamie's snowsuit when she heard the front door open. Pushing the stroller, she'd taken the little girl down the boardwalk to feed the ducks, and they'd been gone about half an hour. She could hear Fitz vacuuming upstairs, so it had to be Aaron, the only other person who had a key. But it was only four in the afternoon.

Aaron walked in, shrugged out of his leather jacket and greeted them both, taking Jamie and hugging her to him.

"Is everything all right?" Kate asked, thinking he seemed a bit nervous.

"Yeah, why?" He kissed Jamie's chilly cheek and placed her in the playpen.

"I don't know. You look as if you have something on your mind." And it worried Kate. The sadness she'd lived with for weeks was lifting from her little by little, mostly due to the child she'd grown to care for more each day. She steadfastly refused to think of having to turn Jamie over to someone else one day. But Aaron's face was so serious. Was he going to let her go? The thought of having to leave had her heart thumping.

"I do." Wondering where to begin, Aaron pulled out a kitchen chair and sat down. "I need to ask you something."

Her eyes on the snowsuit she was folding, Kate braced herself. "All right."

Aaron cleared his throat and plunged in. "I've been working on a special project for months, a shopping mall I've designed. We're about to unveil the scale model of the design tonight at a presentation to the corporate officers who commissioned the work. A lot of people will be there—financiers, underwriters, investors, the board of directors, even the press. It's going to take place tonight at seven at the Seabreeze Inn."

He saw that she'd scarcely moved since he'd begun his recitation, her expression a mixture of anxiety and curiosity. He imagined she was wondering what all that had to do with her. He wasn't sure himself.

It was his father's fault. William had stated this morning that he felt it would be a good idea if Aaron brought a date to the presentation, and he'd suggested Kate. Not as in a real date, but as a platonic, supportive friend. Wives and significant others would be present at the black-tie event, and his dad thought it wouldn't hurt if he had someone at his side. Family men tended to respect other family men.

He could have objected, Aaron was aware. It hadn't been presented as an order, by any means. But he could see the value in his father's suggestion. And he knew that Kate would be an asset to any gathering. He'd wanted to object on other grounds, the ones his father knew nothing about. That being in close proximity to Kate for hours would set his nerves humming and his hands to sweating.

Naturally, he couldn't tell his father that. Instead, he'd decided to ask Kate and, if she said she'd go, he'd make the best of the evening. And he'd pray he could keep his mind on the presentation instead of the woman who even now was looking at him with huge, hesitant eyes.

Aaron ran a hand through his hair. "I'm telling this badly. The fact is, I'd like you to come with me." There, he'd finally gotten it out.

She stared at him, dumbfounded. "Go with you? You mean you're taking Jamie and you want me along to watch her?"

"No, this has nothing to do with Jamie. Fitz will stay with her, I'm sure. You would be with me. Dad will be there. He's very impressed with you."

This invitation had come out of the blue, and Kate didn't know what to make of it. Aaron hadn't made it sound like a date. More as though she was to accompany him to a company function. Surely, he knew lots of women. Why her? She searched his face and almost asked out loud.

Then the answer came to her. She was safe. She knew him fairly well, knew he wasn't ready for an involvement. So being with her was easy. Also, probably his father had suggested her. Fine. It wasn't exactly the invitation she'd dreamed of, truth be known, but why not go? She hadn't been out among people at a formal gathering in months. She adored Jamie, but a part of her longed for an evening of adult conversation.

It might even turn out to be fun.

She'd been quiet an awfully long time. Aaron hoped he hadn't somehow hurt her feelings. "Aren't you going to say something? I mean, I..."

"I accept."

His expression changed from worried to surprised and finally pleased. "You do? That's great." Now that the hard part was over, he smiled. "I'll go ask Fitz if she can handle things here, but I'm sure she'll agree. Can you be ready about six-thirty?"

Her mind was racing. Four-thirty now. She had two hours. She'd take a bath, fix her hair. "Yes," she said, realizing he was waiting for her answer.

"Do you have something, you know, formal-like, to wear? We can run into town if you don't and—"

"No problem."

Of course she would. She'd grown up in Grosse Pointe, a very wealthy city, the daughter of a doctor. Even around the house, she dressed in expensive clothes, name brands. He felt like an idiot for having asked. Chagrined, he touched her arm. "I didn't mean to insult you."

The man was a dichotomy, sometimes so strong and in control, other times as hesitant as a small boy. She smiled at him. "You didn't. I'd better get going if you want me ready on time. Will you get Fitz to come down to Jamie?"

"Right away." He started to leave, then turned back. "Thanks, Kate. I appreciate you helping me out."

"Sure." She watched him dash off. Helping him out. A business meeting, that was all. *Don't make too much of it,* she warned herself.

* * *

Willie's on the Waterfront was a seafood restaurant situated at the east side of Port Huron overlooking the St. Clair River. At ten on a weeknight, only three tables were occupied. The one in the far corner was where Aaron and Kate sat finishing a late supper of shrimp, clams and oysters.

Kate wiped her hands on the snowy white linen napkin and sat back with a sigh. "That's positively the best seafood dinner I've had in years."

Aaron dipped his fingers in the small bowl with a floating lemon slice and reached for his napkin. "I thought you'd like this place. You know the food's good in a restaurant the locals discover and want to keep quiet about. You rarely see a tourist in here."

And he was glad the restaurant wasn't crowded tonight. He enjoyed being alone with Kate, looking at her. She was wearing a black cocktail dress with a single long strand of pearls, the simplicity of the classic look a perfect complement to her blond beauty. He'd had trouble keeping his eyes off her all evening.

Sipping her hot tea, Kate studied him over the rim of her cup. Lord, but he was handsome. Some men looked like undertakers in a tux, and others like fat penguins. Aaron looked as if he'd been born to wear one. The oil lamp on the table flickered, reflecting in his dark eyes, which had seemed never to leave her face all evening. It was almost as if he hadn't really noticed her until tonight.

The presentation had been most impressive. The large red-and-gold room had been decorated with fresh flowers, while strolling musicians had played softly in the background. Businessmen in formal attire and their wives, dressed to the nines, sipped champagne and applauded when the mock-up of the planned shopping center had been unveiled. Modestly, Aaron had accepted congratulations from everyone. She'd been proud to be at his side.

And he'd kept her there, nearby but not quite touching.

Aaron pushed back his plate and leaned forward. "Have I thanked you yet for rescuing me from what would have been a truly dull evening if you hadn't come along?"

She set down her cup. "I didn't find it all that dull."

"Probably because half the people in the room knew you." He'd been floored when more than a dozen had come up to Kate, many offering condolences over her parents' death, others just glad to see her and asking where she'd been hiding. "I had no idea you have so many friends up this way."

Kate had seen how surprised both Aaron and his father had been that she'd known anyone, much less quite a few. "My father owned the Pine Street cottage since before I was born, and some of the people I spoke with tonight also have homes in Grosse Pointe. Dad wasn't crazy about the social scene, but Mother thrived on it. I met most of them through parties she gave, plus I went to school with their sons and daughters. It's sort of a cliquish community."

Until tonight, Aaron had been too self-absorbed to have much interest in Kate's background other than what he already knew. But her popularity had aroused his curiosity, especially in one area. "You can tell me to mind my own business if you like, but I'm curious about something. Obviously, Dr. and Mrs. Spencer were well-off, ran in a monied circle and probably owned several homes and so on. How is it, then, that you, their only child, aren't living in their undoubtedly lovely Grosse Pointe home with all that went with it?''

Kate kept her eyes on her plate. "It's a long story and not a very pretty one." She hated talking about what had happened, hated even thinking about it.

"If you don't want to say, it's all right."

She supposed he deserved to know, living as they were in such close quarters. He'd been pretty up-front with her. "I don't know if you're aware that most doctors, men like my father was, are truly devoted to their patients and deeply involved in medicine, always studying new procedures and keeping up with changes. The running of their practice is the last thing they want to do. So, most often, they turn that and the management of their investments over to an office manager, often their wives or someone they trust implicitly."

"I've heard doctors are notoriously bad money managers."

"Dad was like that, so he let his brother, my uncle Tom, handle everything. But there was a problem, something Uncle Tom was careful Dad never knew. He didn't like me, nor had he been in favor of them adopting me. Tom's wife died years ago, but he has a daughter, Pam, who's my age and a terrific person. Tom does okay as an accountant, but he couldn't hold a candle to Dad, moneywise. I'm sure he envied Dad's easy spending. He also wanted Pam to inherit everything. However, I was later told, when they adopted me, Dad told Tom to add my name to all their holdings. The trouble is that, unknown to Mom or Dad, Tom never quite got around to it."

Aaron raised a shocked brow. "Are you saying that, behind your parents' back, your uncle cheated you out of your rightful share of the estate?"

"Worse than that. He put *his* name and Pam's on everything."

"How'd he manage to do that, forge the signatures?"

"Didn't have to. Dad had trusted his brother and given him power of attorney over his investments. So, after the funeral when we all met at the attorney's office for the reading of the will, I was truly shocked. Tom was hatefully smug, and Pam ran out of the office crying. Her disappointment in her father was clear, but she hasn't found the courage to stand up to him. He manipulates her like he did my father, with practiced charm and empty promises. Tom even saw to it that his daughter owns the bookstore that Dad had meant to be mine. Quite a mess, eh?" Her mouth felt dry and her heart heavy. Kate took a drink of water.

Aaron was incensed. "You can't take this lying down. There are things you can do, challenge the will, hire an attorney who can prove what Tom did. Get witnesses who heard your father's intentions and would testify on your behalf. Surely, you're not going to let him get away with this."

Kate let out a ragged sigh. "I don't want to fight. I loved my parents but, as Tom pointed out, I'm not related to them by blood. He and Pam are. Let them have everything. I'll manage."

Angry on her behalf, Aaron leaned closer. "This isn't about getting by. It's about justice and fair play."

Her hands were trembling, as they always did when she had to think about it all. "Please, let's drop this. I don't want to do anything more about it."

Aaron disliked being pushed, so he wasn't about to push Kate. He would drop it for now. Perhaps later, when the death of her parents wasn't still an open wound, he'd talk to her again. "All right." He looked around and signaled the waiter. "Looks like we're the last ones to leave."

While he settled the bill, Kate composed herself. There was no point in dwelling on the past, she reminded herself. By the time they walked to the car across the graveled parking lot in the cool night air, she felt better.

Aaron opened the door for her and stepped aside. In the dim light from the street lamp, he thought she looked so beautiful and so vulnerable. "I didn't mean to make you sad all over again."

"You didn't. I had a lovely evening." She stared up at him and saw his head start to bend toward her. She waited, guessing his intention. She wanted him to kiss her, had for some weeks. But suddenly, he straightened quickly, catching himself. Kate turned away, disappointed but understanding. Ducking inside, she pulled her coat around her chilly legs.

But they weren't nearly as chilly as she felt inside at that moment.

## Chapter Five

It was becoming a habit, and Aaron wasn't certain that was all to the good. He glanced at his watch and saw that it was three-thirty in the afternoon, and he was already heading for home. He'd been in meetings all day with a management team at Metropolitan, discussing a banking center that they were planning. The project was in the early stages, but they'd accomplished a great deal today, laying the groundwork for the initial drawings. When they'd finished, Aaron had seen no point in driving clear across town back to the office so late in the day.

Or so he'd told himself.

The real reason, he grudgingly admitted in the car, was that he looked forward to going home to Jamie and Kate. His home was once more warm and inviting. The stereo was often playing, the house filled with music. Once he'd caught Kate with Jamie in her arms, dancing to a Bea-

tles tune on the terrazzo floor of the den as his daughter
laughed joyously.

Another time, he'd found them both sprawled on the
family-room floor in front of the television set. The big
purple dinosaur was strutting his stuff, while their two
blond heads were bent over a coloring book. Still another day, he'd arrived home to find Kate icing cupcakes
in the kitchen and Jamie adding the colored sprinkles,
which tumbled to the tiled floor with increased regularity. He'd laughed out loud at his daughter's face smudged
with icing.

And it had felt good. Spontaneous laughter had been
missing from his life for long, long months. He noticed
that Fitz was back to humming while she went around
dusting and polishing—another nice change. He could
tell that the woman who'd raised him and whose opinion he valued liked Kate.

Fitz was one of the few who'd never let him down,
who'd always been there for him and Johnny. All those
years after his mother had walked out on her young
family and Dad had traveled extensively, trying to forget
his wife's desertion by working night and day, Fitz had
been there, steady as a rock.

Aaron liked to think that, under Fitz's guidance, Kate
would be the nanny to his daughter that the older woman
had been to them. Since Jamie's mother was gone and he
worked long hours, at least Kate was there so his daughter didn't feel that sense of abandonment that could
devastate a child. Hell, it could devastate an adult. Nannies, the really good ones, instilled a feeling of security
in children that helped them through the rough times they
faced as adults.

Now, if only he could think of Kate as a nanny and not
as a woman.

He'd almost kissed her that night of the presentation in the parking lot after dinner. She'd looked so lovely, and he'd wanted to hold her so badly. But he'd caught himself in time. For a second there, he thought he'd seen in her eyes a need as great as his own. But he had to have been mistaken. Kate Spencer had been raised in a home with all the advantages. She had a good education and would undoubtedly want to do something more challenging once she got over the shock of her parents' death and her uncle's betrayal. He only hoped that her departure wouldn't come before Jamie was more able to cope, when she was older. Much older.

But he wouldn't think about that just now, Aaron told himself as he parked the car and let himself in the front door. He rarely called out when he arrived, thinking it more fun to catch Jamie and Kate unawares at play.

He could hear Kate's voice coming from the direction of the family room as he removed his coat. Quietly, he walked toward the sound, his steps muffled by the thick carpeting and the drone of cartoons on the television.

"You did it!" Kate said with delight to the smiling child she scooped up in her arms for a big hug. "I just knew you were going to take those first steps any day now." She set Jamie onto her feet, holding one small hand for balance. "Now, let's see you do it again."

Kate stepped back several feet and crouched down, watching, encouraging. "Come on, now."

Unafraid, buoyed by Kate's praise, Jamie started out, taking a hesitant step, then three more, almost running at the end right into Kate's arms.

They both squealed with delight at the momentous occasion. "What a smart little girl." Kate hugged the child, nuzzling her neck.

"Listen, that was wonderful, Jamie, but we're going to have to do it all over again when Daddy gets home." She brushed back a blond curl from the little face as Jamie watched her. "You see, he'd be terribly disappointed if he couldn't see your very first steps. So, when he comes in, we'll set up the scene and you walk to him. It's a thrill we can't cheat him out of, so we'll just pretend we didn't have this little rehearsal, okay?"

Not understanding a word of what Kate had said, but glad she was happy, Jamie grinned at her and crawled over for another hug.

Affected by what he'd just witnessed, Aaron quietly backed up all the way to the foyer. Kate's consideration, her empathetic gesture, moved him far more than he'd expected. She didn't want to rob him of any of his daughter's firsts. Amazed, he shrugged on his coat, opened the door, then slammed it shut before calling out, "Hello. Anyone home?"

Immediately, he heard Kate answer from the family room.

"We're in here."

Aaron walked to the doorway. If he was going to play this game, he had to do it right. As always, he greeted his daughter, scooping her up in a big bear hug and kissing her fragrant cheeks.

"You're home early. I haven't even started dinner." Kate had noted his early return several days lately, and wondered if perhaps he was checking up on her for some unknown reason. She couldn't think of anything she'd done that would make him distrust her with Jamie.

"No hurry. I had a late lunch." He set Jamie down and removed his coat, then strolled to the couch and sat down. "Maybe we should order Chinese tonight, for a change. The Dragon Inn has good food and they deliver. Do you like Chinese?''

As if playing her part the way they'd rehearsed, Jamie maneuvered to her feet and took a halting step toward her father. She squealed, wanting him to notice, then took three more steps before sinking to her padded bottom.

"Hey, look at you!" Aaron played along, glancing at Kate. "Did you see that? She walked."

"I had a feeling it would be any day now." Kate smiled at Aaron's obvious pleasure while she lifted Jamie into a standing position. "Let's see you do it again, sweetie."

And Jamie did, to the applause of both adults. She grinned and clapped her hands, probably wondering what she'd done to get such attention. In her father's embrace, she laid her head on his shoulder and looked at Kate.

Over his daughter's head, Aaron looked at Kate, too, thinking he'd never seen such beautiful eyes. A man could drown in their blue depths. Then there was the fact that she was utterly unselfish and giving. He kept on staring, unable to think of a thing to say, noticing color move into her face.

The ringing phone broke the look and the mood. Aaron handed Jamie to Kate and left to answer the call.

Kate was left stroking the baby's silken hair, wondering why merely staring into Aaron Carver's eyes could weaken her knees.


It was a typical autumn Saturday morning in Michigan with the sun shining, a nip in the air and leaves covering a good deal of Aaron's large back lawn. He'd stood at the kitchen window sipping his coffee thinking it would be a fine day to rake leaves. And he'd thought that, now that she was toddling about, falling often but nonetheless walking, Jamie would enjoy helping.

So he'd mentioned his idea to Kate, who'd said she'd love to help, too. The two of them bundled up the little girl and went out to find rakes and bags to fill and a little red wagon that Jamie's grandfather had given her. When Jamie had tired of being pulled around the patio, Kate found a big ball and coaxed her onto the grass to roll it about while Aaron raked. Which was almost a losing battle, since the leaves continued to fall from the five maples planted around the yard's perimeter.

"It's raining leaves," Aaron said, leaning on his rake for a moment. He'd already filled three big plastic bags and hardly dented the accumulation.

"You want some help?" Kate offered.

"No, thanks. You two have fun." He went back to work, thinking he'd take a break later and play with Jamie. For now, he set aside the rake and left to get more bags, leaving the gate open as he walked around to the side door of the garage.

"Here it comes, Jamie," Kate called out, rolling the large red ball in her direction.

With uncertain steps, Jamie ventured forth, reached out toward the moving ball, then sat down heavily as it came to her. She laughed out loud and tried to get up, but the ball had her tumbling sideways.

Joining in the merriment, Kate went over and mock-tackled her, rolling over and over in the crunchy leaves. She'd put Jamie into her snowsuit, so she knew the child was plenty warm, and Kate had on her leather jacket over a sweater and jeans. There was only a mild breeze, and the sun shone through a few vapory clouds. Kate couldn't keep her eyes off the beautiful baby, who was now trying to take off her knitted cap.

"Leave it on, sweetie. We don't want you to catch cold." Kate tied the strings of the cap again, then jumped up to retrieve the ball, hoping to distract Jamie from her hat. She spotted it at the back of the yard and ran over. She'd just reached the fence when she heard Jamie's frightened cry.

Kate turned and saw a white chow that must have entered the yard through the open gate. He was a mere two feet from Jamie, eyeing her, his blue-black tongue hanging out as he cocked his large head, his thick gray ruff indicating he was full grown.

"Hey!" Kate called out as she jogged across the damp grass. "Get away!"

The dog swung toward her, his dark eyes watchful, and let out a throaty growl. Jamie cried out again, instinctively afraid, for she'd never been close to a live dog, much less one so big.

Just as Kate reached Jamie, the chow set himself between her and the little girl, who didn't know what to do so sat down and started wailing loudly.

"Get out. Leave now!" Kate told him, wishing she had a stick or something. The rake was across the yard, and she didn't dare leave Jamie to get it. The dog had a broad face and muzzle, and mean little eyes. Where was Aaron? "Aaron!" she called out as loudly as she dared.

Enough of this. She'd heard that dogs could smell fear. Maybe she could outfox him. She moved around the dog and scooped up the baby, deciding to make a dash for the back door. With Jamie safely in her arms, she turned just as the chow gave out a loud bark and lunged at her. He was big and heavy, knocking Kate down easily. Protecting the baby, Kate fell to the ground and screamed for Aaron.

Too late. The dog was on her, managing to sink his teeth into her thigh, ripping through the jeans. Again, Kate cried out, shielding Jamie's small body with her own as she heard Aaron shouting and running toward them.

"What the hell?" He grabbed up the rake, holding it high. "Get out of here!" Still snarling, the dog circled wide before running out through the open gate. Aaron rushed over to fasten the gate, then hurried back to where Kate was struggling to get up.

"I don't know where he came from," Aaron explained, helping her up, finally taking a sobbing Jamie from her. "I'm so sorry. I had to go down to the basement for more bags and— Good Lord! You're hurt."

At first, he hadn't seen the tear in her jeans or the blood. "Did he bite you or did you hurt yourself falling?"

"He jumped up and bit me." Favoring her right leg, Kate took a limping step, trying to see behind her at the back of her thigh and assess how much damage the dog had done. She couldn't see much and only knew that it hurt like hell.

"Come on, lean on me. We're going in." He slipped his free arm around her waist and led her into the kitchen. "Fitz!" he called out over Jamie's cries. The frightened child still hadn't calmed down.

Fitz came around the corner frowning. "Saints alive, what's the commotion about?" She took the baby from Aaron, wiping her tears and soothing her in a rocking motion as she looked to the other two, finally noticing Kate's wound. "How'd this happen?"

Aaron ripped the fabric over the injury as Kate stood by the sink. "A damn dog got into the yard and bit her."

"He was going for Jamie," Kate explained. "I had to stop him."

That stopped him. Aaron stared at her in amazement. She'd risked herself to keep his daughter from injury. All the more reason for him to take extraspecial care of her. He bent to peer at the wound, saw the broken skin, the bruise marks. "I'm driving you to the hospital. I think you'll need stitches. When was the last time you had a tetanus shot, Kate?"

"I don't remember. A year or two ago, I think." She flinched, the ache throbbing. "I don't know what came over that dog. I've always gotten along well with animals. We had a sheepdog on the farm. Rex. He slept in my bedroom."

"Some dogs are vicious, that's all." Aaron grabbed his keys from a dish on the kitchen counter and slipped his arm around Kate. "Can you walk?"

"Yes, of course." She was feeling almost as much embarrassment as pain. "Look, I don't think it's more than a deep scratch."

"You can't see it. It's more than that, and I want you looked at." He turned to Fitz, who'd managed to calm Jamie. "Will you look after Jamie and call Dr. Benson? Have him meet us at the hospital." He'd been told he was paranoid, but he couldn't help himself. Ever since Stephanie's illness, no illness or injury seemed trivial. The Emergency staff was very efficient, he was certain, but he trusted Ron Benson more.

"Of course." Fitz patted Kate's arm. "Aaron'll see to your care, dear."

"Aaron," Kate said, "I don't think I need to go to the hospital."

But Aaron was in his take-charge mode. "The dog wasn't wearing a collar, Fitz. We've got to trace him somehow to see if he's had rabies shots lately."

Rabies. That she hadn't thought of. She'd heard those shots were very painful. That thought upset her far more than having a few stitches.

"What was the dog like, Aaron?" Fitz asked, wearing a worried frown.

He described the chow. "Have you seen him around before?"

"I believe so. I think he belongs to the owner of the auto garage on Fenton. I can't be certain, of course."

"I'll look into it from the hospital." He touched the back of Jamie's silken head, very aware of what a dog bite to his daughter's small body might have done. "We'll be back soon." Bracing Kate, he led the way to the car.

"All right, Hector," Aaron said into the phone in the hospital waiting room. "I'm glad Conan's had all his shots. But damn it, man, you'd better see to it that you keep him in your yard. As I told you, his bite is requiring four stitches."

"I sure am sorry, Mr. Carver," Hector told him. "I had him in my yard, but he jumped the fence."

Aaron wasn't buying the man's excuse. "Then chain him, Hector. I don't have to tell you how serious this could have been if your dog had turned on my daughter."

"I understand. I just don't know why Conan went for the lady. He's usually not like that." Hector gave a nervous cough. "Listen, I'll pay her bill there at the hospital. I don't want no hard feelings."

"Never mind. It's taken care of. Just see to your animal." Aaron hung up. The good news was that the dog was current with his shots. The bad news was that Kate's wound was still going to take a while to heal. He walked back through Emergency, where Ron Benson was finishing up.

"The wounds are deeper than I'd thought," the doctor told Aaron as he applied a bandage to Kate's thigh. "She can't feel it now because I numbed the whole area, but it's going to hurt plenty later. I'll give you a prescription for some pain pills. I also gave her a tetanus shot because she couldn't remember when she'd had her last one. Better safe than sorry." He adjusted the half sheet over Kate's leg and helped her sit up. "How do you feel?"

"Fine. Sorry to trouble you on a Saturday." Although she knew Aaron and Dr. Benson were friends from years ago, she hadn't thought her injury serious enough to call him in. But Aaron had insisted. "Hope we didn't mess up your plans."

"I was just watching football on TV, Michigan State losing. No big deal." He glanced at Aaron. "What'd you find out about the dog?"

Aaron updated both of them and noticed how relieved Kate was. "Hell of a thing to have happen. Do you think she'll have a scar?"

"Maybe a little one. We'll see."

A muscle in Aaron's cheek clenched. "She got hurt protecting Jamie," he told Ron, feeling responsible. If only he hadn't left just then, hadn't gone down to the basement for those damn trash bags.

"Which is exactly what anyone else would have done," Kate said, sliding off the table. "Can I get dressed?"

"Sure thing." Ron Benson led his friend out of the cubicle, giving her some privacy, and walked him toward the admitting desk. "Quite a lady, your nanny."

"She's nuts about Jamie," Aaron explained as he turned to the clerk. "I'll handle Kate Spencer's expenses." Since she no longer worked at her father's bookstore, nor would she be covered under any policy George Spencer might have carried before his death, chances were that she didn't have any insurance.

"Fine, Mr. Carver," the clerk said. "We have the form you signed. Billing will mail you the charges."

"Thanks." He turned to shake hands with his friend. "I appreciate you coming over so quickly. It turned out okay, but I was worried the dog was a stray and she might have had to endure that series of rabies shots."

Looking faintly amused, Ron Benson smiled. "No problem. What are friends for? Maybe one day, you'll design me a new house."

"Anytime." Kate hadn't come out of the cubicle. "I think I'll go see if I can help her put on her shoes. She might already be in pain."

"You go ahead, but that shot's not going to wear off for another three or four hours." Benson clapped him on the shoulder and left.

Aaron headed for the curtained cubicle just as Kate stepped out, walking a bit gingerly. This was all his fault, he thought as he took her arm. "Are you hurting?"

Kate was grateful for him at her side. "No, I can hardly feel my leg, which is why I'm afraid to walk without holding on. Even my ankle's numb."

"Just hang on to me and you'll be fine."

For some reason, that thought comforted her greatly.


"Okay, two cheeseburgers, coming up, plus a small hamburger with just catsup." Aaron walked into the family room carrying a plate of fragrant sandwiches, bringing with him the chill of the outdoors, where he'd been grilling. "It's getting downright cold out there."

"Well, it is November," Kate reminded him. She was seated at the far end of the leather couch, pillows propped behind her back and an afghan spread over her legs. In her bouncy chair alongside Kate, Jamie sucked on a pretzel, watching her father place dinner in the center of the large coffee table. "Mmm, they sure smell good."

"I just hope they are." He sat down on the floor to fix Jamie's plate first, cutting up her hamburger and adding a small pile of french fries. He set the plate onto the tray of her chair, pulling it closer so he could keep a close eye on her. "Here you go, honey." He put her sippy cup within reach and turned to Kate. "And just what will madam have on her cheeseburger?"

She couldn't help smiling. He'd insisted that she rest when they'd returned from the hospital, but Kate hadn't wanted to go to bed. So he'd settled her in the cozy family room and even built a fire for her to watch. In no time, she'd fallen asleep from the medication and had awakened to find him just entering the room, telling her they were going to have a picnic.

"Mmm, everything except onions."

"You mean lettuce, tomatoes, pickles, special sauce— the works?"

"You bet." Kate was surprised that she was hungry.

Aaron fixed her a generous plate, then one for himself, and poured everyone a glass of milk. "Aren't we the wild ones, spending Saturday night at home, drinking milk?"

Guilt rose in Kate, stopping her. "You shouldn't have given Fitz the night off to go to her daughter's tonight. She could have watched Jamie for one evening, and I could rest in my room so you could go out."

Aaron swallowed a juicy bite and frowned. "Who said I wanted to go out? I'm enjoying this a great deal." He found he meant every word. He loved listening to his daughter jabbering away as she ate her dinner. And he savored the sight of Kate with the firelight dancing over her features and turning her hair golden. He truly couldn't think of another place he'd rather be tonight.

There was that family thing again, Aaron thought as he chewed on a french fry. He'd been eight, and Johnny six, when their mother had left. They'd been well taken care of by a younger, more energetic Fitz. And yet his mother's desertion and his father rarely being home during those important years had affected Aaron to such an extent that it still bothered him and he still felt that sense of abandonment occasionally.

Which was why moments like this, when he could pretend that Jamie, Kate and he were sharing a quiet Saturday night at home like any other family might, meant so much to him. Oddly enough, Johnny had gone the other route, turning from most family pursuits, always relocating, unable to settle down, pursuing one venture after another. Two boys raised the same yet turning out truly different.

The problem was that his way was merely a pretense.

Kate set her empty plate on the table, amazed that she'd eaten so much while Aaron had merely nibbled. "You're a million miles away," she said softly. "Penny for your thoughts."

Looking subdued, he glanced up. "Not worth that much. I was just thinking about when my brother and I were young, seven and nine or so, and left alone with Fitz for months at a time. She used to drag our heavy coffee table off the Persian rug in the family room, spread out a blanket and make us a picnic. One summer day, she even brought in half a dozen ants to make it more real since it was raining out and we had to stay in."

"She really loves your family. Now you've got me curious. Why were you alone with Fitz so much?"

Enough years had passed that the telling shouldn't bother him, Aaron thought. She'd confided her past, so he felt he owed her a minimal explanation. He gave her the bare facts, leaving out the unhappiness his mother's abandonment had caused her two sons and the husband who still loved her. He let Kate fill in the blanks.

She didn't say anything for several minutes after he finished. He hadn't given a reason for his mother's desertion, and she didn't feel she had the right to ask. "It seems we've both had our share of difficult adjustments. I suppose you could say we're survivors."

"Yeah, I guess you could say that." How had he gotten on this track? He glanced at her empty plate, wanting to change the subject. "Well, I guess you don't like my cooking, eh?"

Kate laughed. "I think those are appetite-inducing pills I've been taking, not pain pills."

"You could stand to put on a few pounds," he told her as he helped Jamie take another bite.

She raised a brow. "Are you saying I'm too thin?"

"Far be it from me to *ever* discuss a woman's age or weight." He finished the last of his burger and held out a fry to Jamie. "Or are you fishing?"

"Fishing?" She was growing tired and sleepy again.

"For compliments. You needn't. You're beautiful and you must know it." He knelt to wipe his daughter's face and hands, since she was obviously full and just playing now.

How could she answer that? No one had ever told her she was beautiful. Dad had looked at her with admiration, but knowing how vain his wife was, George Spencer had been very careful with his compliments, unwilling to upset his wife by seeming to favor his adopted daughter. Certainly Evan never had said any such thing, but then, they'd grown up together so their relationship had lacked the fire some of her friends spoke of. The kind of excitement a person feels when they just look at someone who arouses their interest.

Like she felt in looking at Aaron.

Aaron noticed Jamie yawning. "I think someone's tired. Maybe two someones." He picked up his daughter just as Kate stifled a yawn. "I'm going to put her to bed. Then I'll come back and help you up the stairs."

Kate threw back the afghan as she shook her head. "I'm fine. She needs a bath and..."

"Not tonight. She won't perish if she misses one bath." He tucked the afghan back around Kate's legs. "Don't argue with me. Wait right there, and I'll be back."

She watched him go and decided she'd let him pamper her for one evening. She flexed her leg and felt a twinge of pain but nothing unbearable. Still, stretching out under the warm covers, it was nice being spoiled a little. Turning, she shifted her gaze to the fire.

Twenty minutes later, when Aaron came for her, she was sound asleep.

She was restless and couldn't pinpoint why. It was after nine in the evening a week after her injury, and Kate felt fine physically. But her nerves were unsettled. It had been a somewhat trying day with Jamie being uncharacteristically whiny, probably because she had another tooth coming in. She had hardly eaten a thing and refused her night bottle. Unable to sleep, Kate slipped on her robe and went to check on the baby.

Jamie was sleeping soundly. Her forehead when Kate touched it seemed a little warm, but some children had mild fevers when they teethed. She'd keep a close eye on her tomorrow, Kate told herself as she wandered downstairs.

She made a pot of tea, having gotten used to the stuff from Fitz, and carried it to the library, where she turned the stereo on low. Needing to hear a familiar voice, she phoned Pam.

"Sounds like you love your work," Pam said after Kate had gone on and on about her adorable young charge. "And Fitz sounds a lot like I remember Glynis being."

Kate curled her feet under her on the couch. "She is. She's a housekeeper now, but she was nanny to Aaron and his brother when they were quite young. He's very fond of her."

Pam thought she detected an odd note in her cousin's voice. "And what about you? Is this Aaron fond of you, too?"

Kate frowned at the phone. "No, of course not. He's my employer, for heaven's sake, and nothing else." And that's the way he wanted it to be, more's the pity. "How are things with you?" A change of subject was definitely called for.

"Terrific. Wonderful, in fact." Pam's voice was almost musical.

"Uh-oh. Does this mean what I think it means? A man in your life at long last?"

"Oh, Kate, he's really special. His name is Eli Knowles, and he's a reporter for the *Detroit News*. A staff writer right now, but he'll move up soon, I'm sure, and get his own byline. He's *so* intelligent."

"I see."

"He's thirty. You don't think that's too old for me, do you? He's got this thick brown hair and these gorgeous eyes and..." Pam drew in a deep breath. "I want you to meet him. When can you come?"

Kate was smiling, happy for her friend but a little hesitant. Pam was her age, but she hadn't dated much and she was extremely vulnerable. That, plus the fact her father had a great deal of money that would one day be Pam's. Kate feared that someone would take advantage of her naive cousin, yet she didn't want to burst Pam's bubble. "Maybe next week on my day off." She wanted a look at this paragon of virtue.

"Great. I just know you're going to love him." Pam suddenly sobered. "Oh, Kate, Dad told me to ask you to sign some papers when you come visit." She hated being her father's messenger, but she had little choice. Tom Spencer had her financially under his thumb.

Kate felt herself tense at the mention of her uncle. "What kind of papers?"

"I don't know, just papers. You can read them when you get here." Getting off that subject, she returned to Eli. "I'll make sure he can come when you visit. When's your next day off?"

"I'm not sure. I'll call you the first of the week." They said their goodbyes, and Kate hung up thoughtfully. What papers could Tom Spencer need her signatures on? Couldn't be too important, or he'd have sent them to her or had his attorney call. Could there be a problem in settling her folks' estate? Could he possibly need her help? Perversely, she hoped so, for she wasn't going to make it easy for him. Tom deserved a rough time for what he'd put her through.

Hearing a sound behind her, Kate glanced over her shoulder. Aaron stood in the doorway barefoot, wearing only jeans. The breath backed up in Kate's throat.

"I see you couldn't sleep, either." Aaron carried the book he'd finished to the bookcase along the far wall, found the spot where it belonged and shoved it in place. He hadn't thought she'd be downstairs or he'd have grabbed a shirt. Oh, well, he was hardly dressed indecently and he was in his own house. Noticing the tea tray, he sat down at the far end of the couch. "Is there enough for two?"

"Sure, plenty." Leaning forward, she poured him a cup. "Did you check Jamie before coming down? Her new tooth is really giving her fits." Kate refilled her own cup before curling back up in the corner.

"I went in her room, and she seemed fine." Relaxing, he stretched out his long legs.

Kate swung her eyes to the dying embers of the fire Aaron had built earlier, unwilling to stare at him in his half-undressed state. She'd seen men at the beach wearing far less, yet they hadn't made her feel so uneasy. She'd also lived with Evan for six months, so it wasn't that the male body was unfamiliar to her.

Yet for some inexplicable reason, this particular male body had her hands shaking enough to make her set down her cup.

"Are you a reader?" Aaron asked, trying to think of a noncontroversial subject. She seemed nervous somehow, and he wanted to put her at ease.

"Yes, I love to read. Mysteries, mostly."

"Like Stephen King? You like to be frightened?"

"No, more like Sue Grafton and Sara Paretsky."

He sipped his tea. "Your taste runs to feminist P.I.'s."

"Not always. I like Parker's Spencer, John D. Mc-Donald's Travis McGee. What do you prefer?"

"Oh, Ludlum, Clancy, Grisham. I like courtroom dramas, too." Bored with small talk, he saw that her robe had opened, revealing a section of leg. "Fitz told me you had your stitches out today. How's it feel?"

Suddenly aware of his interested gaze, Kate pulled the folds of her robe more closely around her. "Much better. Dr. Benson says he doubts there'll be a scar."

He reached to touch her hand as it lay on the couch seat between them. "If there is, you let me know. I'll take you to a dermatologist I know who'll remove the scar. I don't want you to be marked because of something that happened here."

Kate kept her eyes on their clasped hands, his so tan and large, hers pale and slender. Why had he touched her? She wished he hadn't, because it made her feel awkward, made her want more.

"Kate, have I thanked you properly for what you did that morning for Jamie? If you hadn't put yourself between her and that dog, Lord only knows what might have happened. That damn chow outweighed Jamie by probably fifty pounds."

"There's no need for further thanks." She wished he'd go, wished she didn't feel so...so anxious around him lately.

"You're very good with her. She adores you, you know." It was only the truth. Jamie's whole face lit up whenever she spotted Kate no matter what she was doing. No one else could get her to eat everything on her plate the way Kate could, either.

"The feeling's mutual. She's a wonderful little girl."

The song coming from the stereo was low and kind of bluesy, something familiar by Kenny G., yet he couldn't think of the title. He glanced over at the terrazzo floor, wondering if he dare ask her for a dance. What could be wrong with one simple dance?

But before he opened his mouth, the frantic cry of a baby came to them from upstairs.

# Chapter Six

The crib was a mess. Jamie had gotten sick and was crying with a raspy sound. Although Aaron had told her he'd go upstairs to check on her, Kate had hurried alongside him, recognizing Jamie's cry as more than just a fussy wail.

"There, there, sweetheart, it's all right," she murmured to the frightened child as she lifted her onto the change table.

"What can I do to help?" Aaron asked, unsure where to begin.

"Stay with her here," she directed him. "I'll get you a wet washcloth to clean her with and some fresh jammies." Kate rushed to the bathroom, then grabbed a change of clothes from the dresser drawer. "Here. I'll change her bed."

"Must have been something she ate," Aaron commented. He struggled to tug off her soiled pajamas, then found another mess. "Looks like she may have diarrhea, too."

Kate abandoned the bed for now and took over Jamie. With soothing words, she quieted the child and hurriedly changed her. "I don't think she has just an upset stomach," she told Aaron. "She's quite warm. I thought she was just teething, but it might be something else."

"You think she's got a fever?" Aaron ran a hand through his hair, always nervous when facing any illness. "I'll get the thermometer."

Jamie did have a fever, a hundred and two, alarming Aaron further. "I think I'll call Ron. This doesn't look good."

"Let me get her something to lower the fever first. Perhaps it's just a mild flu. We'll give her some liquids and—"

"No!" Aaron's voice was rough with worry. "I know you think I'm overreacting, but Stephanie's illness began this same way. Mild flu symptoms."

She should have remembered, Kate realized as she saw his jaw clench, his face turn pale and anxious. "Whatever you say. I'll hold her while you call."

Jamie was no longer crying, was in fact quite lethargic, her head resting on Kate's shoulder as she sat down in the rocker with her after getting one dose of medicine in her. Kate crooned to her gently, stroking the damp hair back from the baby's hot little face. Aaron was right. She did feel awfully warm.

He returned, carrying his jacket. "Ron's going to meet me at the hospital. He agrees that we shouldn't take a chance." He glanced around the room, finally spotted Jamie's snowsuit.

"I'll go with you and hold her while you drive. I'll put the seatbelt over both of us." Kate saw the relief on his face and knew that he appreciated her help. Aaron loved his daughter more than anyone on earth and he was deathly afraid of losing her. Plus, he hated hospitals and distrusted most of their personnel. He definitely needed someone by his side just now.

In minutes, they were bundled into Aaron's Mercedes with the heater blasting away. It was a cold November night, but the sky was clear and there was little wind. Kate held the baby slanted across her lap, the belt restricting both their movements. Jamie didn't mind, for she'd fallen asleep. Kate saw how badly Aaron's hands trembled as he turned onto the deserted street.

"I should have known better than to take her outside this afternoon," Aaron admitted, gripping the wheel. It was Saturday, and he'd spent the morning working in his study, but after Jamie's nap, he'd taken her out into the backyard to run around a little, chasing a ball, rolling in the leaves. She'd laughed and had a great time. How could he have known she'd catch something?

"If she has the flu, then you probably know that it's caused by a virus, which is airborne, passed on from other people. Besides, it was a beautiful fall day, no wind, lots of sun. You shouldn't blame yourself. Children get sick."

*Not this child,* Aaron thought. *Please, not this child.* With a squeal of the wheels, he pulled into the hospital's Emergency parking lot.

Dr. Ronald Benson's relaxed manner and pleasant smile were nowhere to be seen, replaced by a grim expression as he entered the waiting room where Kate and Aaron had been alternately pacing and staring out the window at the faint hint of dawn. He took in his old friend's deeply worried expression and wished he could deliver better news. "It's a virus, Aaron, a damn stubborn one."

Aaron swallowed down a huge lump of fear. "What exactly does that mean?"

"It means she's dehydrated at the moment, but we're replacing her fluids. The fever hasn't broken yet. It's good that you brought her in when you did."

"But she's not in any real danger, is she, Ron?" Aaron heard his voice break with emotion despite his best effort.

"I'm not going to lie to you," Benson said. "She's a very sick child. We have every hope of getting her illness under control. The next twelve or so hours are critical."

*Critical.* That was the same word Ron had used when Aaron had brought Stephanie in that horrible night. Brought her in and never taken her home again. His teeth nearly cracked as he clamped his jaw tightly, struggling not to break down.

Kate felt the tears well up, for the little girl fighting in there to live, for the father who surely couldn't handle losing her. "Is there anything we can do, Dr. Benson?" she asked, wanting desperately to help.

"It can't hurt to pray," the doctor suggested. He placed a comforting hand on Aaron's arm for a few seconds, then was gone in a rustle of his white lab coat, the door to the intensive-care unit swinging shut behind him.

Kate wasn't sure just how much Aaron would tolerate in the way of support, for she didn't know him all that well. She'd never had to be there for someone like this while her own heart was hurting for the child she'd come to love.

His back ramrod straight, Aaron walked to the window and stood looking out, seeing nothing but the feverish face of his daughter. He closed his eyes. This couldn't be happening, not twice in one year. Just hours ago, he and Jamie had been running around, laughing and playing. What kind of cruel joke was this that everyone he loved was to be taken from him? How could he go on without his baby?

Her eyes damp, Kate went by instinct, moving to his side, touching his arm to let him know he wasn't alone, that she understood.

"I can't lose her, Kate," he said in a hoarse whisper. "I *can't!*"

She squeezed his arm. "You won't."

"I know you love her, too." There was nothing they could do but wait.

She looked so tiny lying in the hospital crib, hooked up to an IV and several monitoring machines. Kate pressed her fist to her mouth as she took in the flushed little face, the damp hair, the listless body that shifted restlessly as the fever worked through her.

Dr. Benson had said that the diarrhea had stopped, which was a good sign. Her body fluids were slowly being replenished. Everything known to modern medicine was being done. Now, as Dr. Benson said, all they could do was pray.

Kate looked up at Aaron, who was standing on the other side of the crib. He'd picked up Jamie's little hand and was holding it between his own two much larger ones. His face was set, determination readily visible.

"You're going to be fine, sweetheart," he said to his daughter, his voice low but firm and strong. "You're going to get well, and we'll go home. We'll sit by the fire and have another picnic." He leaned closer to tuck Elmo into the crook of her arm. Kate had thought to bring it along, even as worried as she'd been.

He raised his tired eyes to Kate and saw fatigue and worry on her face. They'd been at the hospital for about ten hours, and she hadn't once stepped away from her vigil outside the ICU doors. Gratitude washed over him as he let go of Jamie's hand and reached to touch Kate.

Wordlessly, they locked eyes and hands. He never could have made it this far without her. She looked small and fragile, but she was a rock of strength when the going got tough. And things couldn't get much tougher than having your child in critical condition.

This wasn't the time to tell her, but he thought she understood how much her being here meant to him. He squeezed her fingers and felt that quick response as she returned the pressure. It was something unique, something special, to be able to communicate without words. Later, when this was all over, he'd thank her for the support he'd never expected from her.

The child in the crib made a sound, and they both turned to her. But it was only an involuntary moan as she thrashed about from the fever. The ICU nurse beckoned them from the doorway, indicating that their time with Jamie was up for this hour. Because Ron had left word, they'd made an exception and allowed both of them to go in to Jamie for five minutes every hour.

Aaron bent to press a kiss to his baby's flushed cheek, as did Kate on the other side. Feeling the need for contact, he took Kate's hand again as they walked out to the waiting room and sat down together. Lost in his thoughts, he sat that way, cradling her hand, his mind focused on willing Jamie to get better.

Kate felt that he hardly knew whose hand he was holding, that she was merely a warm body offering the comfort he so badly needed. True, during the long hours, he'd occasionally look at her in a way that made her feel he was really seeing *her*. But mostly, he was too wrapped up in his own thoughts to acknowledge his surroundings.

She shouldn't have expected more. After all, the main concern for both of them was Jamie and her recovery. It was just that, with both of them loving her so much, it would have been nice to be able to cling to one another for the added strength of getting through this together.

Aaron did seem to reach out to her at times. But every time he felt her getting too close, he pulled back. Kate didn't know if he did that with everyone, or just her, because he feared involvement, especially after the sudden, brutal loss of his wife. She wondered, too, if she was doing herself a disservice by staying on at the Carver house, by learning to love Jamie more every day and by being attracted more and more to the man who seemed disinclined to begin a new relationship.

She heard Aaron sigh, watched him lean his head back and close his eyes, yet he kept her hand trapped in his. As she herself was trapped in a situation she couldn't control yet couldn't seem to leave. Kate, too, leaned back, shifting her thoughts to Jamie, wishing that Dr. Benson would come out any moment wearing a broad smile and bringing good news. Prayers couldn't hurt, he'd said. Kate agreed. Closing her eyes, she prayed for Jamie.

"Wake up, you two," Ron Benson said, shaking Aaron's arm.

Startled, Aaron straightened, then rose, feeling disoriented. Then he remembered where he was—napping in the ICU waiting room with Kate sleeping alongside him. Fear skittered up his spine. "How is she?"

Ron's smile wiped the fatigue lines from his face. "Jamie's over the worst of it. The fever's broken, and she's out of danger."

Aaron's relief was a physical thing, causing him to sag back into his chair. "Thank God."

Kate blinked back grateful tears. "And thank you, Doctor. That's the best possible news."

But Aaron needed more. "Are you sure? She won't relapse or take a turn for the worse, will she?" False hope was devastating.

Benson shook his head. "Very doubtful. She's drinking on her own and keeping it down. We'll try some bland solids soon. I wouldn't take her out on the town just yet, but she's on her way."

"Can we see her?" Kate asked.

"In a few minutes. The nurse is changing her before we take her out of ICU and over to the children's wing. I'll tell her to let you know when Jamie's ready for visitors."

Aaron reached to shake his friend's hand. "Ron, thank you, for everything." He'd made rounds and seen other patients, but Aaron knew that Ron Benson hadn't left the hospital since they'd brought Jamie in. "I owe you, big time."

Ron had been the doctor in attendance when Stephanie Carver had been admitted and died so unexpectedly. And he'd seen what her death had done to his schoolboy friend. Ron had done his share of praying over Aaron's daughter, as well. "Seeing Jamie recover, that's all the thanks I need." With a wave, he left them.

Aaron turned to Kate, his eyes lighting up. "Did you hear? Jamie's going to be fine." Unable to stop himself, his arms went around her, and he drew her close. "We've got her back, Katie."

"I know. How wonderful." She hugged him back, tears of happiness blurring her vision.

He felt like shouting, like singing. He'd been so afraid, but it had all turned out well. Grinning, he swung Kate around and buried his face in her neck, inhaling her special scent. "Everything's going to be all right now."

"Yes." Kate felt Aaron squeeze her until she thought her ribs might crack, then he shifted his head, and his mouth was on hers. Shocked, she didn't resist, couldn't. Her response was swift and instantaneous, her blood heating, her pulse beginning to throb.

All was right with his world once more, Aaron thought as his lips sought Kate's in celebration. She tasted like sweet victory, like a sunny day, like a field of flowers. Then something shifted, clouding his senses. Suddenly, he came alive, his heart hammering in his chest as he deepened the kiss.

Forgetting where they were and that this was probably the wrong man to want, Kate's arms slipped around his neck, and her body moved closer to his. She didn't want to think, just to feel, the hard muscles of his shoulders, the soft hair on the nape of his neck, the wonderful sensations he was awakening within her.

What had begun as celebration became a sensual exploration as he changed the angle of the kiss, his tongue moving inside her mouth to explore, to investigate. A jolt of heat spread through Aaron as he molded her slender body more intimately with his. It had been so long, so very long since...

Heavy footsteps on the polished tile floor startled them apart like two guilty teenagers caught in a parked car. Still breathing hard, Aaron glanced toward the doorway to the ICU lounge and saw his father looking somewhat embarrassed at having interrupted what obviously was a private moment.

Clearing his throat, Aaron felt his face flush as he stepped away from Kate and faced his father. "Have you heard? Jamie's out of danger."

William Carver wore a slightly amused look as he nodded. "Yes, I ran into Ron Benson on the way up. I'm so glad, son. You two must have spent a terrible night."

"Yeah, it was awful." Aaron shoved back his hair in a nervous gesture. How could he have lost control like that? Whatever had he been thinking of? He hadn't been thinking at all; that was the problem. It was the emotional relief that had caught him off guard. Needing to share his joy, he'd reached out to the only other human being in the room.

From under lowered lashes, he glanced at Kate, hoping she hadn't read more into the kiss than was there. She had high color in her cheeks but otherwise looked the same as always except for slightly swollen lips.

What must his father think of him? Aaron wondered. His wife not dead a year, and here he was locked in a passionate kiss with his sick daughter's nanny. Regret had him frowning. "I didn't think you'd come," he told his father lamely. Twice he'd phoned to update him, as well as several calls to Fitz, telling them both to stay put, that they wouldn't be allowed in to see Jamie anyway. Naturally, his headstrong father had done things his own way.

"She's my only granddaughter, Aaron," William told his son. "Of course I wanted to be here. Is it possible to see Jamie now that she's out of danger?"

"Ron said they're moving her to the children's section and they'd let us know when we could go up." He stole another glance at Kate and saw that she looked as disconcerted as he felt. Maybe he could ease things for both of them. "Listen, Kate, I'd like you to take my car and go on home. Get some rest. You've been here for hours."

Kate tried to keep her expression even, despite the sudden stab of pain. He wanted her out of here because he was embarrassed that his father had stumbled in on them kissing. She loved Jamie and she'd spent a very long vigil, yet he would rob her of the chance to see for herself that the baby was really going to be all right. She swallowed down her disappointment and made a stab at changing his mind. "I'm not that tired, really."

But Aaron was not to be deterred. "You're dead on your feet." He dug the keys from his jacket pocket and held them out to her. "Dad will drop me off later. Please give Fitz the good news for me."

Kate took his keys, unable to meet his eyes, quickly said goodbye to William and hurried off.

Yet not before William Carver had seen the hurt on the young woman's face. Annoyed with his son, he turned to face Aaron.

The day nurse stuck her head in the door at that moment. "Mr. Carver, you can follow me to your daughter's room."

Relieved that he wouldn't be interrogated by his father, Aaron led the way, knowing that William would have his say before long. But not today.

It was the Monday of Thanksgiving week, but Kate felt thankful for very little. Of course, there was Jamie, who, like most children, recovered with astonishing speed from her frightful ordeal. She was once more the laughing, happy little baby, toddling all over the house, none the worse for what she'd gone through.

And, Kate reminded herself, she had a lovely home to live in and a generous salary she was banking each week, for she had nothing to spend her money on except the occasional gift for Jamie. She also had Fitz, having grown fond of the older woman with her quaint philosophy delivered in the Irish accent she'd never quite lost.

But what Kate didn't have was any improvement in her relationship with her employer. If anything, Aaron had cooled considerably since he'd acted out of character by kissing her at the hospital that night. He was once more avoiding her, no longer arriving early most evenings, and now spending the hours at home either quietly playing with Jamie or holed up in his study with paperwork. Quite often, he attended business dinners and various presentations, something he hadn't done very often before.

Kate pulled Jamie's door half-closed after putting her to bed for the evening and thought that Aaron needn't bother to think up excuses to avoid her. She'd stay clear of him, since he no longer desired her company. He rarely made eye contact with her, had shared only two meals with all of them recently and hadn't touched her even accidentally since the incident at the hospital.

Restlessly, she went back downstairs, wondering what to do with her energy. She wasn't much for watching television, which Fitz loved to do, already in her room with one of her favorite programs. Kate loved to read, but she'd read herself to sleep nearly every evening for over a week. Here it was seven, and the long evening stretched before her.

She wandered to the family room, picked up a few toys she'd missed earlier, then walked over to stare out at the already darkened sky. It was chilly out, but they hadn't had snow yet. Used to Michigan winters, she didn't mind the cold. Perhaps a walk along the river would clear the cobwebs from her muddled mind and tire her enough to sleep.

That decided, Kate slipped on her heavier shoes, grabbed her jacket and scarf, then went to let Fitz know to listen for Jamie while she took a walk. She might have guessed that Fitz would warn her about strolling around in the dark, but Kate wasn't afraid. The boardwalk was well lighted most of the way with old-fashioned lamp-posts, and she was certain she wouldn't be the only soul outdoors needing a little air.

She set out, a scarf she'd knit hanging around her neck, her hands stuffed in the pockets of her leather jacket. The light wind felt good ruffling her hair. Reaching the boardwalk, she saw only one freighter slowly moving down the river. Soon, there'd be none when the water froze over. Winter was such a forbidding time, when so many things ceased due to the cold. Or perhaps it was her mood, which was a sad one.

Why was it that she always wound up alone? Kate couldn't help wondering. She scarcely remembered her original family, her parents and Michael and Hannah, when they'd lived on the farm in Frankenmuth. One day, everything was wonderful, or had she just viewed it with the eyes of a six-year-old? The next day, her father was dead, her mother taken away, her brother and sister gone, too.

But the Spencers had taken her into their home, and while it hadn't been the same, she'd felt cared for and safe. Now they, too, were gone, and Uncle Tom had robbed her of everything. She had only Pam as a cousin and friend. Yet Pam was suddenly in love and would likely be forming a family with her newspaper man. Leaving Kate alone again.

And then there were the Carvers. She adored Jamie and would be content mothering the child the rest of her days. But the father was another problem. She'd grown to care deeply for Aaron, but he'd made it abundantly clear he wanted no woman in his life, certainly not her.

Yet he'd responded to that kiss that had started out small and exploded into a startling revelation. For both of them, she was sure. He felt it, too, Kate knew. It hadn't been her imagination. But he would deny it. He was a man who would turn from his desire, his needs, because he was afraid of losing again. She'd seen his anguish at the hospital at the thought of Jamie being taken from him. She was no psychologist, but Kate felt that Aaron was afraid of involvements because the one time he'd committed, things had ended badly and much too soon. Then there was the trauma of his mother's departure and his father's absence, so much for a boy to have to deal with. Early fears, she knew only too well, stayed with a person into adulthood.

The wind picked up as she strolled. Kate wrapped her scarf about her neck and walked on. The sky was filled with heavy clouds, and the river was choppy this evening. There was the smell of rain in the air, but it didn't seem imminent. She wished it would snow instead.

It occurred to Kate that she'd never really been in love before. Evan didn't count, for although she'd thought at the time that he was the one, she'd soon realized that he wasn't the man she'd made him out to be in her mind. So here she was in love for the first time at twenty-four, only to find that the man wasn't interested in keeping her in his life. She wouldn't be surprised if Aaron found a reason to let her go soon, for her very presence in the house was upsetting to him, she could see.

The problem was, he wanted her. She wasn't vastly experienced, but she knew desire when she saw it in a man's eyes. But Aaron didn't *want* to want her. And he was a man of iron control when he made up his mind.

Lost in thought, Kate was scarcely aware that she'd ambled past the lighted area of the boardwalk and onto the dim riverbank. The pebbly ground crunched underfoot as she trudged on, wishing she could change a future that loomed ahead as lonely and grim. She disliked feeling sorry for herself and rarely gave in to self-pity.

Squaring her shoulders, Kate decided it was time to discontinue these gloomy thoughts. If Aaron didn't want her, it was his loss, damn it. She would stay on despite his indifference to her and concentrate on Jamie, who loved her unconditionally. If he wanted her gone, he'd have to fire her. She was someone of worth, and if he couldn't see that, then that was his problem.

Head held high, chin up, she walked on with a determined step, scarcely noticing that the wind carried with it the first drops of a cold rain.

Aaron parked his car in the garage, got out and pulled up the collar of his coat. Nearly eight o'clock, a hell of a time for a man to be getting home, especially one who'd left at seven that morning. And to add to his annoyance, it was raining heavily, a blustery downpour cold enough to turn into snow eventually. Hurriedly, he dashed inside, setting down his briefcase and shrugging out of his coat. The house was quiet for early evening.

Rubbing his hands together, he checked and found a plate in the fridge that he could warm up for dinner. Fitz's lamb stew. Apparently, Kate hadn't cooked today. He had little appetite for Fitz's meal, especially having to eat all alone. Maybe later. He wasn't very hungry just yet.

Restless was what he was. He grabbed a small bottle of juice, screwed off the top and drank deeply.

If Stephanie had been waiting for him, he'd have built a fire in the library and they'd have sat together, sipping a glass of wine, discussing their day. Was it *that* woman he missed or merely the remembered ritual, the need to share an evening with a loved one?

Annoyed with his thoughts, Aaron walked toward the front of the house. He could hear television voices coming from Fitz's room at the head of the stairs. He went up, deciding to change clothes before warming his solitary meal. He pushed open Jamie's door, went inside and saw that she was lightly snoring on her back, wearing a pink blanket sleeper. He touched the backs of his fingers to her baby cheeks and found her warm but not overly so. Again, he was overwhelmed with gratitude that she was well and at home, safe in her own bed.

He strolled on down the hallway, pausing at Kate's door. Surprisingly, it was open, but the room was dark. Curious, he peeked inside and saw no one. He snapped on the light and verified that the room was empty. He'd passed both the library and family room downstairs, and she hadn't been in either. Odd, because her car had been in the garage.

Growing concerned, he retraced his footsteps and knocked on Fitz's open door, calling out her name.

She clicked off the TV and rose from her recliner. "Would you be needing something, Aaron?" she asked.

"I'm just wondering where Kate is."

"She went for a walk a good hour ago." With the television off, Fitz could now hear the rain splash against her windows. "Oh, my, will you look at it out there. I got so involved in my story I didn't notice the storm come up."

Aaron frowned. "Where was she headed?"

Fitz shrugged. "She didn't say. Just a walk. She's been a bit on the melancholy side, as I'm sure you've noticed." She peered at him through the glasses that she seldom wore, certain that if he had noticed, he'd chosen to ignore the young woman he was treating so poorly. Keeping her guessing was what he was doing, and her growing fonder of him by the day.

"A walk? Who in their right mind would go walking in the rain when it's pitch-black out?" Swearing under his breath, Aaron stomped out and hurried down the stairs. Damn-fool woman. What could she have been thinking of?

That was all they needed just now, another rush to the hospital, this time with a case of pneumonia, he thought as he pulled his fleece-lined jacket from the back closet. He stopped only long enough to change shoes, then hurried out the door.

From her upstairs bedroom window, Fitz watched Aaron drive off, the rain pelting against the windshield. If only she'd noticed the weather turning bad earlier, she might have called him to go after Kate then. She wasn't certain just how long it had been raining, but by the look of the puddles in the backyard, it had been a while.

The poor child would be soaked and sure to catch cold. She'd best put on water for tea and find more blankets for her bed. Purposefully, Fitz left her room and went downstairs.

*Michigan—Fall 1982*

*It is with a mixture of joy and sadness that I write in my journal today. The joy is boundless, for I hold in my arms our tiny baby, Emily. Sloan's first daughter is beautiful. We are truly blessed.*

*But the sadness lives within me, for we still haven't located my three lost children. Sloan has diligently worked toward that end and we have learned much but not enough.*

*He discovered that a careless judge in Michigan had done some poor record keeping years ago, and my little ones slipped through the cracks of the system. No one in the adoption centers, the Child Protective Services or any other agency, nor in the court system, could tell us for certain what happened to them. My heart breaks all over again.*

*Through Sloan's persistence, we uncovered some facts. Michael, my oldest, had run away from his last foster home at age sixteen, while I was still in the hospital. We've checked military records, police files and advertised in major city newspapers, but so far, we've found not a trace of Michael. But we will not give up.*

*Hannah we traced back as far as her high-school graduation in Lansing, but the last foster family she lived with moved out of the area, and we can't seem to locate them. Thus, we've been unable to learn more. God willing, we will one day.*

*My youngest, Kate, disappeared from the records almost immediately after she was taken from the farmhouse at age six. Apparently, she was privately adopted through an attorney. The lawyer died, and the records are sealed. At this time, we're at a dead end, but I know Sloan will find a way to locate my baby.*

*In the meantime, I fill my hours with Christopher, who is eleven now, a handsome boy who loves me as his mother. And now we have this precious little one. Emily has dark hair, big brown eyes and a dimple in her chin the same as mine. It feels so good to hold an infant again.*

*But still there is an ache, an emptiness in my heart that can only be healed when I once again hold Michael and Hannah and Kate in my arms also. I know that one day that will happen. I pray it will be soon.*

*Chapter Seven*

The lamps along the riverbank were dim under the best of circumstances. In a heavy downpour, they did nothing but illuminate the rain as it fell. Discouraged with trying to drive and search out a particular someone at the same time, Aaron pulled off onto a side street and parked the car. Leaving it, he hunched his shoulders and jogged toward the boardwalk, his thick soles squishing in the wet grass.

There was very little traffic on the boulevard street and even fewer pedestrians. He saw the lights of a freighter way downriver, hazy in the foggy night. Peering ahead, north on the wooden walkway, he could see no one. Yet that was probably the direction Kate had chosen. He remembered it was the path she'd mentioned taking several afternoons when she'd wheeled Jamie in the stroller to feed the ducks. A flash of lightning lit up the night sky, followed by a rumble of thunder. An older man carrying a shopping bag passed by, and an impatient horn blasted from the corner. In the distance, he could hear a dog barking steadily.

He started out, his steps rapid, alternately angry with her and worried over her. Whatever had possessed her to stay so late? To his knowledge, it had been raining since around half past seven. Fitz said she'd left the house about seven, an hour ago. She should be thoroughly drenched by now, the little fool.

Melancholy. Fitz had told him Kate had been melancholy lately. If so, she wasn't alone in her feelings. How did Fitz think he felt, sleeping in the same house with Kate night after night, wanting her yet knowing he shouldn't touch her again? His father's face in the hospital waiting room when he'd walked in on them haunted him. He'd seen shock and disbelief. He'd disappointed William. And small wonder, groping a woman in a public place with his child gravely ill and his wife dead only a short few months.

Water beaded in Aaron's hair and trailed down his cheeks as he hurried on. Fitz seemed to think he was the cause of Kate's melancholy because he hadn't been around much. The housekeeper was trying to lay on the guilt, as she'd done when he'd been a boy. But it wasn't guilt alone that kept him from spending more time with Kate. It was a sense of fairness. He knew he'd never marry again, could never risk being hurt like that again. Loving and then losing that love was the worst nightmare he'd ever lived through. Which was why he felt that it was grossly unfair to lead Kate on. The explanation fell a bit short of perfect, but he didn't have time to think it through more thoroughly just now.

Where in hell was she? he asked silently, trying to discern human shapes from the vague shadows up ahead.

All he saw was a skinny dog darting out of the trees on his way to the road, barely sparing him a glance. He stopped and called out her name, but the wind took the words and whipped them out across the churning river water. Aaron forged on.

He was well past the last of the lampposts when he spotted a lone figure standing alongside a cluster of tall pines, huddled with her back to the river as if trying to avoid the wind-driven rain blowing in from the east. He picked up his pace and waited until he was a hundred or so feet away before again calling out her name.

The figure separated itself from the shadows and stepped out onto the dim path. He rushed forward and saw that it was Kate. Kate with her hair plastered to her head, a wet scarf dangling from her neck, her clothes saturated, her face streaked with mud.

"Thank God it's you," Kate said, recognizing him.

"What are you doing out here?" Aaron drew a folded white handkerchief from his pocket and stepped closer to wipe the worst of the muddy streaks from her face.

"I went for a walk and wound up much farther away than I realized. The next thing I knew, rain was coming down in buckets. I was trying to hurry back when I fell on the slippery walk right into this muddy hole." More annoyed than hurt, she drew in a breath. "I lost my shoe, couldn't find it anywhere in the dark."

"Forget the shoe. Why were you standing just now in those trees? Don't you know that's the last place you should be when it's lightning out?" Concern had him sounding sharp, critical.

Kate felt like grinding her teeth. Here he was, interrogating her in the driving rain. "I *know* that but I didn't know who was coming toward me." She took the sodden handkerchief from him and wiped her eyes.

"Lucky it was me."

She felt him slip an arm around her, but she started shoelessly limping ahead of him. "Yeah, lucky," she muttered. She didn't feel very lucky just then.

Aaron followed, wondering at her strange mood. "What's the matter?"

She hated saying it out loud. "I feel so stupid."

"Well, don't. The storm came up unexpectedly and caught you off guard." As if for emphasis, another bolt of lightning slithered across the sky and disappeared in the dark, whirling river water. The echoing thunder seemed farther away now.

Despite his reasonable explanation of her careless behavior, Kate was embarrassed. The man must think she didn't have a working brain. Children wandered off and got caught in storms, not adults. Well, this would be the excuse he could use to fire her. A woman who didn't have the good sense to come in out of the rain obviously wasn't fit to watch over his child. Kate felt a hopeless shiver take her.

Aaron hustled her across the street. Just as they reached the curb where his car was parked, the other muddy shoe dropped off. Impatiently, he picked it up before opening the door.

"I'll get your car all wet and dirty," Kate said, shoving her hair off her face with the back of a wet hand.

"I'll have it washed. Get in." He waited while she did, then went around to get behind the wheel. In minutes, he had them at his back door.

Kate hurried into the warm kitchen before the shakes took over. She stripped off her ruined scarf and removed her favorite jacket, thinking it would never be the same again.

"Sit down over here," Aaron told her, pulling out a kitchen chair, "and let me help you."

She obeyed, too cold and shivery to protest, then watched him remove her muddy socks as Fitz came bustling in.

"There you finally are. Heavens, child, you've no doubt caught a fierce cold." She poured hot water into the teapot. "Not to worry. We'll have you warm as toast in no time."

There was a scolding tone to Fitz's voice that made Kate feel even worse. "Please, I don't want to be any trouble." She looked up and saw that Aaron was preparing a pan of hot water to soak her grimy feet. The last straw. "I'm going up to take a shower." A bit unsteady but determined not to show it, she rose.

"Sure, you do that, dear, and I'll bring your tea up shortly." Understanding Kate's embarrassment, Fitz touched Aaron's arm and gave a quick negative shake to her head, then took the bowl from him. "You might want to get out of your wet things, as well."

Instead, he went after Kate. "Are you sure you're all right?"

As if in answer, a deep sneeze shook her, followed by a second. "I will be, but thank you." She sniffled into his damp handkerchief, thinking she'd have to launder it tomorrow. But now, all she wanted was to stand under a hot spray until she stopped shivering. She left the kitchen, hoping her soiled feet weren't leaving tracks.

"I'll check on you later," Aaron called after her, then slipped out of his own soggy shoes. "We've messed up your floor but good. Sorry, Fitz."

She took his jacket from him. "Don't you worry about the floor, just go clean up."

At the top of the stairs, Aaron heard Kate's shower already going. Unbidden, the image of her standing beneath the spray, the water spreading through her blond hair and sluicing down her slender limbs, came to him so sharply that he sucked in a quick breath. He could actually picture the texture of her skin, smell the soapy fragrance, almost taste the smooth, wet skin.

Disgusted with himself, he shook his head, banishing the vision, and went into his room.

He waited an hour before going to her, telling himself he just wanted to be sure she was all right. After all, she was an employee in his home. He'd allowed her plenty of time to shower and change and for Fitz to fuss over her. He'd heard the murmur of voices and the clink of the spoon to cup as she'd taken hot tea in to Kate and stayed to make sure she drank some. Probably laced it with Irish whiskey, Aaron thought, recalling Fitz's favorite remedy for colds. It had been quiet in the hallway for some time now.

Slipping a sweatshirt on with his jeans, he stepped across the hall to Kate's room and saw that Fitz had left the door ajar, so she could hear Kate if she needed her, he supposed. His bare feet were quiet on the thick gray carpeting as he went inside. An old-fashioned lamp his father had given him years ago sat on the nightstand, its yellow glass base serving as a night-light. He noticed the empty teacup and the aspirin bottle on the table, as well.

Moving closer to the bed, he saw that she was lying on her side, her legs curled up as if for warmth, one hand holding the edge of the quilt close to her neck. Her breathing was slow and even, indicating she was asleep. Still, he didn't leave.

She looked so small under the mound of covers, her lovely blond hair fanned out on the blue pillowcase. He could smell her shampoo in the room from the adjoining bath and some sort of fragrant lotion. Her face was pale, the skin almost translucent, her lashes dark against her cheeks. Aaron drew in a deep breath and took a chance, sitting down on the edge of the bed.

She seemed not to notice, so he stayed, relaxing a fraction. He wanted to touch her but was afraid she'd awaken and he wouldn't know what to say to her. He hadn't needed Fitz to tell him that he was sending mixed signals to this fragile woman. That he wanted her was evident to both of them. Maybe to all three of them. But it would be unfair of him to start something that would end badly.

She was so lovely, he couldn't help thinking. She smelled so feminine, like the room she slept in. He'd missed that, missed the softness a woman brought into a man's life. Although he'd been annoyed with her tonight for forgetting the time and getting caught in a storm, he'd also felt protective and strong when he'd found her—something he hadn't felt in a long while.

Kate was the sort of woman who made a man feel powerful, made him want to fight dragons for her, to shield her from harm. Yet she was gutsy enough to stand firm against a large dog that had threatened his child. And she'd gone for a walk alone on a cold, wintry evening in the dark, ignoring Fitz's warning, unafraid of either the elements or anyone she might encounter. He smiled at the small container of Mace he'd found in her jacket pocket. Fat lot of protection that would have been.

She'd refused his offer to let him help her clean up. Had it been because she didn't want him to touch her, or because she wanted his touch too much? Without his permission, the kiss they'd shared in the hospital waiting room floated to his mind. Looking down now at her

generous mouth, it was all he could do not to lean down
and press his lips to hers again. He imagined waking her,
seeing her smile filled with surprised pleasure, her arms
reaching for him as she turned back the covers and invited him to join her.

Aaron quickly stood, reaching to rub the back of his
neck with tense fingers. What in hell was he doing to
himself with these fantasies? He had no business here in
the bedroom of his child's nanny, no business wanting
this young woman, no business hurting her. Angry, annoyed, frustrated, he left Kate's room and returned to his
own.

She waited until she heard his door close before she
dared open her eyes. Kate had been dozing when she'd
heard him come in, and had kept her eyes closed because she didn't feel up to any further explanations of her
silly escapade. But apparently, he hadn't come to talk.

What had he been thinking as he'd sat looking at her
for so long? She inhaled the lingering fresh scent of the
soap he'd used and even stuck out a hand and touched
the indentation where he'd sat on the bed. Just to make
sure she hadn't dreamed the whole episode.

She'd thought that her own emotions were a confused
jumble, and realized now that Aaron's were, too. He
wanted but wouldn't allow himself to have what she
would freely give for the asking. She wanted and was denied because of his stubbornness, his refusal to let himself love again.

Time, Kate thought. Perhaps he just needed time. On
that thought, she closed her eyes.

Kate had always loved Thanksgiving. Ever since her
teens, the dinner preparations had been hers alone. Carol

Spencer had never learned to cook, too busy to waste her talents on something she could hire someone to do. But on Thanksgiving, their cook had had the day off, and Kate had taken over.

Which was why she'd talked Aaron into letting Fitz go have dinner with her daughter's family—she would do it all. Just as in years before, she rose early and was in the kitchen with Jamie contentedly fed and playing in her playpen while Kate worked on making the stuffing. Macy's Thanksgiving Day Parade was trumpeting away on the small television set on the counter, the windows were steamed from the warmth of the oven and the tempting aroma of mincemeat and pumpkin filled the room as Aaron walked in.

"I had no idea you'd begin so early," he commented as he poured himself a cup of coffee.

Kate shoved back a lock of hair with the back of her hand as she set the bowl of dressing aside. "It's not so early by now, nearly ten." She nodded toward the TV. "Santa should be putting in an appearance any minute."

"Then I'd better behave." He sipped his coffee as he walked over to greet his daughter. She laughed up at him, jabbering away in her own language, then went back to chewing on a doll's plastic arm. She was teething and chewed on anything handy, including his finger. After a couple of minutes, he turned back to find Kate wrestling with the turkey, trying to balance it with one hand while shoving in stuffing with the other. "Here, let me give you a hand."

"All right. You hold and I'll stuff."

Standing over the sink, he held the bird open as she expertly crammed in stuffing. "You look to be an old hand at this."

"I am. Thanksgiving dinner's my specialty." She glanced over her shoulder to the far counter where the two pies were cooling. "I made both since I don't know which your father prefers." That was the one thing she was nervous about, that Aaron's father was coming to dinner.

"He's not fussy. Fitz used to do kitchen duty when I was young, but now I think he eats out more than in." Carefully, he shifted the bird so she could fill the neck cavity. Of necessity, she had to stand close to him, a fact that Aaron both enjoyed and worried about.

"I like to eat out, but I'd tire of it if I did it daily." She scooped up the last spoonful, but instead of adding it to the rest, she held out the spoon to him. "Want a taste?"

"Mmm, I was hoping you'd ask." He managed to get his mouth around the large spoon and made appreciative noises as he chewed. "Delicious. What's in there?"

Kate bent to sew shut the cavity. "A secret recipe. Can't tell. Must take it to my grave."

"I won't press, then, especially since we just got you well again."

She realized he was referring to last Monday when she'd gotten so wet. "Well again? I sneezed twice, and that was it. The predicted cold never arrived. I come from sturdy farm stock, you know."

"Yeah, you're tough, all right. You must weigh a hundred pounds."

She put a knot in the seam. "A little more than that." She straightened, shifting back and all but slamming into him. "Sorry, I didn't realize you were so close." Which was a lie. She'd felt him moving closer and had wondered why.

Caught, Aaron thought as he stepped back. How was it that being around her had him acting out of character so frequently? "Are you ready to put him in the pan?"

"Her. Hens are more tender." She set the pan on the counter.

She was tossing out straight lines that were hard to ignore. He decided to relax and enjoy the day, not overthink things too much. "Is that a fact?" Playfully, he tested her arm in a two-finger grip several times from wrist to shoulder. "Yeah, pretty tender."

Surprised at his light mood, Kate smiled up at him. "I told you. Okay, put her in place."

He did so with a minimum of fuss, then watched her tent foil over the bird. She stepped out of the way, opened the oven door for him and he shoved the pan in. "I can't wait. I love turkey." But he thought of something that had him frowning. "I'm glad it's a big one. We're going to have one more guest."

Rinsing her hands, Kate glanced at him. "Oh?"

Coffee cup in hand, he leaned against the counter, crossing his ankles. "Dad called a while ago. Woke me up with the good news. My brother, Johnny, is back in town. Do you mind?"

"Of course I don't mind. It's your home." Reaching for the towel, she studied him. "You're not terribly fond of your brother?"

Aaron sighed. "You could say that. He's caused Dad a lot of grief. Can't seem to settle down. He's got wanderlust, I guess. Maybe you know the type."

Kate took bacon out of the fridge and set about making breakfast. "Do I ever. They're irresponsible, think mostly of their own needs, but utterly charming."

"That's for sure. Johnny thinks of himself as an entrepreneur. He's always got some big investment he's working on, some exciting venture that's going to pay big. Of course, he'll need a little seed money to get it off the ground. So he comes home and hits on Dad." Aaron shook his head.

"And does your father go along with his schemes?"

"Sometimes. Most times. I know that Johnny's squandered quite a few so-called loans. But he always assures Dad that when his ship comes in, he'll pay him back. So far, the ship's nowhere in sight."

"He doesn't live here in town, then?" she asked as she turned over bacon slices.

Aaron spoke as he refilled their coffee cups and handed Kate hers. "Only when he needs more financing. Let's see, he's invested in shrimp boats in the Caribbean, a couple of oil wells in Oklahoma a while back and then there was the computer operation in California."

She took a sip of coffee, then pushed down the toast and started the eggs. "Computers are big these days, so maybe he made it with that."

Aaron busied himself setting the table. "I'd be willing to bet that Johnny's the only guy who could lose money even on a sure thing." He paused, trying to be honest. "I want to be fair. He's not a bad guy. He just doesn't believe in working his way up the ladder. He grabs on to every scheme that comes along, absolutely certain that one day he's going to show us all and make a killing. But when things don't work out, it's never his fault, always the other guy's."

She glanced up from buttering the toast. "It certainly doesn't seem as if the two of you came from the same family. You're so solid and reliable, so dedicated to your work."

He thought that over a moment. "Maybe, but in a way, I've always envied Johnny. I can't charm the birds out of the trees like he can."

Carrying the plate of bacon to the table, she flashed him a smile. "Oh, I wouldn't say that."

Watching Jamie happily mangle a crust of toast after having eaten her second breakfast, Aaron sat back to finish his coffee. He'd enjoyed the morning, helping in the kitchen, the companionship of cooking together, talking over breakfast. He didn't want their new closeness to end and didn't want to ask himself why. He remembered something Kate had said earlier and decided to pursue it. "When I first mentioned Johnny, you said you knew the type. Care to elaborate?"

It was no big secret, so she saw no reason not to tell him. "I grew up with a man very much like your brother. Evan Falkner was a neighbor's son, a couple of years older than I. We were both only children and sort of gravitated together, attended the same schools, had the same friends and so on. Later, friendship sort of evolved into an engagement, and everyone told me how lucky I was, how charming Evan was, how much fun he was, always willing to try new things."

Kate folded her napkin, remembering. "He was all that but he also bored very easily. He was always looking for adventure, new thrills, excitement. I found it very difficult to live in that charged-up atmosphere."

"You didn't notice this about him before the engagement?"

She gave a short laugh aimed at herself. "You'd think I would have, since I'd known him since I was about eight. In my defense, he was very good at smoothing over my worries, but his wanderlust increased as he got older.

Then one day, I came home from picking out my wedding dress, and he was waiting for me. Months before, he'd applied for a job with the State Department without telling me and he'd just gotten word that he'd been accepted. He was leaving for Paris the following week."

"Just like that?"

"Mmm-hmm. He said he was sorry but he'd have made a rotten husband anyhow. He simply had to get this out of his system. When he did, he'd return and, if I was still available... Well, you know."

Aaron threw away Jamie's soggy toast and offered her a drink of juice. "I hope you told him to go straight to hell."

"Actually, I didn't. It was partially my fault for not having seen the man for what he was and for deluding myself that I could change the faults I did find. But you know, except for my pride, I wasn't really hurt. We'd drifted together more or less because our families expected us to be a couple, not because of some grand passion." She rose to get a washcloth to clean up Jamie. "I talked with his parents at my folks' funeral. Evan is still unmarried, still traveling, still as irresponsible as he was three years ago. And he will be as long as they keep bankrolling and excusing him."

"Exactly what I always tell Dad about Johnny. But you have to admit, charming guys like those two do hold a certain appeal for women."

"For *some* women, perhaps." She lifted Jamie from her high chair and kissed her cheek.

Aaron stood, his eyes seeking hers. "You never loved this Evan?"

Kate couldn't help wondering why he wanted to know. "No, I never did." She turned to Jamie, who was rubbing her eyes. "I think it's someone's nap time. We've been up since six."

He smiled at his daughter and stroked her soft cheek. "Sleep well, Jamie." To Kate, he said, "I'll clean up here and help you with the rest of dinner when you come back."

"You don't have to."

"I *want* to." He turned to clear the table.

Bouncing the baby on her arm, Kate found herself smiling as she went upstairs.


Aaron opened the door to admit his family, punctual as always, arriving at four on the dot amid a flurry of snowflakes just beginning to fall. "Come in, come in."

Jamie, in his arms and wearing a pretty green jumper, squealed as her grandfather's cold hands framed her chubby cheeks. She'd picked up a few pounds since Kate had taken over the cooking, giving her a healthy glow.

Next, William Carver shook hands with his son, but his eyes were on Kate, who was wearing a soft wool sweater and matching slacks in the same shade of green as his granddaughter's outfit. He couldn't help but think how much the two resembled one another. He greeted her warmly, thinking how inviting the house looked with a wreath made of autumn leaves and Indian corn hanging on the door. And inside, wonderful smells came from the kitchen, and a crackling fire was going in the grate. Without Kate's touch and presence, he doubted that his eldest son would even have celebrated the holiday.

Aaron handed the baby to Kate while his father hung up their coats and he waited for his brother to park the car. Then Johnny was striding up the walk in his usual confident manner, carrying flowers and wearing a cocky grin. Aaron forced himself to smile.

"Hello, big brother," Johnny said, giving Aaron a quick hug before hurrying in.

No coat for his macho brother, Aaron thought. Instead, a cashmere pullover that had to have cost several hundred dollars. He wondered who had bought Johnny the sweater as he closed the front door. "Make yourselves comfortable," Aaron invited, moving to the sideboard to line up several wine decanters.

"No Scotch, bro?" Johnny asked.

Frowning, William sat down on the couch near the fire. "It's a bit early for the hard stuff, Johnny."

"Hey, Dad, it's five o'clock somewhere, isn't it?" Then he apparently rethought his position. "Just kidding. Wine it is." Next, he zeroed in on Jamie. "Look at you, sweetheart. You were just a little munchkin the last time I saw you."

Shy with strangers, Jamie clung to Kate, watching the newcomer warily.

"Look what Uncle Johnny's got for you." He held out a pink-polka-dotted pig wearing a silly green hat and purple boots. No ordinary brown bears from this uncle, evidently.

Jamie's brown eyes grew wide and she cautiously reached out, took the pig, then buried her face in Kate's neck. Her grandfather laughed.

"I don't think she remembers you, Johnny," his father said as Aaron served the wine.

But Johnny's attention had shifted to the woman who held his niece, his dark eyes sliding over her features approvingly. "Well, big brother, you've been holding out on me. We didn't have nannies like this when we were kids." He touched her arm and squeezed it with long, slender fingers.

He was nearly as tall as Aaron, with the same dark hair worn considerably longer and deep dimples in both cheeks. Though he was beautifully dressed and trying to be affable, his smile was arrogant and his manner too bold for just having met her. Johnny Carver didn't exactly remind her of Evan Falkner, for they looked nothing alike. But the dapper self-assurance was all too familiar.

Moving to her side, Aaron introduced them. "Kate, my brother, Johnny. Kate Spencer." Unaware his jaw was clenched, he waited.

"Kate." Johnny's smile widened. "What a beautiful name." He held out the bouquet, shoving aside the green florist's paper to reveal a dozen red roses. "For you, lovely lady."

She couldn't be rude in front of Aaron's father, so she put on a smile. "Thank you. I'll get a vase." But when she tried to hand Jamie to her father, the baby tightened her arms around Kate's neck. She sent Aaron a helpless look.

"I'll put them in water," Aaron said, taking the flowers. What he'd like to have done was throw them into the trash, he thought on the way to the kitchen, then was annoyed with himself for being uncharitable. Johnny was just being . . . Johnny.

He located a vase and added water, his ear turned toward the living room, where he could hear his brother beginning one of his farfetched tales of his trips abroad, painting himself as the hero, naturally. He reached for a rose, and his thumb found a thorn instead. Under his breath, he swore inventively.

What was wrong with him, getting so worked up? If Johnny wanted to fawn over Kate, and if she wanted to let him, it was no business of his. She was free as a bird,

and so was he. He thrust another flower into the vase, his
movements choppy. Even though he'd warned her what
Johnny was like, he was certain his brother would charm
her by evening's end. Fine. It would serve her right if she
fell for that line of bull. He cut his finger again and swore
out loud this time.

Finally finished, Aaron carried the vase of roses into
the living room and set it on a side table. Just as he'd
thought, Johnny was next to Kate on the two-seater
talking and laughing. Jamie was wide-eyed and quiet,
and even his father was listening.

Stepping over, Aaron cleared his throat. "Kate, I could
use you in the kitchen. Dad, will you take Jamie,
please?"

Surprised at his tone, Kate handed the baby over to
William, then glanced over at the flowers. She almost
laughed out loud. They looked as if Jamie might have
arranged them, each rose stuck in at odd angles, the fern
sprouting out of the middle in an unruly clump. Someone's upset, she thought, wisely hiding her smile as she
followed Aaron to the kitchen.

"Kate," William said, leaning back in his chair,
"that's the best dressing I've ever eaten."

"The whole dinner was wonderful," Johnny said,
shoving his chair back and patting his flat stomach. "You
sure don't get meals like that on the road." He leaned
toward Kate, seated across from him alongside Jamie's
high chair. "Do you suppose I could persuade you to
marry me, Kate?"

By the irritated look on Aaron's face, she knew she had
to play down Johnny's frivolous remarks. He hadn't said
much during dinner, but then, none of them had with his
brother holding court. She smiled sweetly at Johnny. "It

seems a lot of trouble to go to. Why don't I just give you the recipe?'' Picking up a dish, she held it out to him. "More cranberries?''

Jamie chose that moment to bang her spoon on her high-chair tray, diverting everyone's attention.

"Ah, I have a taker.'' Kate spooned a tiny mound of cranberries on the baby's plate, grateful for the interruption. Rising, she picked up her own half-finished plate. She'd simply been too nervous to eat much. "I'll just clear these before we cut the pie.''

Aaron grabbed his own plate and stood. "I'll help you.''

In the kitchen, Kate dumped the scraps into the sink and bent to place the plate in the dishwasher as Aaron came up behind her. One glance at his stormy face, and she decided she had to say something before he made a scene. "Is something wrong? You seem a little edgy.'' She noticed he hadn't finished his plate, either. "Was it the dinner?''

"The dinner was fine. Wonderful, in fact. It's my brother. He's such an ass.''

Kate straightened, watching him angrily pace the kitchen. Maybe this dated back to their childhood. Perhaps they hadn't gotten along even then. If not that, she was at a loss. "Look, I know he monopolizes the conversation and he's a show-off and...''

"Do you?''

She frowned. "Of course. Did you think I was believing his inflated version of his travels?''

"Hell, I don't know.'' And more important, he didn't know why the whole day was bothering him. They'd had such a pleasant morning, talking, working alongside one another, laughing. Then they'd sat by the fire while Jamie had napped, watching Green Bay beat the Lions.

He'd felt better than he'd dared dream he would on any holiday this particular year. Then Johnny had arrived and he'd become . . . become jealous.

The truth hit him like a fist to the belly. How could he be jealous? You have to care a great deal for someone to become jealous of another man's attention toward her. No, he was merely protective of his employees. He'd have done the same if Johnny had carried on over Fitz. The fact that that mental picture didn't compute was something he didn't want to dwell on just now.

Aaron walked over to Kate, his expression still angry—at his brother, himself and maybe even her. "You know he's making a play for you?"

"What?" *That* she found ridiculous. "Oh, come on. He's just a blowhard. He can't resist bragging, and I'm someone new to try to impress. The rest of you know him too well."

"You're wrong. Wait and see. He'll make his move."

She'd had about enough. "What if he does, Aaron? Do you think I'm incapable of handling your brother?"

Deliberately, he relaxed his clenched fists. "Do what you want." He left the kitchen.

Aaron helped his father with his coat, his smile forced. They were finally leaving, and he could have cheered. He honestly couldn't recall ever feeling this way before.

Kate stood off to the side holding Jamie, who'd spent most of the evening in her arms or on her lap. Now she watched Johnny come over to them and braced herself.

"It was a great pleasure meeting you," he said, his eyes caressing her face.

"Thank you. Same here."

Johnny lowered his voice. "Listen, I hope I'm not out of line here, but are you dating anyone special?"

She sensed Aaron listening, even though he appeared to be in a conversation with his father. Still, she couldn't lie. "No, not really."

"Good. I'd like to see you again. We could drive to Detroit and catch a play. You must get days off. How about Saturday night? I'll get the tickets. Dinner first?"

Kate wasn't surprised by his invitation, but she wondered if he was doing it because he wanted to be with her or because he knew he was annoying Aaron. However, she'd known what her answer would be before he'd asked. "Thanks, but I don't think so."

He was undaunted, and his smile didn't waver. "Another time, then." He turned to his father, taking out his keys. "Ready to go, Dad?"

"Yes. Again, thank you both for a wonderful dinner." He smiled at Kate, kissed the baby's cheek and hugged his son before walking out the door Aaron held open.

Johnny stepped up, grinned at Aaron and clapped him on the shoulder. "Yeah, thanks, big brother. The food was great, but the company was even better. See you around."

Silently, Aaron closed the door after them. Slowly, he turned to see Kate watching him. "Do I win the cigar?"

"I didn't realize there was a contest. And frankly, I don't know why you care either way." She snuggled the sleepy little girl closer. "Come on, Jamie. Let's get you ready for bed."

Aaron watched her go upstairs and wanted to hit something hard. He'd boxed in college and wished now that he'd saved his punching bag. It would get rid of some of his pent-up frustrations, both mental and physical.

He moved to the picture window and stood looking out at a light snowfall. *I don't know why you care either way,* Kate had said. Did he care? Aaron asked himself.

*Chapter Eight*

The Saturday after Thanksgiving brought with it an overnight snowfall that measured eight inches by early morning, highly unusual for so early in the season. The weather forecasters, caught by surprise, blamed it on a cold front rolling down from Canada. The few adults who had to work grumbled and groaned that every year the small city of St. Clair was paralyzed by just such a storm, and why wasn't the highway cleanup crew more prepared with trucks and salt at the ready?

The children didn't blame anyone; they just cheered, then went out to play in the powdery white stuff.

Standing with Jamie in her arms at the big kitchen window looking out at the huge mounds piled up in the backyard, Kate laughed with pleasure. "Look over there, sweetie, the rock garden's buried, and the shed looks like a drunken tower leaning to one side."

The little girl picked up on Kate's enthusiasm and clapped her hands together delightedly.

"And the trees," Kate went on, "look at their big arms all white now, no more leaves." She hugged the baby to her. "Maybe later, we can go out there and play, build a snowman."

"Or have a snowball fight," Aaron said, coming into the kitchen. "We could each build a fort and stockpile our ammo, then may the best man—or woman or child— win." Sipping coffee, he joined them at the window.

"Is that what you and Johnny used to do when you were young?" she dared ask. His brother hadn't been mentioned by either of them since two days ago when he'd left after dinner. Kate hated subjects that were off limits.

"Yeah, we did." Aaron was in too good a mood to let even the mention of his brother upset him. Besides, in thinking things over, he'd realized he'd gotten annoyed for nothing. Johnny had probably been trying to test him, and after all, Kate hadn't accepted his invitation.

The question she'd brought up about why he should care hadn't been addressed, but he didn't feel like thinking too hard just now. He'd spent all day Friday at his office and had gotten a great deal accomplished. He and Kate had decided separately to get along and they had, so well that he'd called Fitz and told her she could stay on at her daughter's longer if she liked. Fitz had agreed quickly. Too quickly. Was she really needing more time away or was she trying to matchmake? Aaron wondered.

They'd spent a quiet Friday evening eating leftovers and avoiding controversial subjects. He'd decided to spend the weekend getting caught up on a few things that needed doing around the house. But the unexpected snow had changed those plans.

He turned to Kate, deciding he'd show her how flexible he could be. Next to his dashing brother, Aaron had a feeling he came across as stodgy, set in his ways, maybe even dull. Perhaps he'd let himself get that way over the past few months, turning too inward. He remembered a time when he'd been fun, impulsive, spontaneous. He liked to think he could be that way again.

"Who won?" Kate asked.

Aaron frowned, his thoughts causing him to lose track of the conversation. "Won what?"

"The snowball fight when you and Johnny were boys?"

"I did," he said, truthfully, not boasting. "I was always bigger even back then. Johnny had a bout with rheumatic fever that set him back, so his spurt of growth didn't occur until he was about fifteen. He still has trouble keeping weight on."

She saw no animosity or resentment in his eyes this morning. Perhaps his peculiar behavior on Thursday had been a one-time thing. Little did he know he had absolutely no reason to be jealous of his brother or any other man. He was the one she wanted, the one she would have if only he'd give her the slightest encouragement.

Aaron drained his cup and reached for his baby, who immediately pulled his hair in a game they often played. "Ouch!" he said, pretending she was getting the best of him. He reached to gently tug on the little topknot that Kate had arranged on her head, gathering up the baby-fine hair and wrapping an elasticized band around it in the same bright red as her corduroy pants. Kate had picked up bands in several bright colors when she'd gone shopping on her own and surprised him. He had to admit that, guided by Kate's fine hand, his daughter looked sweetly feminine.

Again, she pulled on his hair, and he ducked his head. "Owie! You're giving Daddy an owie." He kissed her before setting her down to toddle off. "Maybe I should get a haircut."

"I'll cut it if you like. I cut my own."

"You do?"

"Mmm-hmm.

"Who taught you, your mother?"

"Oh, no, not Mom. She had a *standing* appointment every Friday morning at a very chic beauty shop. My nanny, Glynis, taught me. She'd been a professional hairdresser before coming to work for us."

It had taken Kate until her teens to fully realize just how vain her adoptive mother was. She'd often thought that Carol Spencer should have chosen a boy instead of a girl, for when Kate began to blossom, her mother had had difficulty handling the competition of a much younger and prettier female in the house. Kate had taken her father's lead and downplayed her looks to avoid setting Carol off. The situation had caused endless problems and was the real reason she'd drawn closer to George.

Bringing her thoughts back to Aaron, she was amused at the skeptical look on his face as she watched him try to decide whether or not to let her near him with a pair of scissors. "Well?"

Kate's hair certainly looked lovely, the cut expertly done. "All right, if you're sure you don't mind."

"I'll go get my scissors."

Seated in a kitchen chair with a large towel draped over his shoulders and his head bent, Aaron decided he now knew what the Chinese water torture felt like. Kate worked slowly on his hair, snipping here, cutting there, combing to check. Meanwhile, her small but strong hands were touching him—his ears, his neck, his scalp. He couldn't have guessed her touch would affect him so obviously, he thought as he squirmed in the chair.

"You have to sit still or you're going to wind up looking very funny," she warned him, unaware of the cause of his restlessness.

Now she was leaning down close enough that he could feel her warm breath on his neck. He felt color rise in his cheeks and his jeans becoming uncomfortably tight. Again, he moved, trying to conceal his problem.

Kate nearly nipped his ear with the sharp shears before she caught herself. Exasperated, she faced him. "Is something the matter? I can stop if you'd rather. Do you wiggle around like this in your barber's chair?"

"My barber's a man," he said through clenched teeth.

Suddenly, it dawned on her. She'd truly had no idea. "Oh," she said softly. "Well, now that we've started..."

"Just finish. I'll be fine."

"I'll try to hurry." Hiding a smile, Kate went back to work. So her touch was exciting him, was it? Here she'd been enjoying the feel of his thick hair in her fingers and stroking the strong muscles of his neck. It had been pure pleasure, not necessarily arousal. However, it could turn that way if...

"Da-da," Jamie said, standing at Aaron's knee, her innocent little face beaming at him.

Aaron broke into a smile. "What did you say, pumpkin?"

She shook her head, unwilling to repeat herself, and toddled off clutching Elmo.

Aaron swung around. "Did you hear what I did?"

"Yes. She said da-da." Pleased for him, she wouldn't reveal for the world that she'd been practicing with Jamie for days now.

"That's one smart little girl," Aaron said with pride.

"And she's going to have one bald father if you don't sit still," Kate warned again.

"Yes, ma'am." His daughter had defused the situation, diverting his uncontrollable thoughts about the woman who seemed oblivious to what she could do to him. "After this, why don't we go out back and build a snowman with Jamie?" It would be safer, much safer, outside in the cold.

"Fine by me." Kate went on snipping.

After half an hour playing outdoors, Jamie looked more like a snowman than the one they'd built, her yellow snowsuit covered from head to toe. She didn't mind a bit, laughing as she rolled around on the soft white stuff, her brown eyes dancing, her cheeks red from the cold.

"I hope she doesn't get sick again," Aaron said, watching her flop down and try to make angels the way Kate had showed her.

She knew why he was constantly so worried about his daughter, so Kate was patient. "She had a virus, Aaron. She can't get that out here. She's bundled up and plenty warm. This is both healthy and fun."

He pushed back the memory of his daughter lying so still in the hospital bed, and bent down to stick another small stone onto the snowman's belly for buttons. "Now for the hat." He picked up the old felt hat he'd found in the basement, then gathered Jamie into his arms. "Here, sweetheart, you put it on."

Misunderstanding, Jamie jammed the hat on over her hood, causing both adults to laugh. She laughed with them, then let her father show her that he meant for the hat to go on the snowman. Finally, she managed it, if a bit crookedly. All three stepped back to admire their work of art.

"Not bad," Kate commented. "What shall we name him?"

"How about Frosty?" Aaron suggested.

"Very imaginative, but I think it's been done." She cocked her head at the snowman, considering. "How about Rupert?"

"Rupert? Where'd that come from?"

"I don't know. I just like it."

"All right, Rupert the Snowman it is." He tipped an imaginary hat to him and bowed. Before straightening, he scooped up a large handful of snow and formed a ball. Noticing that Kate had started to walk away, he took the opportunity to whirl the snowball into her back.

Swiveling, she narrowed her eyes at him. "So, that's what you're up to now, is it?" Making sure that Jamie was occupied trying to climb into a small red wagon Aaron had brought out, she bent to gather snow with her gloved hands. "Be prepared to say uncle, Carver."

Grinning, he fired off another shot, catching her on the shoulder. "Is that right, Spencer? Put your money where your mouth is." He yanked off his gloves, disliking their cumbersome weight, and scooped more snow.

The battle went on until Kate, her hair generously doused with snow and her jacket riddled with hits, ducked around a tree decked out in white and found herself slipping. She fell into a mound of snow Aaron had shoveled earlier to make a path for Jamie's wagon. Laughing, she rushed to regain her footing, but was

pushed back when a heavy body landed on hers, pinning
her to the ground.

"Give up?" Aaron asked, panting from the dash over
to her.

"Never." With her free hand, she scooped snow, then
thrust it down his back collar.

"Whoa!" he said, shivering as the cold, wet stuff made
its way downward. "The lady doesn't play fair." Bracing both knees on either side of her, he grabbed her
hands, hauling both up over her head and holding them
there.

"All's fair in love and war," she muttered, wiggling,
trying to free herself. But he was too strong, too heavy.
Still, she struggled until finally she ran out of steam.

"Say uncle," he demanded.

Instead of defeat, her blue eyes reflected challenge.
"No. I hate that word. Besides, you didn't win fair. You
outweigh me and—"

Whatever else she was going to say was cut off quickly
and completely as his mouth covered hers. Stunned, Kate
didn't move, couldn't have, and not because he held her
captive.

This wasn't the relieved kiss they'd shared in the hospital. His mouth was hard and hungry, as if he'd run out
of patience and suddenly had reached his limit. The in-
dependence she valued so dearly might have had her
struggling to push him away because of the way he held
her down, but the need, the hot, fierce desire, propelled
every other thought from her mind. Yearning for more,
her straining body inched closer to his, closer to the fire.

She felt him release her hands, then felt his fingers in
her hair and on her scalp, massaging as hers had earlier
when she'd cut his hair. She inhaled the clean smell of
pine and the dusky scent of passion as his mouth ground

into hers. A moan she couldn't suppress seemed overly loud in the wintry quiet as she kissed him back with all the need she'd dared not show him before.

He never should have started this, Aaron thought even as his tongue gained entry and dueled with hers. It had happened so quickly, the look in her eyes defying him, her beautiful mouth smiling a challenge, one he could no longer resist. And he'd forgotten the snowball fight, the cold ground and his own name. He'd taken her mouth before he'd realized he'd moved.

It had been so long since he'd let himself just feel, since he'd lost himself in a woman's softness. Yet she was no hothouse flower who would cringe from the hard-edged passion he was unable to disguise. She matched him, demand for demand, the power of the kiss causing him to tremble.

He'd vowed to stay away from her, for her sake so as not to lead her on, for his sake to save his sanity. He'd promised himself they'd have a casual, fun-filled weekend with Jamie, doing nonthreatening things like building snowmen and hauling out Christmas decorations for the house. He'd sworn he wouldn't kiss her again, because if he did, he wasn't sure he could ever stop.

It wasn't too late. He could pull back, claim the kiss was merely a prize to the winner of the snowball fight, laugh it off. But suddenly, she shifted, her arms going around him, dragging him closer, her body movements even through their heavy clothes driving him closer to the edge. And he was reeling.

She tasted so sweet, so fresh, yet she wasn't a spoiled girl who needed pampering and praise. This was a woman made for a man, who would work beside him, lie with him, laugh with him. This was a woman who represented home and hearth, children and forever-after.

This was a woman who made him long for all he couldn't allow himself to reach out for again. For if he lost this time, he'd never recover.

As abruptly as he'd leaned down to her, he drew back and rolled from her, leaving Kate jolted and numb. She lay still, breathing hard, blinking until her hazy vision cleared.

Gritting his teeth, Aaron jumped to his feet and looked around. Jamie, oblivious to what they'd been up to, had finally managed to seat herself in the little red wagon. Not meeting Kate's eyes, he gave her a helping hand up, then turned. "The baby must be cold. It's time to go in." With long strides, he walked over and picked up Jamie before heading for the back door.

Kate gazed up at a pale, wintry sky. Inside, she felt as cold and forlorn as it looked.

When, she wondered, was Aaron going to stop fighting himself?

"I'm not sure it's such a good idea, Dad," Aaron said, looking across the desk at his father.

William Carver crossed his long legs. "Certainly it is. I'm not asking you to attend the entire architectural conference. But Saturday night is the farewell dinner-dance, and since it falls on the fifteenth of December, we're combining it with a Christmas party this year. All the wives and significant others will be there."

Aaron knew that his father had been involved for years in putting together the annual conference. But last year, Stephanie had been very pregnant and they hadn't attended. He'd planned to skip it this year, too. But apparently, Dad had other ideas. "I don't know. Kate's been a little testy lately."

William thought he knew exactly why Kate Spencer was testy. Any fool could see she was in love with Aaron and he was holding her at arm's length. He was impressed with the young woman's devotion to Jamie, her homemaking abilities and the love in her eyes each time she looked at Aaron. William felt sure Aaron loved Kate, too, but he knew that his son was wary of letting himself care again. The guilt of the survivor could keep a man in a stranglehold if someone didn't come along to free him, to make him see. William felt he was that someone.

"Aaron, I think Kate's wonderful with Jamie. But she spends all her time in that big house with only Fitz and a baby for company, with you working so many hours. Give her a break and ask her to this party. She's a woman any man would be proud to have on his arm, and you'd be doing her a favor by getting her out of the house." Pleased with his argument, one he'd thought out carefully, William sat back, watching his son consider what he'd said.

Aaron toyed with his pen, his expression noncommittal. "The part I don't like is that we'd have to stay overnight at the hotel after the evening ends. I don't know if Kate will go for that."

"For heaven's sake, I wasn't suggesting you share a room. We'll reserve two rooms, naturally."

"Yes, I was sure you would. But it just seems so . . . so odd to ask her out to dinner and then tell her we won't be returning till morning."

"Nonsense. Everyone in Michigan knows you can't trust the weather at this time of year, and the evening usually doesn't end until around one. Some of our attendees drink, and I won't be responsible for them driving long distances after such an event. That's why the committee decided it'd be best to reserve the rooms. Kate strikes me as a reasonable person. I'm sure she'll see the reasoning behind our plans.'' He steepled his fingers and moved in for the kill. ''If you like, I'll call her for you.''

Aaron frowned. ''I think I can handle the invitation, Dad.''

''Good.'' William rose, trying to keep from looking too pleased. ''Then we're all set. I'll see you both at the Woodward Arms on Saturday evening.''

He'd gotten roped in, Aaron thought after his father left. It wasn't that he didn't want Kate to go with him. It was more that he thought they both might feel awkward, especially after the way he'd lost his head that Saturday morning in the snow.

They'd been excruciatingly polite to one another since, not avoiding as much as ignoring the other's presence in a room. It had worked, to a degree. They hadn't had anything but the most mundane conversation since and had included Fitz and Jamie in whatever they did. However, Aaron realized he'd learned one thing for certain: the effect of the kiss, the memory of that long, long kiss, didn't go away because he tried not to think of it.

Instead, he found himself recalling that special moment like a teenager reliving his first real kiss. Nights were the worst, when his mind would stroll down memory lane and he'd wake up reaching out for her. For Kate, not Stephanie. No longer Stephanie. Then he'd lie awake drenched in guilt.

One reason probably was that he spent more time with Kate on a daily basis than he ever had with Stephanie, because Kate was home all the time and Stephanie had spent long hours at the hospital working. He'd often worked late, too, and they'd gotten in the habit of turning in early because they both had to be up before dawn. This hadn't left much time for just being together.

Stephanie had worked until two weeks before Jamie was born and had planned to go back, which had been a source of contention between them. But Kate's work was done at the house.

Aaron scrubbed a hand across his face. He hated these moody spells when he'd start thinking about what had been and what couldn't be again. It was far easier to concentrate on his work and not his home life. Which brought him back to his father's request that he ask Kate to the dinner-dance.

All right, so it wouldn't kill him to spend the evening with her. If it was like last time, half the people there would know Kate, maybe even more, since these attendees were from all over Michigan. They'd have dinner at a large table for ten or twelve, maybe he'd dance with her once and, if things got uncomfortable, he could always end the evening early. He'd walk her to her room and say good-night. The next morning, they'd drive home. And that would be that. His dad would be happy, and Kate would have an evening out.

Or maybe she'd turn down his invitation and not go. Bracing himself, Aaron picked up the phone. Three minutes later, he hung up and stared out the window for a long while.

Kate had accepted.

Aaron, his face screwed up, struggled to knot his black bow tie, watching his mirror image. He wore a tux several times a year to various functions, yet he always had trouble with his tie. Lining up both ends, he tugged once more, then stood back, examining the overall effect. Not bad, he told himself.

He walked over to the dresser and gathered wallet, change, handkerchief and keys, placing them in his pockets. He stepped away, then turned back, grabbing his package of breath mints. Better safe than sorry.

Nervous. He was thirty-three years old, and his palms were damp as he dressed to go out with a woman. Ridiculous. He couldn't remember the last time that had happened to him. Maybe in high school.

Three days ago, Kate had accepted his invitation, yet other than to ask if the dinner was formal or informal, she hadn't spoken of it. Of course, he'd made sure that Fitz was willing to watch Jamie while they'd be gone. He'd kept busy most of the day in his study, but he'd noticed that Kate had gone to her room to dress some time ago. She was probably already downstairs.

He glanced at his watch and saw that it was nearly five. Cocktails were to be served at seven, with dinner at eight-thirty, though he never liked to arrive early. The drive would take them about an hour and a half, so they had plenty of time. With a last pat to his hair, Aaron went downstairs.

He found Fitz in the kitchen feeding Jamie in her high chair.

As she so often did these days, his daughter looked up at him and called out, "Da-da."

Her new word never failed to get a smile from him. "How's my girl? You had a long nap, didn't you?"

"It's the fresh air," Fitz commented. "Kate had her out in the snow. A regular little snow bunny is what she is."

"That's good, sweetie. First chance I get, we'll get a sled and, when you get bigger, we'll try you out on some skis."

"Aaron, would you mind helping me with these earrings?" Kate asked from the archway.

He hadn't heard her come down. "No problem." He turned and stopped in his tracks, his breath backing up in his throat. Later, he was to wonder if his mouth had actually dropped open.

"My, my," Fitz said, "don't you look lovely."

An understatement if he'd ever heard one. *Smashing* would have been more fitting. She was wearing a long red velvet sheath with a high neck and long sleeves, the soft material of the dress fitting her like a glove, clinging to every curve. There was very little skin showing, only her hands and face, yet it was the sexiest outfit he'd ever seen. On her feet were some strappy little red heels that definitely weren't meant for hiking in the snow.

Maybe if she hadn't dressed so conservatively around the house for the past three months, he mightn't have been so stunned. Even the evening he'd taken her to his presentation, she'd worn a simple black dress. But this, this was a side of Kate he hadn't even suspected. Aaron's gaze traveled back up to find her amused blue eyes watching him as she held out a gold hoop earring.

"It hooks in back, and I can't seem to get it right," Kate told him, enjoying his discomfort.

Aaron swallowed hard and walked over to her.

Holding her hair back out of the way, Kate pushed the post through and angled her head toward him. "Ready."

He'd suddenly sprouted eight more thumbs, he realized as he tried to anchor the thin post into the small catch. Her scent, something new and heady, wrapped itself around him, fogging his mind further. It took him three tries, but he finally got it. He took a large step back and almost sighed in relief.

Kate shook back her hair, which had grown longer and now hung a little past her shoulders. "Thanks. Are we ready to leave?"

"Yes, sure." Aaron took his time saying goodbye to his daughter and giving Fitz a few last-minute, totally unnecessary instructions in order to regain his composure. Odd how Kate could look so motherly holding the baby while dressed in slacks and sweater and look so...so different tonight.

"You two have a wonderful evening and don't you worry about a thing," Fitz said. She was holding Jamie as she walked to the foyer with them. "We'll be just fine."

Aaron helped Kate with her black cape before putting on his own coat and picking up their two overnight bags. "I left the number where you can reach us by the phone," he told Fitz.

"Fine." Fitz held Jamie up so they could both kiss her.

Kate paused to stroke the velvety baby cheek. It was the first time since she'd moved in that she'd left Jamie overnight, and it felt odd. "Bye, sweetie." She followed Aaron out.

Aaron's mouth was a thin line. "You didn't tell me he'd be here," he told his father.

William frowned as he watched Johnny whirl Kate around the dance floor. "It was a last-minute thing, actually. Guests are welcome, you know, and Johnny asked if he could bring a date. What could I say?"

Aaron saw that Kate was listening attentively to his brother as they danced, Johnny talking nonstop, and he wondered what farfetched tale he was spinning for her benefit. All through cocktails, dinner and the speeches, Johnny had all but ignored his own date and concentrated on charming Kate. The redhead his brother had brought along looked as annoyed as he felt.

William was annoyed, too. He loved both his sons, but Johnny never had liked to play by the rules, and that bothered his father. "I have two words of advice for you, son," he said to Aaron. "Cut in." With that, he walked off.

Not only did it feel peculiar to be on a date again, Aaron thought, after so many years away from that scene. But here he was on the sidelines while another man danced with his date. Of course, he'd invited Kate with the best intentions, so she'd have a night out after being stuck in the St. Clair house for weeks on end with very little social life, as his father had pointed out. But somewhere along the way, possibly when he'd first seen her in that knockout of a dress, all thoughts of his noble gesture had fled. He was simply a man out with a beautiful woman he didn't wish to share.

Weaving between dancing couples, he reached them and tapped Johnny on the shoulder. For a moment, his brother ignored Aaron, then put on a smile and turned. "I believe your date's looking for you," Aaron said, and reached for Kate.

She came into his arms happily, willingly, and suddenly, his tension eased. As if on cue, the band moved into a slow, romantic tune and he found himself holding her close. When she didn't protest, he urged her a fraction nearer, his face in her hair, breathing in her scent. "I hope you didn't mind my stealing you back from him."

"Mind? What took you so long?" Kate was exactly where she wanted to be. She'd decided when Aaron had invited her out that she'd seize the moment, use the opportunity to let Aaron know, if not by words then by whatever other means at her disposal, that she wanted him and only him. By the look in his eyes when he'd seen her in the kitchen, by the way he'd been watching her all evening with that dark, hooded stare and by the way he was holding her so very close, she thought he might be getting the message. She certainly hoped so.

She hadn't deliberately sought love, Kate thought as she felt his warm breath on her cheek. She'd wanted only a job and a place to live until she could regroup. Instead, she'd found a man who needed loving as much as she did, and a baby who'd come to mean the world to her. In the early years, she'd been bathed in love, yet after having to leave the farmhouse, she'd never quite felt she belonged with the Spencers. With Aaron, she felt at home, at peace.

If only he'd recognize that they had something very rare and special between them.

The song ended, and he gazed down at her. It felt so good holding her. He didn't want to let her go. "Do you want to go back to the table and listen to more boring architectural discussions or do you want to dance some more?"

She smiled up at him. "No contest." She snuggled into his embrace and let him lead her around the floor.

Johnny bided his time, then stepped up to them just as the last dance was announced, giving Kate his most dazzling smile. "I believe this one's ours."

She smiled back but didn't let go of Aaron's hand. "I'm afraid I've promised this dance to your brother."

Johnny's smile slipped a bit, but he decided to be a gentleman. "Then I'll say good-night and hope we meet again, very soon."

Aaron guided them around the floor, his mind still on Johnny. "He's nothing if not persistent. I'd say he's got a real case on you."

"I outgrew his type years ago," she said, then tightened her hold on him.

Aaron returned the pressure as he held her close.

They were among the last to leave, saying good-night to William Carver by the elevators. Johnny and his date were nowhere to be seen. They stepped off the elevator on the sixth floor, where their rooms were located, Aaron wishing the evening didn't have to end. At her door, he inserted the key, then turned to her. "Thank you for coming with me."

She looked up at him with luminous eyes. "Thank you for inviting me."

Conflicting emotions warred inside him. He wanted to pick her up, take her in to that big double bed and lose himself in her. He wanted to love her all night long and wake up with her reaching for him.

But he couldn't do that to Kate. It wouldn't be fair to lead her on when he was so uncertain about his own feelings, about what was right and what was wrong, about what the future held for both of them. He needed time.

Gently, he kissed her cheek. "Good night," he whispered. Disappointing them both, he turned and walked across the hall to his own room, quickly going inside.

Keyed up, angry, tense, Aaron tossed his key onto the dresser and took off his jacket. He hadn't been able to meet Kate's eyes as he'd left her, knowing what he'd see there. He held out his hands and saw they were trembling. He'd never been an indecisive person. What the hell had happened to him?

Just as he loosened his tie, he heard a knock on his door. He walked over to open it.

She stood there in her bare feet, half turned to show him her back. "I'm sorry to bother you, but my zipper's stuck. I can't get it up or down. Could you help?"

He saw smooth flesh and the edge of a red satin bra. Aaron grabbed her hand and pulled her into his room.

## Chapter Nine

"What are you doing out in the hallway half-undressed?" Aaron demanded.

"I told you," Kate said in her most reasonable tone, "my zipper's stuck and I need help."

"Anyone could have walked by and seen you half-naked outside my room, banging on the door to get in. Someone we know, even."

"*Banging* on the door? Half naked? Hardly. Besides, I don't know too many people who'd be shocked to catch a glimpse of my bare back. Can you think of one?" She was being maddeningly and deliberately obtuse.

"You know, I have a certain reputation to uphold." Aaron had no idea why he was ranting about; he just knew if he stopped talking, he'd be in big trouble. "Besides, anyone seeing you alone out there, especially in that dress, might get the wrong idea. What if some guy happened along and really came on to you?"

Kate pretended to consider that. "I've never thought I was the type to drive a man wild, but I guess you can never tell." She cocked her head at him, enjoying herself tremendously. "Are you going to just stand there or are you going to help me?"

"Turn around," he ordered, wiping his damp hands on his trouser legs, then bending to the task at hand. She really did have a problem. A tiny scrap of material was caught in the zipper's teeth. Carefully, he tried to move the tab upward. The pressure only seemed to ensnare the material further. Shifting his hold on the seam, he tried to pull the zipper tab down. It wouldn't budge. His fingers brushed her warm skin and found it smooth as silk, distracting him. Annoyed, he lashed out at her. "How in hell did you get this so jammed?"

He was definitely getting testy, Kate thought. "Accidents happen, you know."

He wasn't sure about that. Her voice held a hint of amusement that annoyed him further. And she kept wiggling around, deliberately diverting him. "Will you hold still?" Irritated to the max, he yanked at the zipper harder than he meant to. The pull tab came off the track, the two sides of the dress parted and her back was revealed from neck to just below her waistline.

"Uh-oh," Kate murmured.

Aaron found his eyes riveted to a swatch of red satin panties. "Damn," he muttered, turning away. "I'm sorry. I'll pay for the damn thing." He grabbed his jacket. "Here, you can put this on to go back to your room and— What are you doing?" While he'd turned to get his jacket, she'd swung around and let the dress flutter to the floor and pool around her bare feet. She stood before him wearing red panties, a low-cut red bra and a very female smile.

"It's ruined anyway." She kicked it aside, her heart hammering crazily in her chest, but she kept her eyes steady on his. She was taking the biggest risk of her life. But someone had to make the first move, and apparently it wasn't going to be Aaron. If he rejected her now, she'd lose everything. But she'd taken that first step in coming to his room, and there was nothing to do but go for it. "I've never thrown myself at a man before," she told him.

Foolishly, he stood with his jacket dangling from one hand while trying to keep his eyes on just her face. "This isn't a good time to begin, and I'm the wrong man to try it on. I'm not what you need, Kate."

"I haven't asked you for a commitment." Although that was what she longed for, what she'd prayed for. "I haven't asked for promises or declarations of undying love."

"Good, because I don't have any to give you." Somewhat unsteadily, he tossed his jacket on the chair and thrust his hands into his pockets. "I've been down that road. Marriage isn't for me."

"I'm not asking you to marry me. I'm asking you to make love with me." The hardest words she'd ever said.

"No!" A helpless need had his heart pounding and his mouth dry. He wet his lips, knowing he had to get her out of his room and fast, before his body took charge of his mind and banished his resolve. "I don't want that."

"Is that right?" Kate slowly slipped a bra strap off one shoulder.

His eyes widened. "Now what are you doing?"

"Seeing if you really do want me." She took a step closer and lowered the other strap.

"Damn it, Kate, don't do this. I'm not in the mood." He quickly turned his back on her before his hands reached to take what she was offering.

"Really?" She moved behind him and, with two fingers, yanked down his suspenders.

Turning around as he pulled the suspenders back into place, he scowled at her. "This is crazy. You're not like this."

"I'm not? Let's find out." She stepped closer, slipped his tie from beneath his collar, opened the next two studs and slid one hand beneath his shirt, touching his bare chest. Thank goodness he couldn't read her mind, Kate thought, and realize how frightened she was of the huge gamble she was taking. She wasn't without some experience, but she'd never played the seductress, never had to. She was flying by the seat of her pants on this one, and deathly afraid of a crash landing.

Aaron's strong fingers closed over her wrist as he removed her hand. "You're playing with fire. You're going to get hurt."

"I like to take chances." Which wasn't really a hundred percent true, but what the hell. She eased her hand from his grip and ran her fingers over the shirt covering his chest, then up over his shoulders, caressing, exploring. As her hand roamed back, she felt his heart thudding beneath her touch and decided he wasn't as unmoved as he wanted her to believe.

It took every ounce of willpower that Aaron possessed to resist, to not reveal what he was feeling. He would hold firm until she tired of her silly game. When she finally realized he wasn't going to respond, she'd feel humiliated at her feeble attempt and leave. He hated hurting her that way, but it was every man for himself in the war of the sexes.

He was strong; she'd give him that. She had to pull out bigger guns. Rising on tiptoe, she brushed her mouth across his, lightly at first, and met resistance. She licked his lips slowly, thoroughly, then pressed her mouth to his again, coaxing a response. She felt him quiver with tension, but he didn't kiss her back.

He didn't move, hardly blinked. It was becoming a contest of wills, and Aaron knew that Kate had no idea how close he was to throwing in the towel. His muscles ached from the tension of holding back, and his pulse pounded, echoing in his head. She was better at this than he'd ever dreamed, and he was, after all, only flesh and blood. Quivering flesh and heated blood, at that.

He saw that she was about to kiss him again and decided to let her know the score. He grabbed her arms and held her away, his eyes wanting to linger on her full breasts heaving with every breath she took, his mouth trembling with the need to taste her. "Making love isn't a game with a winner and a loser, Kate. I'll admit that I do want you, but I haven't been with a woman in nearly a year. It could be over in seconds. Is that what you want, a quickie?"

She wouldn't allow him to bait her or to insult her. The room was dim, with only the bedside lamp glowing softly. Yet she could see his face clearly, the fear warring with the need. "It'll do for starters. After all, we have all night."

Aaron ground his teeth. "You don't know what you're asking for."

"I think I do." Defiantly, her eyes challenged him. "What's the matter, are you afraid?"

That did it. Aaron's control snapped. "No, but you should be." He took her mouth with all the stored-up need he'd had simmering since she'd walked into his life.

Tonight, he'd wanted to protect her, to give her a chance to save face, go back to her room and no harm done. But she'd refused to back down and finally she'd pushed him too far. Every man had a breaking point.

His hands weren't terribly gentle as they roamed over her, molding her slender form to his yearning body. His mouth on hers wasn't soft, but hard enough to make his every desire known. His fingers found satin, slippery and soft, then the silken flesh of her thigh, arousing him further.

Unable to resist, he slipped his hand beneath the waistband, seeking and finding. He swallowed her moan as she tensed, then dug her fingers into his shoulders. Steadying her with one arm, he drove her up, higher and still higher, until she jolted, then went limp against him. He picked her up and moved them both to the bed.

Kate's breath was coming out in gasps as her wide eyes stared up at him. He'd toed off his shoes and was struggling to remove his pants, his gaze never leaving her face. Still, he had to ask. "Are you sure you want to go through with this, lady? Because we've only just begun."

In answer, she held out her arms to him. Wearing only briefs, he came to her. With mouth and teeth and tongue, he feasted on her, teasing, tormenting, driving her to heights she'd only dreamed of. Kate could merely hold on and let him take her where he would. Eager for each new move, she found herself more aroused than she'd ever been, more needy than she'd thought it possible to be.

His hands—they were so clever, knowing exactly where to touch, how to pleasure. His mouth—it was everywhere, tasting, provoking, torturing. His teeth nipped, skimmed, nibbled along her earlobes, the tendons of her neck. He had her breathless, begging, bordering on insanity as he denied her searching hands access so they could end this madness.

"Too soon, little lady," he whispered, his voice husky. She murmured a protest he ignored as he found a new pleasure point and delighted in the discovery. With sureness of purpose, he tossed aside her bra and skimmed off her panties, reveling in the beauty he'd uncovered.

She'd never been touched like this before, Kate knew, not so knowledgeably, so completely, so urgently. She'd never been kissed with such expertise, his lips drinking from her, his tongue driving her wild and still wilder. She'd never felt like this, incredibly alive, yet her limbs were so heavy and her head so light. She'd never truly made love before, she realized.

His mouth on her breast had her drawing in a deep, shuddering breath that pleased him to no end. She tasted sweet, exotic, elementally female. It strengthened him to know he could make her shudder, make her plead, make her moan out loud. He eased off, letting up for moments at a time, then with renewed energy went back to work his magic on her again.

Kate was strung so tight with need, desperate to have him inside her, and still he took his time, kissing the inside of her elbow, the skin of her abdomen and returning to her waiting mouth. Determined and made bold by desire, her hands reached again to shove off his briefs, and this time he let her. At last, her fingers closed around him, and she sighed in undisguised pleasure.

Aaron knew he had no time to waste. Shifting them both, he joined with her, plunging to the depths, and heard her cry of stunned response. As he began to move, her hands tangled in his hair, and she pulled him to her, kissing him deeply. In moments, they found the rhythm, hearts beating together as they climbed.

But Kate had one more need. She angled her head back, breaking the kiss. "Open your eyes," she demanded, and watched while he did. She saw the hazy passion in his, the dark intensity that was such a part of him. But more important she saw that he knew who was making love with him.

Breathing hard, moving fast, he saw her smile and knew why she'd wanted him to look at her. In a hoarse whisper, he spoke her name a moment before they catapulted over the edge of the world.

Regrets were for the morning after, Aaron thought as he lay looking out at the night sky. It wasn't even dawn, and he was already experiencing them big time.

It wasn't that he regretted making love to Kate. What man wouldn't want her, especially as she was last night? But this particular man couldn't allow himself to get involved again. Loving, caring too much, meant that your heart, body and soul belonged to another. When you gave people that kind of power, everything they did could ultimately hurt you. Whether they left of their own free will or were taken from you by some quick, fatal disease, either way the results were the same. You were left alone and aching. Call it desertion, abandonment or death, you were robbed of a future you'd hoped would be happy.

He'd expected to feel guilty after making love to a woman other than Stephanie, even though his wife was dead. He'd waited nearly a year, and yet it wasn't guilt so much as fear that he felt. Fear that he'd put himself in a position to be hurt again.

He turned his head to look at Kate still curled around him, warm and soft, limbs heavy with sleep, her mouth slightly swollen from his endless kisses. Her hair fanned out on the pillow next to his was like a dream he'd envisioned many a restless night. Her hand lay in his, so trusting. It was easy to believe, with her fingers entwined with his, that neither of them would ever break that trust.

But he knew someone would.

Yet even knowing that, he wanted her again, wanted her still. From the moment she'd touched him and even before, he'd wanted her, wanted to lie just like this with her. It felt so damn good to hold her and it felt so damn right. But he knew it wasn't, that he was deluding himself. There was no such thing as forever. The jealous gods would move in and rip his heart out again.

It was too high a price to pay.

Kate shifted slightly in her sleep, easing her head onto his shoulder, squirming around until she was more comfortable, her eyes never opening. He watched her with a mixture of sadness and pleasure. She was everything good, everything sweet and kind. He would hurt her by easing her out of his life now, but not nearly as much as he'd be hurt when she left him after she already owned his heart. He had to think of Jamie, who was beginning to care for Kate more every day. Better to make a clean break before the bond was too strong. Next time, he'd hire a nanny that was more like Fitz, a grandmotherly type.

Yet he couldn't ask Kate to leave just yet. That would be too cruel, especially at Christmastime. He wasn't Scrooge. He'd wait until the time was right and then he'd find a way. She'd never seen the hard side of him, the tough businessman, the rigid-disciplinarian role he could assume. He'd show that side to her, and she'd choose to leave on her own. It'd be better that way.

But until then, until he could separate them as painlessly as possible, he would indulge himself just a little. He would hold her, comfort and be comforted and hope the pleasure would be enough to last through all the cold days and nights after he'd sent her away.

Tightening his arms around Kate, Aaron closed his eyes.

Kate awoke feeling strange, as if there'd been a sudden noise she could no longer hear, some change in the atmosphere. Her eyes moved about the dim room, but she saw nothing unusual, heard nothing. Beside her, Aaron had his eyes closed, his breathing slow and easy. Yet she sensed that something was different, as if some monumental decision had been made while she'd been asleep and she'd had no say in the matter.

Foolish, she chided herself. Her eyes shifted to the window where neither of them had paused to draw the drapes last night. She couldn't see the clock, but the sky was just lightening with morning. A morning she looked forward to with no small amount of trepidation.

Kate drew in a shaky breath. How would things look to Aaron in the light of day? She felt heat rise in her cheeks as she thought of their night, the way she'd deliberately seduced him. Finally, he'd become a willing participant. More than willing, for he'd taken the lead from her and run with it. She'd fallen asleep in his arms, replete and relaxed, only to be awakened again and again by his renewed desire. Even when she was drowsy, he'd had no trouble coaxing a response from her.

But the day brought reality into sharper focus and regrets back into the picture. Would he feel guilty for being unfaithful to his dead wife? Would he think her too bold for having initiated their lovemaking? Would he be angry with himself that he'd given in to a baser need, overcoming his strong resolve not to become involved again? Kate had no idea, for they'd spoken very little.

Perhaps she was being a ninny, she thought hopefully. Perhaps he'd awaken and smile, pull her into another soul-shattering kiss and want to make love again. Perhaps things would change between them from now on, and Aaron would realize that it was all right to love again, that Stephanie wouldn't want him to live like a monk for the rest of his days.

Perhaps frogs could grow wings and fly.

Carefully, Kate raised her head from Aaron's shoulder and crawled out of bed. She stood watching for several seconds, but he didn't move. With a forlorn sigh, she walked over to pick up the red dress, examining the fateful zipper. She could hardly wear it across the hallway in this condition.

She spotted Aaron's dress shirt and held it up to herself. The tail hung past her knees. She'd take a quick shower, put on her underwear and his shirt and then scan the hallway before dashing across. It would be far easier to face him later over the breakfast table than across their rumpled bed.

In the bathroom, Kate turned the water on to steaming. She felt a little achy, but it was a good kind of soreness, the sort that came with using muscles too long dormant. Before the mist covered the mirror, she studied her face and saw swollen lips and eyes that held a certain satisfaction. She smiled at her reflection. The night had been wonderful, and she had no regrets. If she had to live with only the memory, so be it.

Opening the door to the shower stall, Kate tested the temperature, then stepped in. The heat felt good, and she tilted her head into the spray. She was reaching for the soap when suddenly the door was jerked open. "Oh!" she cried out, surprised at the intrusion.

Aaron stood there wearing only a scowl, his big hands jammed on his slim hips. "Young lady, I want you to answer just *one* question," he demanded, his voice stern.

Kate placed a protective hand to her breasts, her heart suddenly thundering. It was all over—their tenuous relationship, her job, being with Jamie. All gone because of an impulse. She'd taken a gamble and lost. "What?" she managed to say.

"I want the truth." Then Aaron's expression shifted from mock anger to a sensual smile as he stepped into the shower stall, closing the door behind him and gathering her into his arms. "Did you deliberately break that zipper?"

She nearly sagged with relief but managed an answering smile. "A smart woman never reveals her secrets."

"I thought as much." His hungry eyes shifted to her lips, and he bent his head to kiss her, the spray pouring down on both of them.

The water was nearly cold when they finally left the stall.


"I'll Be Home for Christmas" was playing on the stereo on Christmas Eve as Kate hung a lovely old ornament near the top of the huge tree Aaron had put up in the family room, taking advantage of its vaulted ceilings. The lights were strung, the star glimmering on top and Jamie fast asleep. They'd waited until now to decorate the tree, anxious to surprise the baby.

She listened to the sentimental lyrics of the song and sighed. Home, she thought. A word that evoked such deep meanings in people, especially around the holidays.

She had vague memories of Christmases past on the farm at Frankenmuth with her birth parents and Michael and Hannah. She'd told Aaron the story the weekend they'd spent in Detroit at the Woodward Arms, and he'd asked if she'd ever tried to locate her brother and sister. When she'd said she hadn't, he suggested that perhaps they could look into it after the first of the year. It had warmed her heart knowing that he wanted to help her.

From the box on the table, she picked up another antique ornament, this one shaped like a delicate teapot, given to Aaron by his father when he'd been a child. Kate's adoptive parents had given her special ornaments several Christmases, but when Uncle Tom had hustled her out of the house in Grosse Pointe, which had been her home for eighteen years, she'd had to leave so many treasured mementos behind. He'd told her she could come back later for them, but when she'd called to ask, he'd sloughed her off with one excuse after another.

Perhaps it was time she stood up to Tom Spencer, as well. Just knowing that Aaron wanted her had given Kate a certain confidence she'd been lacking. Certainly, he hadn't mentioned love or spoken of a future together. Maybe he never would. But he'd been affectionate and loving with her ever since that first night they'd spent together. For now, Kate was contented with that.

She wasn't sure if she could get anywhere with Tom, for he had a great deal of wealth now and many connections. Perhaps if he realized she wasn't after money but rather things that rightfully belonged to her, gifts and the like, he'd relent. Yes, she thought, placing the teapot in a prominent place, she'd also look into that after the first of the year.

Aaron climbed down from the stepladder he'd been using to hang ornaments near the top of the fourteen-foot tree and paused, gazing up. "Jamie's eyes are going to light up brighter than this tree tomorrow," he commented.

"I can hardly wait until morning when we bring her down." Kate found a miniature church complete with steeple in the same box of ornaments. "These are just beautiful."

Aaron walked over to join her. "My grandmother gave that whole box to Dad, and he handed them to me when I built this house. She was a special lady." He reached to take the church from Kate, memories crowding in on him. So many Christmases that his father had tried to make special for him and Johnny after their mother had left, with help from his own parents. His grandmother had taken them to see Santa, shopped with them to pick out their gift for Dad, then come over to bake cookies alongside Fitz. There'd been love in the home despite the absence of one parent.

Which was what he intended to give Jamie.

"It's great that you have memories of your grandmother. I scarcely recall mine, even though she lived with us for a while."

The story of how Kate had been removed from her home, losing contact with her mother and siblings, at the tender age of six had moved him deeply. That, along with the injustice of what Tom Spencer had done to her, seemed enough to make anyone bitter. Yet Kate wasn't. Only there was a sadness about her when she spoke of the past.

He stepped to her side and slipped an arm around her. Despite his resolve, he had trouble keeping his hands off her. "Let's not think about the past. We can't change our memories, but we don't have to dwell on them." He certainly didn't want to think about last Christmas, which had been Stephanie's last. "Let's concentrate instead on Jamie's *first* Christmas."

Kate smiled in agreement. "Speaking of that, how are we going to keep her from *un*trimming the tree? I've tried to put all the more delicate ornaments near the top, but she's a busy little explorer."

"We'll just have to keep an eye on her. Fitz will help. She'll be back day after tomorrow." Aaron bent to retrieve a small box he'd placed under the tree earlier. "You're going to think I'm as impatient as a child, but I'd like to give this to you tonight." Dad would be over tomorrow, and Stephanie's parents usually drove down from Bay City, where they lived, weather permitting. He didn't want any of them speculating, so he thought it best to do this privately.

Kate backed up to the couch and sat down holding the small wrapped package that gave every impression of being a jeweler's box. Surely not. They'd achieved a certain intimacy over the past two weeks, but this was the man who'd pointedly and repeatedly said he was through with marriage.

"Well, open it," Aaron prompted.

There were many other things that could be inside, Kate told herself as she ripped off the pretty wrappings. Yes, it was a jeweler's box. Heart thudding, she opened the lid. Nestled inside was a lovely pair of pearl earrings. "They're beautiful," she said, silently aware of her disappointment and hoping Aaron was too occupied to see.

"I've noticed the pearl necklace you wear, and the ring, so I thought you might like these."

"I love them. Thank you." That's what she got for being premature. Not even that, for what she longed for was never to be. She needed to give up the idea of permanence with Aaron, Kate lectured herself. He'd made that abundantly clear. Never once, not even in the heat of passion, had he slipped and made even the slightest reference to love or a future together.

It was just that, there for a minute . . .

"Well," Kate said, recovering well, she thought as she reached for the slim wrapped gift she'd placed under the tree earlier, "mine isn't nearly as grand, I'm afraid." She handed him the package. "But I did make it myself."

"I don't know when you'd have time to make anything, considering that Jamie's naps get shorter every week," he said, removing the wrapping. Inside the box was a scarf in shades of gray and blue and made of the softest wool he'd ever touched. "Kate, this is lovely." He turned to her. "Dad always told us that a gift someone makes is far more valuable than one anyone can buy. Thank you." He leaned closer to kiss her.

A touch of his lips on hers—that's all it took, and Kate instantly wanted more. His mouth lingered, savoring, and she gave herself over to the kiss.

Never could he get enough of this, Aaron thought as he set the gift and box aside and pulled her into his arms. He was becoming addicted to Kate, to her special flavors, to all she could make him feel. He'd have to do something about that, and soon.

But not tonight.

Forgetting the unfinished tree, Aaron gathered her into his arms and carried her upstairs to his room.

*I am nervous, so very nervous. My thoughts are a jumble of hope and fear.*

The search for my children has gone on for years now. For a while, I was afraid that Sloan would try to convince me to give up, would tell me that the hunt is fruitless and futile. I should have known better, known that the man I love is not a quitter.

I would get so discouraged, and it was Sloan who would tell me to keep the faith, that one day we would all be together, he and I, Christopher and Emily, Michael, Hannah and Kate. They are not with us yet, but at last, we have another avenue open to us.

Sloan heard of a television program that solves mysteries and reunites separated families. It was worth a try, we thought, so he wrote to the producers and told them the story of our long search. Much to my surprise and delight, they invited us to visit them in Los Angeles, where the series is filmed. We did and had several meetings with them. They agreed to air our plea.

It was fantastic. They took down all that I told them, then set up a reenactment using actors, showing how I was taken to the tuberculosis sanitarium from my farm home in Frankenmuth after Lance's death and how Child Protective Services picked up my three children and separated them, and how when I was released two years later, I could find no trace of my little ones. Watching my story unfold brought tears to my eyes all over again.

Then it was my turn, and the host of the show called me to him so they could film me asking anyone who might know where the Richards children were today to telephone the studio. They rehearsed me a little, but mostly, I told my story from the heart. I tried to stay composed, but it wasn't easy. I prayed that my children, wherever they were, might even see the show, or someone they knew would tell them about it and they'd call.

*With tears in my eyes and hands trembling, I joined
Sloan on the sidelines after the filming. "They'll call,"
he told me. "Wait and see, they'll call you now."*
   *I pray he is right.*

## Chapter Ten

"I swear I think she knows that Santa paid us a visit last night," Aaron said, carrying Jamie downstairs at seven on Christmas morning.

"She must have. She usually doesn't wake up this early, not when it's still dark out." Tying the belt of her new green robe, Kate followed them down, smiling at Jamie, who was laughing at her over her father's shoulder. The baby was wearing a miniature version of Kate's robe, both made by Fitz. Fitz had told them when they'd opened their gifts yesterday morning just before she'd left for her daughter's home, that she'd chosen the color so they could wear green on Christmas morning.

The robe Aaron was wearing was the masculine version in red, only because, Fitz had said, she'd heard that red was a lucky color and it went so well with Aaron's coloring. It surely did, Kate thought as they walked toward the family room. But then, what color didn't? Even unshaved, his hair straight from their bed and not combed as neatly as it usually was, he was so very handsome. Perhaps not to everyone, Kate thought, but seen through the eyes of love, he was gorgeous.

So in love, she thought. She was madly, hopelessly, irretrievably in love with Aaron. Sharing his room when Fitz was gone, making love with him, going to sleep in his arms and waking up feeling cherished with his hand in hers—it was everything she'd ever dreamed a love should be. Today, she would not spoil it by negative thoughts or fears of the future. Maybe, for once, the gods would smile on all of them, and things would work out so that little Jamie could have both a mother and father.

"What do you think, Jamie?" Aaron asked after setting her down and turning on the tree lights.

The little girl appeared awestruck, her brown eyes huge as she stared at this enormous foreign object right inside her home. The many strings of lights started to blink and wink after warming up. Mesmerized, Jamie watched. Then she looked up at Kate beside her and clapped her hands, laughing out loud.

"I guess she likes it," Aaron decided.

"I'd say so. Why don't I put on a pot of coffee for us and get her some juice and a handful of cereal to nibble on? That should tide her over until breakfast."

"Great. Meanwhile, we'll decide which of your presents to open first, right, Jamie?" He took her hand and moved closer to the tree, then crouched down beside her. "Shall we start with that big red box with the striped bow?"

In the kitchen making coffee, Kate realized she had a smile on her face, one she hadn't consciously put there. It was from happiness, sheer happiness that had her feeling like smiling. This would be her best Christmas yet; she was certain of it.

By nine, the family room looked as if a tornado had whirled through. Wrappings and ribbons were scattered every which way, empty coffee cups sat on end tables, cereal had spilled on the carpet and "Rudolph" was playing in the background on the stereo. Aaron had built a fire just because the occasion seemed to call for one. Then he'd sat by the tree with his daughter to help her with the large wooden pieces of a puzzle that she'd selected from numerous other toys, including a new doll complete with small crib, a tricycle and a huge stuffed bear.

"No, sweetie, not in the mouth. Put it here in the circle." He checked the puzzle board. "This one may be a little advanced for her age. I probably should have waited." He looked up at Kate seated on the hearth, her hair backlit from the fire like a gold cloud around her shoulders, her face clear of makeup, her eyes warm on his. She was so lovely that he lost his train of thought.

"What?" Kate asked, frowning as he kept staring. "I can't have lipstick on my teeth since I'm not wearing any. What is it?"

"You're very beautiful," he said softly. "Did you know that?"

Taken aback, she anchored a lock of hair behind her ear. "No one's ever said so."

It was Aaron's turn to frown. "Are you serious?"

How could she explain that she'd been raised in a household where her adoptive mother welcomed no comparisons? "Let's talk about something else. There's a package still under the tree. Why don't you help Jamie open it?"

He studied her as she pointed out the gift. She brushed off praise regularly and seemed not to believe him whenever he complimented her. He wondered why she was so self-effacing.

While Jamie, who'd lost interest in the puzzle, began examining a pull toy that consisted of several quacking ducks, he did as Kate asked and opened the last package. He found a soft angora hat, scarf and mittens for Jamie. "They're lovely. I'll bet you made them, right?"

"Yes. I hope the hat fits her."

"Maybe later, we'll put them on her and take her for a ride on her new sled." He'd found one with a seat and a strap designed for little children.

"I'd like that."

Aaron could no longer resist. He rose to his knees and leaned toward her for a very long, very thorough kiss. Just as he let go, he heard the doorbell chiming. "A little early for visitors," he grumbled as he stood, checking the time on the mantel clock. "Probably someone looking for directions. I'll get rid of 'em and help you with breakfast."

Whistling, he walked to the front and opened the door.

"Aaron, I see we've surprised you," Todd Crandall said, shifting the packages in his arms to shake hands in his usual robust manner.

"Merry Christmas." Behind him, her arms laden with wrapped presents, Millicent Crandall smiled. "We drove down from Bay City last night and checked in at the St. Clair Inn," Stephanie's mother explained. "This time of year, you can never tell about the weather, and we didn't want to miss Jamie's first Christmas." Noticing Aaron's somewhat stunned expression, she became alarmed. "The baby's all right, isn't she?"

Aaron recovered, outwardly at least. "She's fine. Never better. I . . . uh . . . wasn't expecting you so early." He glanced down at his robe, his bare legs, his slippered feet. "I'm afraid I'm not dressed for company."

"We're not exactly company, son," Todd grunted as he moved past Aaron and went inside. A short, ruddy-cheeked man who'd retired as a manufacturers' rep ten years ago, Todd Crandall was everyone's idea of a born salesman, outgoing and friendly. "Pretty chilly out there," he said, setting down the packages and rubbing his gloveless hands together.

"How are you feeling?" Aaron asked his mother-in-law, moving to small talk while he mentally regrouped. For years, she'd suffered migraine headaches, which Stephanie had also had. Aaron hoped Jamie wouldn't inherit the tendency.

"Quite good, actually," Millicent said, following her husband inside. She was a stern-faced woman who'd been a librarian and looked the part. She had two passions, books and Stephanie. Her daughter's death had hit her hard. "You know we're such early risers," she told her son-in-law. "We had breakfast at six when the coffee shop opened and just couldn't wait a moment longer to see our granddaughter." Opening her coat, she gazed around. "Where is Jamie? Surely she's awake."

Of all the times for Stephanie's parents to show up unexpectedly, Aaron thought, his jaw tightening. They had a home in Florida and spent winters there, but flew back to Michigan for Christmas each year. However, with their daughter gone, he hadn't known for sure that they'd bother to make the trip this year. At the very least, he'd thought they'd call instead of just showing up on his doorstep.

"Oh, yes, she's awake." Uneasily, he glanced in the direction of the family room, then toward the neat living room. "Why don't you have a seat in there, and I'll go get her?"

"Da-da," said a little voice, and Jamie came toddling toward her father, dragging the quacking ducks. But when she saw the strangers, she stopped.

"Oh, how adorable," Millicent said, smiling at the child, "the two of you have matching robes." She started toward her granddaughter.

But Jamie was still going through the stage where she feared anyone not familiar to her. Turning tail, she ran back to where Kate stood in the family-room archway and clutched her legs, burying her face in Kate's robe.

With a sinking heart, Aaron watched his mother-in-law's face register surprise, then shock and finally a hurt betrayal. "Oh. I guess we interrupted something. We didn't dream you'd have company this early." Her words were icy cold and directed at Aaron, although her assessing gaze took inventory of the woman Jamie had run to.

Nothing to do but bluff it out, Aaron decided. "This is Kate Spencer. She's Jamie's nanny." A part of him could view the scene as it must look through Millicent's eyes, and he could have groaned out loud. "Kate, Mr. and Mrs. Crandall, Stephanie's parents."

"Another matching robe," Millicent said. "How clever."

"It's good to meet you both," Kate answered, ignoring the woman's comment as she lifted Jamie into her arms. She'd never in her life felt so awkward, so exposed. If only Aaron had warned her that Jamie's grandparents would be dropping in. She knew how this scene must look, exactly as it was—a man and woman looking as if they'd just tumbled out of bed.

Ever the congenial one, Todd came forward. "William told me a while ago when we talked that you'd hired a nanny for Jamie. Mr. Carver spoke very highly of you, Miss Spencer." Aware of his wife's disapproval, he peered past Kate, thinking he'd diffuse the situation by calling in the very proper housekeeper. "Is Fitz in the kitchen? I'll bet she's got some of her great tea brewing."

Deeper and deeper, Aaron thought. He was getting in deeper, and there seemed no way out. "Fitz is visiting her daughter. She . . . she'll be back later."

Swallowing down her simmering anger, Millicent stepped closer to the blonde holding her granddaughter and spoke directly to Jamie. "Hello, darling. I can't believe you're walking already and not yet a year old. Your mother walked early, too. Come see Grandmother, Jamie."

Jamie peeked again at the stranger, and her small arms tightened around Kate's neck as she turned her back on Millicent.

Kate felt she had to say something. "She just needs to get used to you for a bit. We've been opening packages, and she's a little overexcited." She looked to Aaron to help her out but saw that he wore that tight look she hated, the one he hadn't had on for some time now. Damn, why couldn't these people have used the phone?

Hurt at the rejection and furious at her son-in-law and the blonde, Millicent turned her back and walked to the door. "Todd, I think perhaps we should leave. They're obviously busy here." Each word was deliberately cutting.

Aaron ran a hand through his hair, feeling like a teenager caught sneaking a girl into his room. "Look, why don't you both have a seat in the living room, and Kate will make some tea while I get dressed?'' Helplessly, he shot a look at the packages they'd brought. ''I'll sit down with Jamie, and she can open her gifts and—''

''I don't believe so.'' Mrs. Crandall rubbed at her forehead with her gloved hand. ''I believe I'm getting one of my headaches. Todd?''

As a man who'd never stood up to his wife, Todd Crandall wasn't about to start now. He didn't view the scene they'd run into quite the same as Millicent. He'd loved his daughter dearly, but Stephanie had been gone for many months now, and Aaron was a healthy male in the prime of life. Surely they couldn't expect him to live alone with only a small child and a fussy old house-keeper? Perhaps Aaron had used poor judgment in tak-ing his daughter's nanny to his bed, but the man wasn't a monk, and the woman was a looker. Still, he had no choice but to go along with his wife's decision.

Quietly, he shook Aaron's hand, then sent Kate an apologetic glance before escorting Millicent out. There were days when Todd Crandall wished he were still on the job and traveling five days out of seven. Life had been infinitely easier.

Aaron stood with his hand on the door frame. ''Won't you please come back around four? Dad's coming over for dinner. I know he'd like to see you both.'' Which wasn't exactly the truth. Dad had never cared for either of the Crandalls, but Aaron had to try to get past this nightmare somehow.

''We'll see,'' Todd said, unable to make a decision on his own about this, knowing his wife's feelings.

''I doubt I'll feel better,'' Millicent added as she went down the steps. ''First, you put away all of my daugh-ter's photos, and then you bring another woman into the house you built for Stephanie, with her barely gone.'' She dabbed at her eyes as she got into the car.

Todd tossed him a powerless glance before getting behind the wheel.

He had no defense, Aaron thought. His mouth a thin line, he watched the Buick drive away. Shoving the door closed, he stood there wondering what else he could have done.

''I'm so sorry,'' Kate said, coming to his side. ''If you'd have mentioned they might drop in, I'd have—''

''I didn't know myself.'' The words were harsh, clipped.

She set the baby down and touched his arm. ''Is there something I can do? I feel terrible.''

As if sensing the sudden tension in the house, Jamie began to cry.

Aaron bent to pick her up, cuddling her close, his heart a heavy stone inside his chest.

''Shall I make breakfast?'' Kate asked, wanting, needing, to do something.

''I'm not hungry.'' Carrying his daughter, Aaron went upstairs.

Slowly, Kate walked over to stare out at the snow-covered yard. ''Merry Christmas,'' she whispered as tears trailed down her cheeks.

''Aaron, are you still here?'' Nick Chambers, one of the junior architects Aaron's father had taken on last year, stood in the doorway to Aaron's office. ''Everyone's gone home to primp for the party. You're going, aren't you?''

Wearily, Aaron dropped his pen and leaned back in his desk chair. ''Maybe later.''

Young, single and handsome, Nick grinned as he shrugged into his coat. "Your dad really knows how to put on a shindig. Great food, lots of booze. I'll wait for you if you like."

Aaron shook his head. "Thanks, but you go on. New Year's Eve has never been my favorite night." Especially this year.

"All right, but drop by later. I know your dad will feel terrible if you don't at least put in an appearance."

"I probably will." After Nick left, Aaron swung his chair around to stare out at a dark evening sky with a few stars already out, the river unusually calm for winter.

A man who'd lived all his life in a cold climate, yet he disliked winter. Or perhaps it was just his mood these days, disliking everything. He felt like the season—cold, forbidding, frozen inside.

The past week had been plain awful, ever since Christmas Day. He'd phoned the Crandalls later that day at the St. Clair Inn and invited them again to dinner, but Todd had told him Millicent didn't feel up to it and they'd be driving back home as soon as she felt able. Aaron knew that it was just an excuse, but he could hardly insist.

Nor did he really want to. Dad had come over, as he had past Christmases, and immediately sensed the tension between his son and Kate. For Jamie's sake, they'd tried to pretend that things were as usual, but he doubted even the child was fooled. Dad had taken him into the study, and assisted by two glasses of wine, he'd told his father about their morning, leaving out nothing.

William Carver was hardly shocked or even surprised that he and Kate had become lovers. As a matter of fact, he heartily approved. He'd told Aaron to ignore "the old biddy,'' as he had often called Millicent, and forget the whole incident.

But he couldn't. He kept seeing the shock on his mother-in-law's face as Kate had walked out wearing the matching robe, looking tousled and well loved. He had only himself to blame. He had never been one to flaunt things in someone's face, yet that's how it had turned out. He was a grown man who wasn't cheating on his wife, for she was gone. And Kate was free.

Yet he felt drenched in guilt. Guilt over being alive when the Crandalls' daughter was dead. Guilt that he wanted a woman when he shouldn't. Guilt that he would wind up hurting Kate. His life was a mess, and he shouldn't tangle her up in his problems. He'd hardly spoken ten words to her since that day, yet each time he looked at her, he saw the pain in her eyes.

Swiveling around in his chair, he decided he'd had enough of his own pity party. He'd go to Dad's annual New Year's Eve gala and not think about anything. He'd eat, drink and be merry.

Sure he would.

He knew everyone at the party, and they were all nice to him, even though he was moody and somewhat sullen. He didn't deserve their kindness, Aaron thought as he sipped on his third ginger ale. He knew better than to mix alcohol with depression.

For two hours, he'd wandered around his father's house, shaking hands, inquiring as to the health of people he rarely saw, making nice. He'd nibbled at the lavish buffet and watched his father's worried gaze follow him around. He wished he knew what to say to remove the concern from his eyes.

"Hey, bro!" Johnny Carver, glass in hand, sauntered to where Aaron stood on the sidelines watching the festivities. "Dad told me earlier he didn't think you were going to show."

Just what he needed, Aaron thought. Johnny with his insincere prattle and his whiskey breath. "I changed my mind." He checked out his brother's camel-hair jacket and his designer tie. "You look as if you're dressed to go out on the town." And he wished he would go, anywhere but here.

Johnny ran a slim hand down one of his lapels. "You like the new threads? Thanks." He stood back and looked up and down Aaron. "You, on the other hand, look like something the cat dragged in. You need a haircut, your tie's crooked and your shoes could sure use a shine. What's happening to you, bro?"

Aaron hated being called "bro" and felt that Johnny knew it, so he wouldn't give him the satisfaction of letting him see his irritation. "Well, *bro,* some of us have to work for a living, and hard work takes its toll on a man."

"I wouldn't know." Johnny grinned, turning on the charm, then swallowed more of the amber liquor from his glass. "So, where's Katie, the nanny? I thought she'd be here, and you'd be guarding her from all these bright young architects who would undoubtedly know a good thing when they saw one."

He couldn't prevent his jaw from clenching momentarily. "She's home with Jamie, which is what I pay her to do."

Shrewd eyes stayed on Aaron's face. "Uh-huh. Do I detect a little falling-out in paradise?"

"My personal life is none of your business." Aaron drained his ginger ale before he gave in to an impulse to throw it into his brother's smiling face.

"Home, eh? Okay, answer this for me. Are you two an item? I mean, I got the impression you were keeping Kate for yourself."

He had to start sometime to withdraw, to end this pseudorelationship that was tearing him apart. What better way to start the new year? "You've got it wrong. Kate's an employee and nothing else." His throat tightened as the words tumbled out, and he wanted to call them back. But it was too late.

Johnny's handsome face moved into a wide smile. "That's the best news I've heard in a long time, bro. Since Katie's free as a bird, I think I'll pay her a visit." Tipping two fingers to his forehead in a mock salute, he strolled off, swaggering a bit.

Aaron marched over to the bar his father had set up in the family room. "Scotch, on the rocks," he told the bartender.

Kate sat in the dim family room with only the blinking Christmas tree for company. Feet propped on the coffee table, she sipped tea and stared out at the frozen river. In half an hour, the grandfather clock in the marble foyer would chime the midnight hour, and another year would begin.

Last New Year's Eve hadn't been particularly memorable. She'd gone to the country club with her parents and several old friends. It had been nice but not exciting. A couple of weeks ago, she'd envisioned this New Year's Eve as truly wonderful.

Weeks ago, Kate had heard about William's annual party and she'd hoped to attend with Aaron. She'd fantasized that he'd stay by her side, loving and attentive. Then afterward, they'd return here, and she'd greet the new year wrapped in the arms of the man she loved, something she'd never done. But that was not to be.

Fitz had taken the call from Aaron informing them that he was going to his father's party straight from the office. Fitz had hung up the phone and glanced over at Kate, who'd come down after putting Jamie to bed. She'd given her the message and made no further comment. What was there to say?

Aaron couldn't handle people knowing he cared about her. That was the bottom line. Yes, it had been awkward to have his dead wife's parents pop in on them, all three in robes and obviously recently out of bed. But if Aaron hadn't been steeped with misplaced guilt, he could have eased the situation with a heartfelt explanation. She and Aaron were both single, both adults, after all, yet the timing had been terrible. Empathetic as she was, Kate could understand Stephanie's mother's pain and anger. Perhaps nothing they'd have said would have eased the woman's pain.

What had bothered her the most was the way Aaron had reacted, as if he'd been caught cheating on his wife with the help. He'd looked ashamed, which had hurt the most. Was he ashamed of her, of his own actions or of being caught in a compromising situation? She didn't know, for he was barely speaking to her.

Kate had foolishly hoped that the nostalgia of the new year might bring him around. So she'd made a special dinner tonight, hoping he'd arrive home at a decent hour and they could eat together and talk. Since the incident, she hadn't thought he'd attend the party at all.

But only Jamie and Fitz had eaten, for when she'd realized Aaron wasn't coming, even before his phone call, she'd lost her appetite. She'd spent lonely New Year's Eves before, sometimes even in the middle of a happy group of people, but never quite like this. That was because she'd never been crazy in love before with a man who didn't feel the same.

She reached for her teacup just as the front doorbell chimed. Fitz was already in her room, and Kate saw no reason to disturb her. Who on earth would be coming at this late hour? she wondered as she got up. Didn't anyone Aaron knew ever call first?

She swung open the door and immediately regretted not having called Fitz to come down. Hand on the knob, she kept her expression cool. "Hello, Johnny. Aaron isn't here."

"Don't I know it," Johnny said, brushing past her. Inside, he turned around and held up a bottle of champagne in one hand and two fluted glasses in the other. "I've come to help you welcome in the new year."

Leaving the door ajar, hoping he'd get the hint, she just stood there. "I'm not much in the mood to celebrate."

He shrugged off the cashmere coat that he'd had draped over his shoulders. "Then it's up to me to put you into a better mood." He glanced up the stairway. "Fitz and Jamie all tucked in for the night?"

Resigned, Kate closed the door. "Jamie's asleep, but Fitz is watching television. Why don't I call her down and—"

"No, no, no." He grabbed her arm, all but dragging her back toward the kitchen. "Let's let the sweet lady enjoy her evening while we enjoy ours." He set the bottle and glasses on the table and reached for a towel. "This is good stuff. Dear old Dad buys nothing but the best."

Kate could smell liquor on his breath. He'd apparently had a head start, but maybe the drink had loosened his tongue. "You were at your father's?"

"I'm still staying with him. I've got a lot of irons in the fire, but I'm taking my time choosing the right investment. For now, I'm using his place as a central base." He pulled the foil off the champagne, then loosened the wire binding.

Kate tried to sound mildly interested. "How's the party going?"

Johnny draped the towel over the bottle and started easing out the cork, all the while studying Kate. "If you mean how's Aaron doing, he's just fine. Living it up, drinking, dancing. He can be a hell of a lot of fun when he wants to be."

So Aaron was enjoying the evening. Good for him. Kate crossed her arms over her chest. "That's nice."

"Yeah, my brother was quite the party boy until Stephanie came along. She put a crimp in his style, but he wanted her bad enough to stop his drinking and carousing. Man, he really loved that woman. Still does, don't you think?" The cork gave with a little pop, and vapor whirled out of the opening. Quickly, he began pouring.

"I wouldn't know," Kate answered. "Listen, don't pour any for me. I told you, I'm not in the mood."

"Ah, come on, Katie. What's the harm in toasting in the new year? We're just two lonely people here. Let's keep each other company, eh?"

She decided to play along for a few minutes, not to appear rude. She took the glass he handed her, clinked it to his and sipped. It was cold and tart and very good.

Johnny turned on the boyish charm. "Can I see your tree?" He hooked two fingers around the neck of the bottle and carried it into the family room, setting it down on the coffee table. "Big sucker, ain't it?" he commented, gazing up at the tree.

Kate sat down in the far corner of the couch, where she'd been sipping her tea, and put down her glass. It wouldn't do to drink much around Johnny Carver. She had a feeling he was the sort who'd take advantage. She only wished he'd get the message, that she had absolutely no interest in him and it would be best if he left. Still, he was Aaron's brother, and she merely worked for Aaron. She must remember that.

Johnny sat down on the middle cushion of the couch, not too close but not far away, either. "So, what's a nice girl like you doing all alone on the biggest night of the year?"

She shrugged. "It's just another night to me."

He drained his glass and picked up the bottle. "Drink up. The night is young." He poured more and was annoyed when she refused to let him top off hers. "Kate," he began, trying for sincerity, "don't you like me?"

"I don't *know* you," she answered carefully.

"We can change that." He shifted slightly closer. "I'm a nice guy, not a brooder like my brother. We could have some good times together."

This was a discussion she didn't want any part of. "I think it only fair to tell you that I'm simply not interested."

He reached to stroke two long fingers along her cheek. "Why not give us a chance, get to know me?"

Her blue eyes suddenly frosty, she met his gaze. "What part of the word *no* don't you understand?" Quickly, she stood. "I think you should go. I'm tired."

Annoyed with her rejection, Johnny slammed down his glass, ignoring the champagne that sloshed onto the table. "Fine. Your loss." He got to his feet somewhat unsteadily. "You've chosen the wrong brother to fall for, Katie, my girl," he told her as he made his way to the front door. "You're wasting your time waiting for Aaron to come around. He'll never get over Stephanie." He grabbed his coat and yanked open the door, then turned back to her, his handsome face suddenly hard. "All you are is someone handy to warm his bed, but he'll never love you."

Tears sprang to her eyes, but she pushed them back. She wouldn't give him the satisfaction of a reply or a reaction.

With a sneer, he stepped outside. "You're probably a cold fish, anyhow." He got into his car parked on the curved driveway and gunned the engine noisily before racing off, wheels squealing.

Blinking rapidly, Kate closed the door. Johnny Carver was drunk. He was just babbling on because she'd turned him down. That was all, she told herself as she gathered up the glasses, cup and bottle, taking them to the kitchen. She wouldn't pay any attention to anything he'd said.

She'd just finished cleaning up when she heard the front door open. Moving into the front hallway, she saw Aaron taking off his coat. For a long moment, their eyes locked, neither saying a word.

"Was that Johnny I passed outside the gate?" he asked, knowing full well it was but wanting to hear what she'd say. He hated the way she looked, eyes too bright, a sad look about her beautiful mouth. What in hell had Johnny said to upset her?

"Yes."

"What did he want?"

"Me," she said quietly. Turning, she ran up the stairs.

He should go after her, Aaron thought. He should take her in his arms and apologize for his brother. He should tell her it was eating him alive, this distance between them.

But he couldn't. It would only complicate things. He had to do this, had to make her unhappy enough to leave. She needed to get on with her life, find someone who could love her the way she deserved to be loved.

Wandering back to the kitchen, he saw the open bottle of champagne. He guessed that Johnny had brought it to her, probably thinking she'd willingly jump into bed with him. He didn't know Kate Spencer.

Aaron reached for one of the glasses on the drainboard and poured himself some of the bubbly. He hadn't been able to finish the Scotch at his father's, his mind too preoccupied. Now he sipped the champagne and wished he had someone to share it with. Not just any someone. Kate.

He strolled into the family room, gazed out at the frozen river, then at the embers in the fireplace. Like the embers of his life, smoldering, dying. He sipped champagne and tasted bitterness.

Aaron heard the foyer clock chime twelve times. Midnight. "Happy New Year," he said to his reflection in the window. He set down his glass, turned and went upstairs to his large, solitary bed.

## Chapter Eleven

The Book Tree was located in a section of Grosse Pointe known as the Village. Variety stores, trendy restaurants and specialty shops stretched along both sides of a broad, tree-lined street. Kate found a parking space across the street from the bookstore she'd operated for George Spencer for two years and checked it out.

It seemed that her cousin had made few changes since taking over in August. But then, Pam's heart wasn't in bookselling. She'd agreed only to please her father. Kate had phoned her this morning and asked if Pam could spare the time for lunch. It was January 2, and she badly needed to talk with someone. Fortunately, her cousin had welcomed the idea.

So Kate had asked Fitz to watch Jamie for the day, and the older woman had quickly agreed, since Kate rarely took time for herself. Aaron, of course, had left the house early, presumably gone to his office. He'd spent most of New Year's Day behind the closed doors of his study. Jamie had been cranky, with another tooth about to break through, so Kate had put her to bed early and gone to her own room. She hadn't felt like eating dinner, refusing Fitz's invitation to join her in the kitchen. She had no idea if Aaron went down. The year had started out swimmingly.

With a sigh, Kate walked across the street and stood for a moment examining the window display. Decorating had been her specialty, for she'd truly enjoyed changing things around every few weeks, highlighting local authors, building displays around seasonal themes. Pam's window seemed unimaginative and thrown together in a hurry. Perhaps her cousin was too preoccupied to notice or care.

The bell over the door jingled as Kate went inside. A tall young man she didn't recognize was behind the counter ringing up a sale. Glancing about at the various book dumps and postholiday sale tables, she made her way to the back and spotted Pam pulling books from one of the shelves. "You're working awfully hard," she said as she reached her side.

Pam turned, her face lighting with a welcoming smile. "Kate." She pulled her cousin into a hard hug. "Oh, I've missed you."

Kate closed her eyes on an unexpected rush of tears. She'd badly needed to hear that, to know that there was *someone* who missed her. "Same here," she said, pulling back to look Pam over. She'd never been terribly pretty, her face angular and thin, her nose too long and her hair straight as a stick and mousy brown. But things had changed.

"You look wonderful," Kate told her. Pam's face was fuller, her brown eyes bright with a healthy glow and her hair softly permed. She even had a more stylish pair of glasses. "Could love had brought about this change?"

Pam laughed, not the hesitant sound she used to make but a confident chuckle. "Does it show?"

"Does it ever. So, tell me, when do I meet Mr. Wonderful?"

A disappointed frown flickered over Pam's features. "Eli's in Ann Arbor on a story. I so wanted you to meet him." She linked her arm with Kate's and led her into the back room, where her small office was located. "Never mind. This just means you have to come back soon." She paused to study Kate. "How are *you?* You sounded sort of strained on the phone."

Unbuttoning her coat, Kate shrugged. "I've been better. Where shall we go for lunch?" Her tale of woe would wait.

"How about Tomasino's? We can pig out on pizza. Remember how we used to do that nearly every Wednesday night?" It had been their dinner date for girl talk, and Pam had truly missed those chatty get-togethers. She sensed something was bothering Kate, something new. "A back booth where we can talk. Okay?"

"Sounds wonderful."

The root beer was foamy, the cheese gooey and the pepperoni had a spicy tang to it. Pam closed her eyes in ecstasy. "This is heavenly. You know, I haven't been here since you left."

Kate chewed with remembered satisfaction, surprised she was hungry. "I haven't had pizza in months, either." She wiped her hands. "So, tell me all about this Eli who's changed your life."

Eyes dancing, Pam talked for some time about the redheaded reporter who was, of course, perfect in every way. "I realize I'm no expert, but Eli seems too good to be true. He's honest and thoughtful and caring. He makes me laugh, which I think is so important. I'm nuts about him, Kate, as if you couldn't tell. But I'm scared. What if I'm wrong?"

Kate sipped her root beer before answering. "Wrong? What do you mean? You suspect he's an ax murderer with a dozen buried secrets? I don't think so. If he's all you say, and the chemistry's there, too, then go for it. But who am I to say? My track record's abysmal."

"Ah, yes, the chemistry." Thoughtfully, Pam set down her pizza. "There was no chemistry between you and Evan, was there?"

"No. That's why, when we broke up, it was more a relief than anything terribly hurtful. Chemistry's awfully important."

"You mean like your hands get damp when you're with him and your heart pounds when you touch him and when he kisses you, you feel as if your head will blow off?"

Kate laughed. "Sounds more like a case of the flu, but yes, something like that. Is that how you feel with Eli?"

"Mmm, yes. Multiply that by several thousand. But I have a question. If Evan didn't do that for you, how do you know how it feels?"

"I read a lot." Kate kept her eyes on her plate.

"Yeah, sure. Come on, give. Who is he?" When Kate didn't answer, didn't even look up, Pam decided to press a little. "Is he the reason you look so sad?"

Kate let out a trembling breath. Isn't that why she'd come to see Pam, to talk things over and perhaps get some insight in hearing her own story stated out loud? So she told her cousin and dearest friend about Aaron and about the past four months, leaving out the seduction scene and other intimate details. She felt that Pam could read between the lines. By the time she'd finished, the pizza had grown cold and her appetite had fled, mainly because the story lacked a happy ending. "No matter how I wish things were different, I can't win in a contest with a dead woman and all of Aaron's memories and feelings of guilt."

"You think he cares for you, but he won't admit it because it seems like a betrayal to his dead wife?" Pam thought the idea absurd.

Kate leaned back, feeling weary. "I don't know *how* he feels because he won't talk to me about his feelings. Except that one time when he told me quite clearly that marriage wasn't for him."

"What was his childhood like?" Pam asked.

"His mother walked out, leaving his father to raise two small boys. He's never forgiven her, or forgotten, and he feels a sense of abandonment even now."

"I can relate to that. I felt the same for years. Of course, my mother died, but Dad even blamed her for that, since she'd gone walking in the rain and gotten pneumonia. As if she'd *deliberately* gotten sick and died to make his life inconvenient." Pam leaned closer. "But you know, Kate, since talking all that over with Eli, I've come to realize that Dad was wrong to brainwash a child's mind, to try to turn me against my poor dead mother's memory."

Kate couldn't have agreed more. "After the last six months and the way he's treated me, there isn't much I'd put past him."

"That reminds me." Pam opened her purse and handed Kate an envelope containing a folded sheet of paper. "Here's the paper he asked me to have you sign."

Kate read the legal document slowly, then looked over at Pam. "Have you read this?"

"No. What is it?"

"It's a release form relinquishing all rights to my parents' estate. Your father told me that nothing they owned had my name on it and that my adoption papers were lost. Why would he need a release form if that were true?"

"Good question. Listen, Kate, I'm only delivering the darn thing. If you don't want to sign it, don't. I told you months ago that if I were you, I'd get myself a lawyer to look into this whole affair. He's my father, but I'm not sure he has your best interests at heart."

No, Tom Spencer had always had his own interests at heart. And Pam's. But maybe that was about to change. She sensed a new confidence about her cousin. "Don't tell me you're actually standing up to him these days?"

Pam made wet circles on the tabletop with her root-beer glass. "Eli wants me to move in with him. Dad doesn't want me involved with him, says Eli's not good enough for me, that one day I'm going to be a very wealthy woman." Troubled brown eyes looked up. "Kate, what good is money if no one loves you?"

How true. William Carver had money, prestige, position—yet was a lonely man. And his son was following in his footsteps. But Aaron would have to figure that out for himself. "None that I can see. Do what your heart tells you, Pam. It's time that man stopped jerking you around." She glanced down at the document. "And me, too, for that matter. I'm going to keep this and take your advice. I'm going to hire a lawyer."

"Good for you." Pam motioned to the waitress to bring them coffee. "Now, let's get back to your employer-slash-lover. He is that, isn't he?"

They'd always been each other's confidante. "Yes, but I don't know for how much longer. As you said, Aaron cares, but he doesn't *want* to care. I think he's planning to fire me because I make him feel things he doesn't want to feel again."

"He's afraid you'll leave him, like his mother did and his wife, too. Even though the wife had no choice. Do you know why the mother left?"

Kate accepted the coffee and took a taste. With Fitz around, she mostly drank tea, so the brew tasted extra-good. "I don't know for sure, but rumor has it, from what I gather from Fitz, that she left Aaron's father for another man."

"Why? Is he as controlling as my father?"

"No, not at all. But he's a workaholic."

"That'll do it. Is Aaron also?"

"He was when I first moved in. But gradually, he began coming home earlier, spending time with his daughter and with me. We did things together with Jamie. Oh, Pam, she's so adorable. She'll be a year old in a couple of weeks. If I have to leave her, I don't know what I'll do." Tears threatened again, and she blinked them back.

Pam reached to squeeze her cousin's hands. "Confront Aaron, when the time is right. Tell him how you feel."

But Kate was hesitant. "I don't know."

"I'm going to confront Dad. I'm sick of living over the bookstore in that small apartment where he has a key so he feels free to drop in on me anytime without knocking. I'm going to move in with Eli and tell Dad afterward. I'm also going to give him notice that I'm putting the Book Tree and the building up for sale. I never asked him to deed it over to me in the first place. I've always believed he did that to wrestle it away from you, because he knew his brother wanted you to have it. I want to use my degree in library science, to get a job *I* want. There's nothing wrong with running a bookstore. But it's not my choice.''

''Wow. You have come a long way. Eli's good for you.''

Pam smiled. ''Yes, he is. I wish I could say that Aaron's good for you.''

''So do I.'' Kate glanced at her watch. ''I really enjoyed this, but I've got some shopping to do before driving back. I want to get Jamie something special for her birthday.'' Something the little girl could keep to remember her by when Aaron sent her packing.

Pam rose, walking with Kate to the front of the nearly deserted Italian restaurant. ''This has been great, but I wish you were happier.''

Kate gave her friend a sad smile. ''One day, I will be.''

Aaron lay in bed wishing he had a cigarette. He'd stopped smoking after meeting Stephanie. As a nurse, she'd been adamantly against cigarettes, so he'd finally given in. After the first month, it hadn't been too bad. He rarely had the desire anymore.

But tonight was an exception.

Hands behind his head, he lay staring up at the ceiling. Today was Jamie's first birthday, and Dad had come over to help celebrate. Kate, putting all their differences and hurtful silences aside, had baked a beautiful cake with pink-and-white frosting. Aaron had taken pictures of Jamie in a pretty party dress opening her gifts. And later, he'd snapped her in her high chair, her brown eyes huge as the first piece of cake was placed in front of her, then the next shot showing her diving into it with both hands. They'd all laughed.

Only, the laughter, at least on his part, had been forced. Even such a special occasion as his daughter's first birthday didn't thrill him. Nothing seemed to anymore. Because of Kate.

He had only to look at her to want her. But her eyes no longer lit up when he walked into the room, and her real smiles were reserved strictly for the baby. He'd hurt her, all but ignored her and still she hung on. Any day, he expected her to say she was moving on, thereby freeing him to get on with his life, such as it was. But she didn't.

He wasn't sure why. He could see she was unhappy. Maybe it was a stubborn streak that wouldn't allow her to quit something she'd committed to. Or maybe she held out some foolish hope that one day things would change. They wouldn't.

She'd given Jamie a beautiful music box for her birthday. When you wound it up, it played "Remember." Fitz's sharp eyes had watched Kate as she played the tune several times, as if trying to burn the song and its message into the child's mind.

Aaron swung both legs off the bed and reached for his pants. There was no use trying to sleep with his mind in such turmoil. Maybe the childhood remedy of a glass of milk would help, or a good book. He left his room and started down the hallway. It was then that he heard a sound.

Jamie, he thought, and went to her room. But no, she was fast asleep, clutching Elmo. He went back into the hallway and paused, ears cocked, listening hard. There it was again, coming from Kate's room. He went to her closed door and waited. He heard the bedsprings as she shifted and then several words he could barely make out. It sounded as if she were struggling with someone.

"No, no, please, no," she murmured.

Hurriedly, he went in. She was wearing a knee-length nightshirt and had kicked off the covers. Her head shifted on the pillow, one way then the other. He stepped closer and saw a fine sheen of moisture beaded on her face.

Her lips trembled, and she murmured again. "All gone. They're all gone. Mom, come back, please."

A nightmare that had her thrashing about, locked in its grip. He sat down and touched her shoulder. "Kate, wake up. You're having a nightmare."

Her breathing was fast, coming out in huffs. "Where are you taking me? Please, no."

Aaron gripped both her arms and gave her a gentle shake. "It's all right, Kate. Open your eyes. You're okay."

Her eyes fluttered open and looked wildly about. Finally, her gaze settled on him, and she just stared, her body trembling.

He wasn't sure if she recognized him. "It's me—Aaron. You were having a nightmare." He brushed back damp strands of hair from her face. "You're safe."

Safe. Then why didn't she feel safe? Kate raised a shaky hand to her forehead. How did Aaron get in here? She must have been crying out and woke him. "I'm sorry."

"Don't be. We can't control our dreams." He felt awkward, out of his league. "Do you want some water?"

"No." What she wanted was for him to hold her, to banish the memory of the nightmare, the same one she used to have years ago but not in a long while. She wanted him to understand, to love her. She wanted a miracle and knew that Aaron didn't believe in them.

"Do you want to tell me about the dream?"

She felt stupid, like a child again. "I don't know why it popped up now. I haven't had it since I was a teenager. It's always the same. These two shadowy figures are making us get into this big car, and someone else is putting my mother into an ambulance. She... she's not moving, and I'm so afraid she's dead, like my father. Then the car starts up, and I'm looking out the back window. We get farther and farther away, and no one will tell me where my mother is." Her hand fluttered to her throat. "Silly, I know, but it seems so real."

"Is that what happened to you back on the farm in Frankenmuth?"

Kate took in a deep gulp of air. "Pretty much. It's the only memory I have that keeps recurring." She moved as if to sit up, and he reached to help her. She felt embarrassed and wished he'd leave. "I'm sorry I woke you."

"You didn't. I was awake. I heard you and I got worried." He touched the ends of her hair, then cupped his hand around her shoulder. "I hate seeing you so upset, Kate."

How was she supposed to answer that? "It's all right. I'm not your responsibility. You can leave. I'm fine, much stronger than I look. I can manage and—"

"Oh, shut up." He pulled her into his arms and felt the tension ripple through her. She stiffened for a long heartbeat, then her arms wound around him and the tears came. He held her gently, murmuring nonsense in her ear to soothe her, acting on instinct. He thrust one hand into her hair, his fingers massaging her scalp, hoping to relax her. She wasn't weeping, just quietly crying, as if the tears were falling without her permission, and yet that seemed more heartbreaking than if she'd sobbed.

Finally, it was over, and Kate felt shame along with embarrassment. Never in her life had she clung to a man while she'd cried her heart out. Too many emotions had piled up over the past months—her parents' death, her uncle's betrayal, her unrequited love for Aaron, the holidays. The floodgates had opened, and for a few moments there, she'd wondered if she'd ever be able to stop the tears.

"I'm sorry," she whispered, her voice thick.

"Don't. Don't say that again." Aaron bent his head to kiss her damp cheeks, then her closed eyes and finally slanted his mouth to kiss her lips, tasting salty tears. The kiss he'd meant to offer comfort turned on him as desire, hot and heavy, slammed into him.

"Why is it I can't leave you alone?" he asked, his eyes glittering in the semidarkness.

"The same reason I can't walk away from you," she answered.

But tonight would be different, Aaron decided. Always before, their lovemaking had been as breathtaking as a storm raging out of control, two people wild to get at each other with precious little time to spare for the niceties. Not tonight. Tonight, he would romance her at his leisure, and the past and future be damned. There was only tonight.

Kate hadn't thought him to be particularly sensitive before. Skillful, definitely. Sexy and devastating and very capable of taking her to the heights. But tonight, his hands moved slowly over her, savoring, relishing, enjoying. He stroked lazily, aroused gradually, kissed tenderly.

He seemed to bring emotion along with desire to her bed this night. There was feeling here, dark and wondrous, but also sweet and loving. With infinite patience, he wooed her, beguiled her, coaxed her to feel along with him. Tears that had nothing to do with nightmares or fear leaked from her eyes as she accepted, as she reacted, as she reveled in his touch.

Aaron found new fascination in every curve and hollow, exhilaration in breasts that quivered with need, excitement in knowing she wanted him desperately. Needing to watch her response on her beautiful face, he sent her soaring with just a touch and swallowed the sound of his own name on her lips.

No man could make love to a woman like this, with such care, with such tender touches, if he didn't love her, Kate thought in a haze of feeling. Aaron did care; she felt it, knew it, deep inside. But he wouldn't admit it, not even to himself, not yet. She prayed she could wait him out.

She was so giving, so selfless. He felt bathed in her goodness, humbled by her generosity. Only in this way could he show how much she meant to him. Only because he could no more stay away from her than he could stop breathing.

Shifting them both, eyes locked with hers, Aaron entered her and, in minutes, lost all sense of self. But what he found with Kate was far more valuable, for she gave him the greatest gift of all—herself.

There was no denying it—when things worked out in the bedroom, everything seemed brighter, Kate thought as she walked into the den. It was late afternoon a week after Aaron had come to her bed, and although life wasn't perfect, it was decidedly better.

They hadn't slept together since, for there was Fitz to consider. Kate was grateful that the woman, who was slightly hard of hearing, hadn't been awakened by their activities that night, although Fitz's bedroom was at the far end of the hallway. By unspoken agreement, they'd shared only kisses since, yet there was a truce of sorts, and Aaron wasn't quite as moody. He didn't join her and Jamie in everything they did, but he did participate occasionally and he seemed happier.

Kate dared to dream the change was the beginning of better times to come. She'd even decided to go forward with her plan to look into the situation with Tom Spencer. Her uncle had phoned her shortly after her luncheon with Pam and brusquely demanded that she "sign the damn paper and mail it to him right away." She'd respectfully declined. She'd told Aaron about the problem just before he'd left this morning and showed him the legal document. He'd encouraged her to pursue the matter.

To that end, she was looking for the address book he'd told her was on his desk in his den. His lawyer, Peter Jeffries, was very knowledgeable, but if he couldn't help her, he'd surely recommend someone who could. Kate hadn't wanted to use anyone she'd known in Grosse Pointe, for the good old boys' club was alive and well, and very protective of its members.

The address book with Peter's phone number wasn't on the desktop. She looked around but couldn't spot it. Aaron wasn't due home for hours, and by then, the law offices would be closed. She was most reluctant to pry into his personal things. Still, he'd told her to go find the book. The desk drawers didn't seem to be locked. Cautiously, she opened the top center drawer. Not there.

Sitting down in his chair, she opened the right-hand drawer but found no book. Next, she tugged on the large bottom one, and when it came open, curiosity took over. The address book wasn't in sight, but several framed photos were, piled in randomly. With a nervous glance toward the door, she removed several.

A wedding picture, Aaron and Stephanie, looking young and happy and carefree. Kate could see her own resemblance to the woman Aaron had married, slight though it was. Next came a studio portrait of Stephanie, probably taken before their marriage, a bright smile on her face, her hair quite long. Very attractive. She could see why Aaron became interested.

The next few revealed Stephanie in her nurse's uniform, and then several of Stephanie as a new mother holding her baby. There was also one of the three of them, mother, father and child. Kate's heart lurched at that one, hurting for the woman who'd lost so much.

Why had Aaron hidden these away so long? Fitz had told her months ago that he didn't want any reminders of his grief. While Kate knew that Aaron still missed Stephanie at odd moments, she truly didn't feel he was still grieving in the heartbreaking sense.

It wasn't right to deny Jamie pictures of her mother, because she should grow up with some sense of who'd given birth to her. Kate certainly could relate to the feeling of loss of her birth parents. She had only one picture of the three Richards children, taken in front of the farmhouse with their dog, Rex, shortly before her world had fallen apart. She'd have given anything growing up to have more photos of her mother and father that would have added substance to her vague memories.

Surely, Aaron would want to do the right thing for his daughter's sake. Pushing in the drawer, she decided she'd make him see, using her own story to hammer home her point. Carefully, she stacked the framed pictures and carried them out of the den.

Another damn snowstorm. Aaron was sick of winter, and it was only late January. At least two more months of the white stuff to go. Grateful to have made it home without skidding into another car, since the roads hadn't been salted yet, he pulled into his garage and heaved a tired sigh.

He looked forward to a glass of wine, one of Kate's terrific dinners and some playtime with Jamie. That would surely chase away the problems of his long day.

Entering through the back way, he stomped snow from his shoes and removed his coat. Turning, he saw Fitz by the stove and Jamie in her playpen, the table already set. "Mmm, smells good. What are we having tonight that smells so good?"

Fitz welcomed him with a smile. "Kate made chicken soup earlier. I'm just cooking the noodles for it." She bent to the cupboard to look for the colander.

Aaron walked over to kiss his daughter. "Where is Kate?"

"Upstairs. In Jamie's room, I believe. Said she had something to take care of." Humming, Fitz stirred.

Curious, Aaron made his way upstairs, removing his jacket and tie along the way. At the open door to Jamie's room, he paused. Kate had cleared off a space on Jamie's chest of drawers and she was standing in front of it, holding up two framed photos as if trying to come to a decision. There was something familiar about the pictures. An alarm went off inside his head as he stepped inside. "What've you got there?" he asked.

Startled, Kate looked up, surprised she hadn't heard him come in. "I found these earlier." She shifted so he could see the pictures. "I thought Jamie would enjoy having one of them in her room."

"What the hell!" Aaron marched over and snatched the photos from her hands. "Just who gave you permission to go pawing through my private things?"

She'd never seen his face so stormy. "I didn't mean to upset you, Aaron. I was looking for your address book with Peter's phone number when I ran across these in your desk. I know that pictures of Stephanie may hold some sad memories for you, but your daughter needs to know her mother. I would've given anything to have a few of my parents. She needs to grow up having a sense of who she is, of her background, her family. I think—"

"Think. *You* think? No one gives a damn what you think."

That hurt, but Kate had come too far to back down. He was annoyed, but maybe she could make him see. "Aaron, please, think about it. Do you plan to raise Jamie and ignore the part her mother played in her life?"

Aaron didn't look at the pictures, just held them in a death grip. "You had no right. You've overstepped your boundaries this time. This is *my* home, and we do things *my* way around here." Not even fighting his rising fury, he turned to leave. "And if you don't like my way, you can leave."

Stunned at the way he'd overreacted, at the depth of his anger, Kate just stood there. She certainly hadn't intended to anger or hurt him. Perhaps if she waited until he cooled down and went to him to apologize, everything would be all right.

Yet even as the thought formed, deep inside she knew that nothing was ever going to be all right again.

## Chapter Twelve

By seven o'clock that evening, Kate had Jamie in bed and her decision made. Saying goodbye to the baby she'd come to love as her own was the hardest thing she could remember doing. She stood in the doorway to Jamie's room, watching the toddler in her crib sucking one thumb while in her other hand she held on to a somewhat raggedy Elmo. Kate had meant to buy her a new one and hadn't gotten around to it. Now she wouldn't have the chance.

Her vision blurring, she finally turned and headed for Fitz's room. She needed to talk with the housekeeper, needed a large favor. Fitz had sensed that something was wrong at dinner when Aaron hadn't come down and Kate hadn't been able to eat a bite. But she'd been too polite to ask, and Kate was grateful. But now she had to confide in her.

"Come in," Fitz said at the first knock. Seated in her lounge chair, she clicked off the television. One glance at Kate as she walked in, and she suspected what was coming. The sadness in the young woman's eyes had been building for weeks while Aaron had waffled between quiet moods, then stormed around like a chained bull pulling at his restraints. "Sit down, dear," she invited Kate, indicating the only other chair in her sitting room.

"Thanks, I won't keep you for long." There was no point in beating around the bush. It was getting late, and the snow was still coming down. She'd already talked with Pam, whose sympathetic understanding had almost been her undoing. She'd immediately assured Kate she could stay with her as long as she wanted. Nervously, she cleared her throat. "Would it be possible for you to watch over Jamie until my replacement can be found?"

There was no surprise on Fitz's thin, lined face. "So you've finally had enough, have you? Can't say I blame you, dear. Aaron's not always an easy man to live with. The good Lord knows I've been praying that things would work out between the two of you."

It would only insult Fitz if she pretended to not know what she was talking about. The woman had two good eyes and had watched them both closely for months. "I'd hoped for that, too."

"I suppose you know he loves you. Just too damn stubborn to admit it."

"I've given him every chance, Fitz. Maybe after I leave, he can find some peace."

"I pray you're right, dear. Of course I'll watch the little one. He'll not find another like you, that's for certain, and I don't mean just as a nanny."

"Thank you for that." She stood, wanting to get under way before the roads became impassable. Impulsively, she bent to hug the woman she'd become so fond of. "Take care of yourself. I'll miss you."

"Not half so much as we'll miss you around here. Will you call now and again, or write?" Fitz found her eyes damp. Damn-fool man, she thought, not recognizing the prize right under his nose. Living in the past was for the very old or the addle-brained, she'd always believed. A man with a growing child needed to focus on today and the future.

"I'll try." She didn't know if she could bear hearing little updates on Jamie, that she was talking and toilet trained and all the rest. Perhaps a clean break would be best.

"Is it still bad out?" Fitz got up and glanced out the window. "Maybe you should wait until morning." Maybe she'd go to Aaron's room and shake some sense into his hard head.

"I really need to go now. I've only a few things to pack." Fighting tears, she smiled. "Goodbye, Fitz. I won't forget you."

Fitz needed one last hug and went over to get it. "Nor I you, child. Be careful. The world's a rough place."

Hadn't she learned that over and over? Kate thought as she hurried to her room.

"Well, Aaron, what do you think?" Fitz asked. "Do you want to give her a trial run, or shall we keep on interviewing?"

Anger sat on his shoulders like a hair shirt he couldn't shrug off. His days were miserable, his nights a living hell. Fitz looked at him constantly with undisguised disapproval and disappointment. His father shared her opinion and had even suggested today that perhaps Aaron ought to take some time off, for he wasn't fit to be around at the office. Two short weeks, and things had gone from bad to terrible.

But the worst was Jamie. He hadn't even known that she knew how to say Kate's name, but he knew now. The child wandered the house, going to the doors, looking out the windows, her face sad and often tearstained. And always she called out, "Kay...Kay." She woke up crying and called for Kate, and went to her crib each evening with the same sad chant. She wouldn't eat very much, just wanted her bottle, even though Kate had very nearly weaned her. She was reverting, and he couldn't think how to stop it.

He heard Fitz clear her throat pointedly and glanced down at the application for employment in front of him. The agency had sent over nearly a dozen applicants. None suited. He'd found something wrong or lacking with each and every one.

He remembered thinking weeks ago that he should hire an older woman as nanny, one closer to Fitz's age, a woman who wouldn't remind him that he was a man with a man's needs. Now here she was, out in the living room after both he and Fitz had talked with her. Madeline Walker was fifty-eight, a widow with two married children and four grandchildren, and she was tired of living alone. She preferred being called Maddy, loved kids, had a pleasant manner and seemed to have plenty of energy. He tapped his fingers on the desktop thoughtfully.

"Aaron," Fitz interrupted, thinking he needed a nudge, "she's the best of the bunch. I can't keep up the house and care for Jamie, too. I'm long past being able to do that. Please, let's give Maddy a try." She was about at the end of her rope with more work than she cared to do, a sullen employer and a baby who moped around all day crying for someone who would never return. If it weren't for Jamie, she'd have given notice, too, Fitz thought, for she was too old for this much tension.

"All right," Aaron finally said, his voice resigned. "Tell her we'll give her a week's trial. You work out the details with her." He swung his chair around and stared out at a bleak February sky. It was turning into a long winter in more ways than one.

"I hope that Jamie likes her," Fitz muttered.

"She will. She'll adjust. We all will." Moodily, he listened to Fitz leave. Damn right they would. Jamie was a baby. She'd formed a slight attachment to Kate, but she needed to expand her horizons and get to know and like all sorts of people. Fitz would probably enjoy having someone around who was closer to her age. And he'd be able to concentrate on work again, God willing.

He'd always thought that March was the bleakest month of the twelve, especially in Michigan. His coat collar turned up against the freezing wind coming off the river and blowing snow everywhere, Aaron struggled his way to his back door. Where was the kid he'd hired to shovel snow? There was scarcely a path, much less a clear walk. Did he have to do everything himself to get things done right?

Walking in, he heard Jamie fussing before he'd closed the back door. Frowning, he entered the kitchen and saw that Maddy was trying to feed his daughter, but Jamie was batting away the spoon at each attempt. Standing at the stove, Fitz turned to him. "Welcome home. We hope your day went better than ours."

Annoyed that two very capable women couldn't manage both his child and his home, he hung his coat up and walked over. "What seems to be the problem?"

Maddy had joined them with a sunny disposition. Gradually, it had disappeared, replaced by an exasperated look. "She just doesn't want to eat, Mr. Carver," she answered.

"Kate used to say that when a child's hungry, they'll eat, and when they won't eat, there's a reason." Her expression bland, Fitz kept her eyes on Jamie.

Growing more irritated by the minute, especially at having Kate's name brought up regularly, he pulled a chair over to Jamie and put on a smile. "Hi, sweetheart. Let Daddy help you." He scooped up a spoonful of mashed potatoes and held it to her mouth. Staring right at him, she shook her head. "Come on, sweetie, just a little bit more. For Daddy?"

Reluctantly, Jamie opened wide and took the potatoes.

Aaron flashed a victory smile at both ladies and scooped in more. Then he got in a third. "Nothing to it," he said.

That was when Jamie puckered up and blew the entire mouthful of soggy mashed potatoes directly into her father's face. While he sputtered and swore under his breath, she stared at him, wide-eyed at what she'd done, then burst into tears.

"I'll just take her on upstairs and give her a bath," Maddy said, whisking the child out of the chair.

Aaron tossed down the spoon and reached for a napkin. This was just the perfect topper to a grueling day in which he'd accomplished far less than he should have. "I give up."

Leaning against the counter, Fitz eyed him. "You're good at that, aren't you? Giving up, I mean. You do it well and quite often."

Aaron scraped the last of the mess from his face, noticing that his tie was stained, as well, and got up. "I don't feel like going into this right now, Fitz." Only her long service to both his father and him kept Aaron from saying more.

"Nor do I, but it appears someone has to speak up, and I don't see any other hands in the air. I'll speak my piece, Aaron Carver, and then you can fire me or do whatever else you wish." She waited until he sat down again, a resigned look on his grim face, before seating herself across from him. Even as a youngster, she'd seldom had to call Aaron to task, unlike his wayward brother. But occasionally, even a good man needed reminding.

"I've tended to you, boy and man, watched you grow up and been as proud of you as I would be if you were my own. I sat with you when your wife took ill and watched you bury her, knowing you loved her still."

Aaron raised his eyes to her face, his expression unreadable, but she had his attention. Fitz so seldom lectured that when she did, he found himself listening in spite of his determination not to.

"You had no choice when you lost Stephanie," Fitz went on, "as I didn't when my Sean was taken from me. You railed against the fates, and I understood all too well. Then a beautiful young woman came into your life, her heart so full of love. She gave that love to Jamie and to you, but you threw it back in her face. Only a fool turns away from the love of a good woman, and I've never thought you to be a fool, Aaron. I know, too, that Stephanie wouldn't want you to be grieving nor her babe to grow up in a household with two old women and a miserable father.'' Intently, she watched him, letting her words sink in.

Finally, Aaron spoke, his voice sounding tired and defeated. ''What if it happens again, Fitz? What if she gets tired of everything, or someone new catches her eye, like with my mother, and she walks away? Or what if something happens, and Kate dies, too? You know the story of her family. The father died, the mother was taken away ill and God only knows where she wound up, her three children scattered to the winds. I don't see why I should put myself at risk for all that again. It's too hard.''

''Dear boy, you're stronger than you think. You can't keep yourself from loving simply because you're afraid of death. Dying's a part of living. As to desertion, I'd stake my life that Kate would never have left if you hadn't driven her away. Are you willing to lose all the years the both of you might have over something that might never take place till you're older than I am?''

But Aaron was stubborn in his thinking. ''You're giving advice you never took yourself. *You* never remarried.''

''No, I didn't, because I never met another man I could love. You don't replace gold with copper. I'm thinking that Kate's as solid gold as you'll find, wouldn't you say?''

He was quiet a long time, scrubbing his hand across his face. ''I don't know, Fitz. I want her back, but it's such a gamble. This way, Jamie's young and she'll soon forget Kate, and so will I.''

Fitz got to her feet slowly. "If you believe that, you're a bigger fool than I thought. Wake up, man. You broke her heart, and now it's killing you, and Jamie, too—all three of you miserable. Forget her? No, you won't. Even the little one can't." She repositioned the chair. "Go after her, Aaron. You're only half a man without her." She left the room then, left him with much to think over.

Seated at his desk in his office, Aaron looked out the window on a sunny April morning. It had rained for nearly a week, but spring was in the air. And spring was a time of rebirth, of hope.

His father had always told him that it takes a big man to admit he's made a mistake. He'd spent a lot of time thinking, working things out in his own mind. He hadn't been able to act until he'd been certain this time. Finally today, he'd had a long talk with William and he'd admitted that he had made a monumental mistake in causing Kate to leave him and Jamie.

For the first time in weeks, Dad had smiled with genuine warmth. Aaron was amazed at how much better he, too, felt in just making the decision. He'd hinted as much to Fitz when she'd served his tea this morning in the kitchen. He'd never known her to be impulsive, yet she'd rushed over and given him a big hug.

The phone rang and he swung back, hoping it was the call he'd been expecting. He didn't know where Kate was, and she'd been gone since the middle of January. The one person she'd mentioned most was her uncle, Tom Spencer, who'd been easy enough to locate. He knew they didn't get along, but he was certain that Tom would know where Kate was. He'd put in a call to the man earlier and was told he'd phone back.

Spencer's voice was curt and businesslike, without an ounce of warmth, but he listened courteously as Aaron explained that he was looking for his niece, Kate.

"Sorry, but I can't help you," Tom Spencer said.

Aaron frowned. "She hasn't been in touch with you?"

"No, she hasn't. Kate and I are not the best of friends, never have been."

"I realize that. All I want is an address or a phone number."

"I have no reason to assist you." Tom Spencer hung up the phone.

Surprised by the man's churlish behavior, Aaron shook his head. That certainly was a dead end. He remembered that when they'd first met, Kate had been staying at a nearby cottage her parents had owned. Maybe she'd gone there. It shouldn't take but a few phone calls to locate the place, on Pine Street, he recalled.

Within half an hour, he learned that the cottage, in Tom Spencer's name, had been sold last November. All right, what next? Kate had mentioned that before her parents died, she'd lived with them on Weber Court in Grosse Pointe. If she went back to that area, she'd probably contacted some of her old friends and neighbors. Aaron went to get the street directory.

Much to his surprise, in nearly two hours of phoning, he'd come up empty-handed. He sat scowling at his notes. Hard to believe that Kate had contacted not a single person in her old neighborhood. One or two had been chatty, but most of the people he'd talked with had been guarded. Undoubtedly a close-knit community.

Aaron was staring off into space, trying to think of the next place to try, when he remembered the cousin Kate had mentioned, the one who was also a close friend. Her name was Peggy. No, Paula. That didn't sound right. Oh yes, Pam. Pam Spencer. Reaching for the phone book, he hoped that Pam hadn't married and changed her name.

There were quite a few Spencers in Grosse Pointe, but no Pam or Pamela. However, there was a P. Spencer listed. Quickly, he dialed the number. After two rings, the answering machine picked up, and a woman's voice came on.

"Hi. You've reached Pam Spencer. Can't talk with you right now, but leave your name and number and I'll get back to you as soon as I can. Thanks."

Aaron left a brief message, stating that he was a friend of Kate Spencer's, which was sort of true, and he needed to get in touch with her about an important matter. He recited both his work and home phone numbers and hung up. Now all he had to do was wait. And worry.

Aaron was exasperated. Two days and half a dozen messages later, he still hadn't had a call back from Pam Spencer. Was she out of town? Had Kate told her not to call him? Was she as nasty as her father? He was at his wit's end when he remembered that Pam worked in a bookstore in Grosse Pointe. But which one?

Again, he perused the phone book, the Yellow Pages this time. He read all the listings twice and settled on one: the Book Tree on Kercheval. Yes, that sounded right, although he'd heard the name only once. Growing desperate, he called that number.

The young man who answered told him that Pam wasn't there and he wasn't sure when she'd be back. Aaron drew in a frustrated breath. "Does she still work there?"

"Work here?" the man asked, oddly hesitant. "I guess so."

Annoyed beyond belief, Aaron hung up. Didn't the jerk know who worked at his store? Calm down, he told himself, and think.

Maybe he should try another avenue. She probably had a doctor, an accountant, a lawyer...wait. A lawyer. He'd referred Kate to his own attorney, Peter Jeffries, regarding looking into her parents' estate. Reaching for the phone, he hoped to hell she'd contacted Peter.

"I don't feel I can help you much, Aaron," Peter said in answer to his question. "Yes, Kate's my client. No, I can't discuss her case, not even with you."

Aaron's impatience came through. "I'm not asking you to divulge some legal confidence, Peter. I just want to know where to find her. We have some unfinished business."

Peter's voice was cautious. "I don't like the sound of that."

His jaw clenched. He hated discussing his personal life with his business attorney, but it appeared he had little choice. "Damn it, I love her. I need to tell her, to bring her back to us."

The lawyer was still hesitant. "If that's the case, why did she leave St. Clair so suddenly?"

"A lot of reasons. Look, Peter, this isn't a breach of client-attorney privilege. I just want to talk with Kate."

"I'll tell her to call you."

Aaron wished he could take the time to count to ten. "Not on the phone. This isn't something I can say on the phone." And he wasn't entirely sure Kate would call him after talking with Peter.

Peter was silent for a long minute. He felt protective of most of his clients, but particularly Kate Spencer. To be cheated and betrayed by a relative was, in his book, truly a cardinal sin. Kate was vulnerable, and he didn't want anything more to go wrong in her life. However, he'd known Aaron and his father for years and knew they were trustworthy. "All right. You can find her at the Book Tree on Kercheval. But be careful, Aaron. She's already been hurt far too much by too many people."

"I know that. I won't hurt her, I promise." Aaron hung up and raced for his keys.

A flower box outside the Book Tree had tiny crocus plants pushing through the dark soil. Aaron wondered if Kate with her love of growing things had put them there. The window display consisted of a large stuffed pink rabbit surrounded by little yellow chicks and baby ducks mingling with dozens of children's books artfully arranged within an area enclosed by a white picket fence. Around the perimeter were potted plants—African violets, tulips, daffodils. He'd forgotten that Easter was coming. Did Kate's job consist of decorating the windows, too, for it seemed like something she'd put together?

He went inside, the tinkling bell overhead announcing his arrival. The store was crowded with people browsing and buying. A tall young man toward the back was up on a ladder getting down a book a redheaded woman was waiting for. Perhaps that had been the one he'd spoken with about Pam. A teenage girl was in the cooking section helping two matronly ladies. And two youngsters were seated in a carpeted area furnished with a child's rocker, small bench and table with chairs, where an older

woman was evidently conducting children's story time.
The store had a homey feel to it, an inviting atmosphere,
a warmth lacking in some of the chain stores. He could
almost feel Kate's fine touch everywhere.

In another moment, his gaze settled on the person undoubtedly responsible for this bookstore's success. She
was standing behind the counter at the register ringing up
sales for a grandmotherly type. Now that he'd finally located her, Aaron stood off to the side, watching.

Kate was even lovelier than he remembered nightly in
his restless dreams. Her hair had feathery bangs that
brushed her forehead, the back longer, falling past her
shoulders. She was wearing navy, the dark color making
her skin appear a pale gold by contrast. She finished the
sale and handed the package to the customer, smiling and
chatting for a moment before turning to the young man
next in line, who was buying reference books.

He decided to wait, to let her notice him. Several minutes later, her eyes making a swing of the room, she did
and she drew in a sharp breath. The smile she'd flashed
for the customer slid from her face, and she gripped the
edge of the wood counter.

Kate waited for her heart to stop thudding so loudly.
She'd thought she'd never lay eyes on Aaron Carver
again, and yet there he was, as heartbreakingly handsome as ever. Why had he come, now when she'd just
about gotten her life back on track? In a move that had
infuriated her uncle, Pam had deeded the bookstore and
the building over to Kate, leaving the small apartment
and moving in with Eli. Then, to add to Tom Spencer's
problems, Kate gone to see Peter Jeffries, who'd filed
a lawsuit on her behalf against the uncle who'd tried to
steal her inheritance.

None of the changes in her life since she'd left Aaron's home had come easily. She'd settled into the apartment over the shop and fixed it up for herself and for the baby who would arrive in the fall. Finding out she was pregnant had been a shock, then an overwhelming pleasure. Together, they'd be fine, and no one —*no one*—would ever take her child away from her.

Kate had worked hard in the bookstore, too, making it more appealing for all ages, and her efforts had been rewarded with good sales and loyal customers. If she still missed both Jamie and Aaron daily, hourly, if at night she still reached out for the man who wasn't there, if the tearful moments still hit her with maddening regularity, it was the price she had to pay for her peace of mind. She'd heard Aaron's calls on Pam's answering machine, for she'd never changed the message. Her first thought had been that something had happened to Jamie, but a quick call to Fitz had reassured her. That worry resolved, she'd sworn the housekeeper to silence and hoped if no one returned his call, Aaron would give up eventually.

She should have known better. Aaron was back, staring at her in that watchful way he had, and she couldn't imagine what it was he wanted from her. With trembling hands, she turned to the next person in line.

Aaron saw Kate, somewhat distractedly, nod to her customer and step out from behind the counter to show him where the book he wanted was. Watching her closely, Aaron felt the shock move through him like a tidal wave as he realized what he was seeing. Pregnant. She was obviously pregnant.

Swallowing hard, he waited.

Story hour ended, and the children and their parents left, as did the reader, who said goodbye to Kate and went out the back way. The young man from the back came forward and asked if he could help Aaron locate a particular book, but he shook his head, his eyes never leaving Kate. Finally, there was a lull in the line of customers, so he walked over to her.

She stood her ground, her eyes unwavering, though her lower lip trembled slightly.

"When were you going to tell me, or weren't you?" he asked, his voice low and sounding a little hurt to his own ears.

Her chin came up in that challenging way she had. "Don't worry. I don't hold you responsible. I'm old enough to know better. The baby's mine and no one else's. We want nothing from you."

She said her say with such quiet dignity that admiration rose in him. Even so, he wasn't about to accept her explanation. In a swift movement that caught her off guard, he dodged the counter and pulled her into his arms, his mouth taking hers in a stunning kiss that effectively stopped any protest.

Kate wanted to remain stiff and unresponsive, wanted to show him he couldn't come waltzing back into her life as if nothing were wrong and overwhelm her. In her head, that's what she wanted. But her heart and her traitorous body welcomed him seconds after he touched her. Her hands fluttered in surprise, then settled on his shoulders and finally pulled him closer when they should have been pushing him away.

Oh, Lord, she'd missed him, missed this, this mindless feeling that only Aaron had ever evoked in her. She found herself kissing him back with all the need that had been building inside her, the desire that had lain dormant until now, the love that she'd hidden in her heart. But it was that love he didn't want, she finally remembered, and drew back.

Eyes hazy but clearing, she looked up at him. Peripherally, she was aware of her two salespeople hovering in the background, undoubtedly wondering what to make of this scene, but she ignored them. "Don't think that that changes anything. I..."

"Kate, I've missed you terribly. So has Jamie. She cries for you constantly."

Pain flickered across her expressive face. "Oh, you know just how to turn the screws, don't you?"

"Not this time. I was wrong. I love you. We both do."

Warily, she studied him. "You're only saying that because of the baby. You don't have to. I can handle this without you." The bluff was weak, and she knew it but she had to be firm.

"Perhaps you can, but *I* can't. I can't manage without you, Kate. I walk around like a zombie, unable to work, to sleep. And it's true, Jamie *still* cries for you after all these weeks." He glanced down at the small but definite proof of her pregnancy. "I didn't know about the baby. That's icing on the cake. I want *you*, I want you back with us, I want to make a home with you. Since you left, it's just a house, a very sad house."

She wanted to believe. Oh, how she wanted to believe. "What about Stephanie? Are you sure you're not still feeling guilty and...?"

"You were right about that. I was being selfish and self-indulgent. After you left, I put one of Stephanie's pictures in Jamie's room and I talk to her about her mother. I don't want her to forget Stephanie, but for me, that part of my life is in the past. You and Jamie and now the baby, that's the future.'' He watched her struggling with her doubt, with unasked questions. ''Please marry me, Kate. I love you. Please tell me you care, just a little?''

At last, she released a trembling sigh. ''A little? I've loved you from the first, from that very first day. Oh, Aaron.'' Moving back into his arms, Kate felt as if she'd finally found the home she'd been seeking all her life.

*Epilogue*

*St. Clair, Michigan—December 1995*

Kate heard the back door open, bringing her back to reality from her nostalgic memories. In minutes, Aaron came into the family room and joined her on the couch, his hands cold as he slipped them around her and pulled her into a hungry kiss.

"Mmm, I've waited all day to do that. You taste scrumptious." He nuzzled her neck.

She smiled at him, welcoming the solid feel of him holding her. "I've missed you. The kids and I played in the snow out back. Fitz even came out with us for a while, but I think we tired her out. She went to her room right after dinner. Jamie kept asking me where Daddy was so she could go sledding." Almost three, the little girl was full of life and curiosity, talking nonstop, delighting both of them.

"I'm sorry I missed the fun, but the meeting lasted longer than I'd hoped. Tomorrow's Saturday. I'll take them both for a ride on the sled. Say, what about Aaron Jr.? Didn't he ask for his daddy?" A running joke between them was that their sixteen-month-old son was jabbering a blue streak in his own language and calling everyone "Mama", even Fitz and the mailman.

Sitting back, Kate smiled at her husband. "Nope. Sorry, Daddy, you're going to have to wait a while longer. Did you have dinner?"

Aaron sat back, toeing off his shoes and loosening his tie. "Yeah, Dad and I grabbed a sandwich on the way to the meeting."

"I'm glad you've eaten, because I have something I want to talk to you about."

Stretching his arm along the couch back, Aaron gathered her to him. "Okay, shoot."

So she told him about Pam's call and the television program "Solutions" and, more important, about seeing her mother and learning that she was not only alive but anxious to locate her three children.

"You're kidding?" Aaron studied her face. "You're not. I can't believe it."

"Neither could I." Kate reached for the pad she'd put on the end table. "I copied down the number to call."

"This is wonderful news, babe." Shifting to the table on his side, Aaron dragged over the phone and held it out to his wife. "Call them now. You can never have enough family."

It took a while to get through to the station and another few minutes of waiting while the person answering the phone put her on hold. Then suddenly, a woman's soft voice came on. "Hello, this is Julia Richards."

Kate blinked back a rush of moisture. "Hello, Mom? This is Katie."

## REUNION:
*Frankenmuth, Michigan—Christmas Eve, 1995*

Julia needed to catch her breath. The day, only half-over, had been the happiest of her life but slightly overwhelming. She stood quietly in the foyer of her recently remodeled farmhouse in Frankenmuth, gazing through the garlands that hung over the archway leading into the family room. Her heart was inside that room, she thought with a catch in her throat.

She'd longed for this sight for so many years that she could scarcely believe her eyes. There was a Christmas tree decorated with hundreds of tiny blinking lights and crowded with lovely ornaments, the star on top almost brushing the high ceiling. Beneath it were enough brightly wrapped and beribboned packages to make any child's heart beat faster.

The fireplace on the far left was ablaze with yule logs, the mantel strung with overlapping red-and-green and striped stockings, waiting for Santa's midnight arrival. The scent of evergreen mingled with the woodsy aroma, and in the background, the stereo was softly playing Christmas carols, filling the house with music.

From the kitchen drifted mouth-watering cooking smells, gingerbread cookies and pumpkin pies and a turkey basting in the oven. There was so much warmth and love that she felt as if the seams of the wonderful old house might split. Sloan had bought the farmhouse over a year ago when he'd heard it was going on the market, as a gift for Julia, and he'd lovingly restored it to where the marvelous rooms combined the old beauty with modern conveniences. At last, there was enough room for their entire family, six bedrooms upstairs and a generous downstairs.

And what a family, Julia thought, never tiring of looking at them, her eyes misty with the tears that kept reappearing, tears of joy. The television program, "Solutions," had worked, thank God. Not long after their segment aired, Michael had phoned, then Hannah and finally Kate. Julia had been shocked to learn that all these years, her children had thought her dead. All that pain and suffering. Ah, but today, she would think no more about the years gone by. She would just enjoy the present at last.

They'd agreed to meet for a Christmas reunion, and when she'd given them the old address of the Frankenmuth farmhouse, none could believe that they'd actually be going back, not just to their home but to their mother who'd been searching so long. A smile on her lips, Julia gazed at her family, one by one.

Hannah looked a great deal like her mother, Julia thought, though prettier with all that thick auburn hair. Beside her on the piano bench was her handsome husband, Joel Merrick, who held their son, nine-month-old Will, on his knee. They were both attorneys living in Boston and had already invited her and Sloan to consider vacationing there next year.

On the couch was Julia's daughter by Sloan, Emily, fourteen years old and fascinated with the youngest member of the family, three-week-old Julie, born to Julia's son, Michael, and his wife, Fallon. They lived in

San Diego and operated a home for runaway teens, which she and Sloan had promised to visit soon.

Across the room, bringing in more logs for the fire, was Sloan's son, Christopher, a tall and handsome twenty-five, the boy Julia had adopted after they'd brought him back from Mexico, where his birth mother had fled after kidnapping him. Julia watched Chris set down the logs, then join the others at the piano. And going from group to group, his tail happily wagging, was Prince, a two-year-old sheepdog Sloan had gotten this past summer.

"Happy, darling?" Sloan asked, coming up behind his wife. He'd been observing her for some time and could only guess at how full her heart was right now. Dabbing at her eyes, she turned in his arms, and he thought again how lovely she was. At fifty-two, she had only a few strands of gray in her dark hair. Now, at last, her eyes were sparkling.

"Never happier, Sloan." She hugged him close. "Thank you for the best Christmas gift anyone ever had."

Glancing up at the mistletoe overhead, Sloan kissed her just as the doorbell chimed. "I believe the rest of your present has just arrived." Together, they went to open the door.

A lovely blond woman stood on the wooden porch holding the hand of a little girl, and a dark-haired man stood behind her, in his arms a bright-eyed boy.

Julia's face broke into another wide smile. "Katie!" Opening her arms, she embraced her daughter.

Kate's husband reached around the two women to shake hands. "You must be Sloan. I'm Aaron Carver, and this little guy is Aaron Jr." He placed his free hand on his daughter's shoulder. "And this young lady's Jamie."

"Welcome, welcome. Come in, please." Sloan guided the newcomers in, taking his turn hugging Kate while Julia got acquainted with another son-in-law and a couple more grandchildren. Ushering everyone into the family room, he began the introductions all around. There were smiles and laughter and happy shouts and hugs to share.

Amid the noise and confusion, Jamie Carver walked over to the tree and stared in wide-eyed wonder at all the gifts. She turned then and found the woman Mommy had told her was her grandmother. Jamie had never had a grandmother before, but she thought she might like this lady. Quietly, she went to her and took her hand.

Julia smiled down at the little girl who'd slipped her small hand into hers. "Hello, Jamie. Are you having a good time?"

"Yes, but when are we going to open the presents?"

Julia's dark eyes skimmed each face in the room, then turned to look at her granddaughter. "Some of us already have."

\* \* \* \* \*

*Silhouette*

SPECIAL EDITION ™ ©

*That's My Baby!*

# "Just call me Dr. Mom....

I know everything there is to know about birthing *everyone else's* babies. I'd love to have one of my own, so I've taken on the job as nanny to three motherless tots and their very sexy single dad, Gib Harden. True, I'm no expert, and he's more handy at changing diapers than I—but I have a feeling that what this family really needs is the tender loving care of someone like me...."

## MOM FOR HIRE
### by
### Victoria Pade
### (SE #1057)

In October, Silhouette Special Edition brings you

### THAT'S MY BABY!
Sometimes bringing up baby can bring surprises... and showers of love.

Bestselling Author
# BARBARA
# BOSWELL

Continues the twelve-book series—FORTUNE'S CHILDREN—
in **October 1996** with Book Four

## STAND-IN BRIDE

When Fortune Company executive Michael Fortune needed help
warding off female admirers after being named one of the ten most
eligible bachelors in the United States, he turned to his faithful
assistant, Julia Chandler. Julia agreed to a pretend engagement, but
what starts as a charade produces an unexpected Fortune heir....

MEET THE FORTUNES—a family whose legacy is greater than riches.
Because where there's a will...there's a *wedding!*

"Ms. Boswell is one of those rare treasures who combines humor
and romance into sheer magic."　　　　　　　　　*—Rave Reviews*

*A CASTING CALL TO
ALL FORTUNE'S CHILDREN FANS!*
If you are truly one of the fortunate
you may win a trip to
Los Angeles to audition for
Wheel of Fortune®. Look for
details in all retail Fortune's Children titles!

## The Calhoun Saga continues...

in November
*New York Times* bestselling author

# NORA ROBERTS

takes us back to the Towers and introduces us to
the newest addition to the Calhoun household,
sister-in-law Megan O'Riley in

## MEGAN'S MATE
(Intimate Moments #745)

And in December
look in retail stores for the special collectors'
trade-size edition of

# THE
# Calhoun
# Women

containing all four fabulous Calhoun series books:
*COURTING CATHERINE,*
*A MAN FOR AMANDA, FOR THE LOVE OF LILAH*
and *SUZANNA'S SURRENDER.*
Available wherever books are sold.

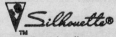

Look us up on-line at: http://www.romance.net

CALHOUN

This October, be the first to read these wonderful
authors as they make their dazzling debuts!

### THE WEDDING KISS by Robin Wells
**(Silhouette Romance #1185)**
A reluctant bachelor rescues the woman he loves
from the man she's about to marry—and turns into
a willing groom himself!

### THE SEX TEST by Patty Salier
**(Silhouette Desire #1032)**
A pretty professor learns there's more to making love
than meets the eye when she takes lessons from
a sexy stranger.

### IN A FAMILY WAY by Julia Mozingo
**(Special Edition #1062)**
A woman without a past finds shelter in the arms of
a handsome rancher. Can she trust him to protect
her unborn child?

### UNDER COVER OF THE NIGHT by Roberta Tobeck
**(Intimate Moments #744)**
A rugged government agent encounters the woman he has
always loved. But past secrets could threaten their future.

### DATELESS IN DALLAS by Samantha Carter
**(Yours Truly)**
A hapless reporter investigates how to find the perfect
mate—and winds up falling for her handsome rival!

Don't miss the brightest stars of tomorrow!

Only from ▼ *Silhouette*®
™

Continuing in October from Silhouette Books...

This exciting new cross-line continuity series unites five of your favorite authors as they weave five connected novels about love, marriage—and Daddy's unexpected need for a baby carriage!

You loved
> **THE BABY NOTION** by Dixie Browning
> (Desire 7/96)
>
> **BABY IN A BASKET** by Helen R. Myers
> (Romance 8/96)
>
> **MARRIED...WITH TWINS!** by Jennifer Mikels
> (Special Edition 9/96)

And the romance in New Hope, Texas, continues with:

> **HOW TO HOOK A HUSBAND (AND A BABY)**
> by Carolyn Zane (Yours Truly 10/96)

She vowed to get hitched by her thirtieth birthday. But plain-Jane Wendy Wilcox didn't have a clue how to catch herself a husband—until Travis, her sexy neighbor, offered to teach her what a man really wants in a wife....

And look for the thrilling conclusion to the series in:

> **DISCOVERED: DADDY**
> by Marilyn Pappano (Intimate Moments 11/96)

DADDY KNOWS LAST continues each month...
only in Silhouette®

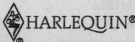 

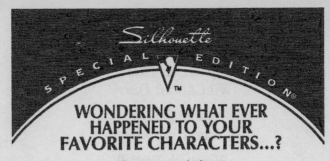

*Silhouette*

SPECIAL EDITION ™ ®

# WONDERING WHAT EVER HAPPENED TO YOUR FAVORITE CHARACTERS...?

Silhouette Special Edition's
SPIN-OFF SPECTACULAR finally gives much-loved
characters their own story. Catch these exciting titles from
some of your favorite authors:

**OF TEXAS LADIES, COWBOYS...AND BABIES:** (August, SE #1045)
Jodi O'Donnell first introduced Reid and Glenna in DADDY WAS A COWBOY
(SR #1082). Now as Glenna begins her life anew—with Reid—she
discovers she's going to have a baby!

**A FATHER'S GIFT:** (August, SE #1046)
In the first book of GREAT EXPECTATIONS, a new miniseries from
Andrea Edwards, a tough cop becomes Mr. Mom when he moves back
in with the family he's never stopped loving.

**DADDY OF THE HOUSE:** (September, SE #1052)
Diana Whitney's new series PARENTHOOD begins with the story
of Cassie Scott—and she's expecting! And the perfect daddy is
Jack Merrill—who's already the father of matchmaking twins!

**THE HUSBAND:** (October, SE #1059)
The popular SMYTHESHIRE, MASSACHUSETTS series by Elizabeth August
comes to Special Edition in October!

Don't miss any of these wonderful titles, only for our readers—only from
Silhouette Special Edition.